Relationships 2

Published by Phaze Books
Also by Piers Anthony

Relationships

PHAZE
Cincinnati, Ohio

This is an explicit and erotic collection
intended for the enjoyment
of adult readers. Please keep
out of the hands of children.

www.Phaze.com

Relationships 2

another collection of stories by

PIERS ANTHONY

PHAZE
Cincinnati, Ohio

A Phaze Production
Phaze Books
6470A Glenway Avenue, #109
Cincinnati, OH 45211-5222
Phaze is an imprint of Mundania Press, LLC.

To order additional copies of this book, contact:
books@phaze.com
www.Phaze.com

Cover art © 2007,2008 Debi Lewis
Edited by Candi Bowen

ISBN-13: 978-1-59426-724-6
ISBN-10: 1-59426-724-3

First Print Edition – March, 2008
Printed in the United States of America

10 9 8 7 6 5 4 3 2 1

Table of Contents

Introduction

This is a sequel collection to the one published in 2006 by the VENUS PRESS republished by PHAZE. Women need to watch what they say, because a man can take the slightest positive word as an invitation to commitment. When the first volume was published, the proprietor of VENUS remarked politely that she might be amenable to more like it. So I pondered—and suddenly was back writing tales of relationships, as it turned out, for another publisher.

The first collection consisted of twelve mainstream stories. This one is seven stories, but is a longer volume, because more of them fall into the novelette length. They range from 1,500 to 23,000 words. More of them also verge into fantasy or science fiction, but they remain focused on relationships; you'll find no spaceships or time travel here. Merely a trans-gender humanoid android, an obliging siren, an exercise machine that projects holograph and tactile images, and a couple of stories involving the Afterlife. Nothing very far out of the ordinary.

As before, I went to my comprehensive Idea File and sorted through notions, then selected those that seemed to be ripening at this time. As before, one came to me on its own, bypassing the file; that is "Friends of Bolivia," a sequel to an inset story in "Hot Game" in the first volume. Two others I remembered from the file, but couldn't locate, so had to write them from scratch, as it were. As before, the stories did not necessarily follow the courses I expected. Like people, they soon established their own identities once animated. Writing is like that. If you want a perfectly predictable product, become a brick maker or literary critic, where the verdict precedes the experience.

As before, these stories generally have strong erotic elements. But again, sex is not the point, merely a significant aspect of the experience. Most of these are romances, with a similar caution: not all relationships are romantic or sexual. Love has many facets.

Faking It

Joe was the last one on the elevator before it started up, and the only black man. The white folk didn't say anything, but they gave him room. That was because he was massive, muscular, and carried the faint smell of garbage. He was used to their reaction and mostly tuned it out.

At each stop, one or more people got off, until only Joe and a small pudgy white girl remained. She stood in the corner farthest from him, facing away as if shutting out awareness of her peril. He was used to that too.

There was a rumble, then a crash. The elevator's light went out as it jolted to a halt. The girl screamed. Joe hung on to the rail, his heart suddenly racing.

Then there was silence and stillness. Joe's breathing slowed as he realized that the scare was over. Except for the complete darkness. He did not like that at all.

There was a sound from the other side, as of someone trying to stifle nausea. "You okay, honey?" Joe asked. "I mean, not hurt?"

She didn't answer. He could guess why. "Honey, I'm scared too. I don't mean you no harm. I just want to get out of here. I get uptight in closed places. Feeling like I can't breathe. There's a word for it."

Then she spoke. "Claustrophobia."

"Yeah, that's it. I like the wide open spaces. I'll be glad when they get the power back on."

There was silence. She was still afraid of him.

He talked because he had to or go crazy. "Honey, I don't like being stuck in here any better'n you do. You don't have to be scared of me. I'm just a city dump worker on his way to get a local driver's license. 'Cause I'm from out of state, and there's only so long they'll let me drive here on my old card. I'm not a—" But that was a wrong direction, because he didn't want to even hint that he might hurt her.

"I'm not afraid of you," she said. "I'm terrified we're going to die."

"Don't say that! It's just a glitch. The power'll come back on soon and we'll be okay."

"It's a tremor. It may be bad."

"A what?" At least she was talking now.

"A tremor. Part of an earthquake. We get them here on occasion. It could be hours or days before the power returns, depending on how close we are to the epicenter."

"Hours or days!" he repeated, appalled.

There was a pause. Then he heard more stiflings. She was crying.

"Honey, don't get me wrong. I'm scared too, like I said. But if you need someone to, well, hold you—" He broke off again. This wasn't a black girl. "I'm sorry. I shouldn'ta said that. I'm just going to sit right here in my corner." He eased himself to the floor, as standing seemed pointless.

"I do need that," she said, surprisingly. "May I come to you?"

"Sure," he said, amazed.

He heard her moving toward him, guiding herself by the railing. When her foot touched his extended leg, she got down, sat beside him, and felt for his arm. He remained still, knowing that she would fear being grabbed. He smelled her faint perfume, a nice contrast to the odor that clung to him despite his best efforts.

"May I?" she asked.

"Sure." He wasn't certain what she had in mind. He just didn't want to frighten her into flight. Things were bad enough without her freaking out.

She leaned into him. "Put your arm around me, please."

He did so, slowly, carefully. In a moment she was half-lying against his chest, her hair touching his neck and chin. He was conscious of the fullness of her blouse against his side. She might be pudgy, but she had a body where it counted. He tried to stifle the ideas it gave him. *She was a white girl.*

Then she was quietly sobbing into his collar. He felt her shoulders shuddering, and the warmth of her tears soaking his shirt. "It's okay, honey," he said. "They'll fix it soon." He hoped.

After a time her emotion abated. "Thank you," she said, not moving. "I needed that comforting."

"Any time, honey." Actually, reassuring her helped him handle his claustrophobia.

"I'm going for my driving license, too. My first. I have to take the eye test, and the written exam. I know the material completely, and my vision is good, but I'm still nervous about failing. I get—" She shrugged against him.

"Uptight," he said. "I know how it is. You know it cold, then you go blank and fuck it up." Oops. "I mean— "

She laughed, slightly. "I know the word. My brother's in the army. He told me about SNAFU: Situation Normal, All Fucked Up."

Now, he laughed. "That's it, all right."

"Are we going to die?"

He had been trying to avoid that notion. "Naw. They'll get the power back, and we'll head up for our tests, just like nothing happened."

"Sometimes it takes weeks to find isolated people trapped in the rubble. What will we eat? How will we eliminate?"

She was getting morbid. He didn't know enough about white girls to be sure of her mood. "Piss in a corner if we have to. I'm used to the smell. I promise not to look."

She laughed more fully. "What would you see, in the darkness?"

"I just mean it's, well, black men are supposed to have a thing about white gals, so you don't want me looking, even if I can't see anything."

"Is it true?"

"Sure, my word is good. I don't got much, but I got that. I wouldn't look."

"I mean about black men liking white girls."

"You yanking my chain, girl?"

"I just want to know."

"How old are you?"

"Free, white, and eighteen. I'll be going to college soon, if I can ever decide on a major. Nothing appeals."

So he couldn't get in trouble for corrupting a minor. "Sure, I guess. It's a cultural thing. A status symbol. A white gal is the ultimate prize. Especially a blonde."

"Is it true for you specifically?"

He hesitated. "I don't want to answer that."

"We're going to die anyway. Can't there be truth between us?"

"We're not going to die!"

"We've got a good chance of it. Whole square miles could be in rubble."

"You got the blues, honey."

"I'm depressive, yes. But we really are in serious danger. An aftershock could break the cable and drop us six floors to the basement. Are you going to answer my question?"

"I don't want you to think I'm on the make for you. We need to get off this subject."

"Is it true for you?"

She would not quit. He surrendered. "Yeah. I felt your—your shirt. It's a turn-on."

"My breast aroused you?"

"Yeah."

"I'm blonde."

"Yeah."

"So you do desire me."

"I never said that!"

"Don't you?"

"Honey, I'm trying to comfort you, not scare you to death."

"Because I'm no beauty. I'm plain, with acne, and about fifteen pounds overweight."

"Honey, you're fine. Those things don't matter.

You're *white*."

"Would you like me to take off my clothing?"

He exploded. "What the hell are you trying to do, honey? I'm trying to treat you right."

"We're going to die. I don't want to die chaste."

"What are you talking about?"

"You are sexually experienced, aren't you?"

"Well, I've had black gals. Maybe fathered a baby or two. I didn't stick around. That's the way of it, for my kind. But I'm not trying to make it with you."

"I told you I wasn't afraid of you. I was afraid of myself. I've got this image in my mind, from a story I read once. It was about a lovely white princess, and she went into the garden, and there came this huge ugly blackamoor. That's what it called him. She dropped her clothing, opened her arms to him, and he threw her and enjoyed her. I always wondered about that. I knew it was sex, but I wasn't sure that black men really preferred white women. I've seen some lovely black women. So I'm verifying that with you."

"Yeah," he said, bemused. "I'm a blackamoor, black as the ace of spades, and you're a white princess, and I'm hot for you. But that don't mean I gets you."

"You could give me that experience, so I don't have to die incomplete. That's what I want."

"You're out of your head. You'd never say it if you weren't halfway freaked out."

"I'm not hysterical. I'm just seeing things with preternatural clarity. I'm going to die, and I don't want to do it as a virgin."

So she was a virgin. He tried to banish the thought, but his member was getting stiff. "Honey, do you know what they do to black men who rape white girls? They start with castration. Then they get ugly."

"I am not proposing rape. But what does it matter, if we both die?"

"Honey, you're scaring me. Say we do it. Then we get rescued. I'll get lynched."

She considered. "Then let it be our secret."

"Naw. My own big mouth would convict me."

"I don't understand."

"Honey, when a couple fucks, the woman usually keeps her mouth shut. But the man's gotta talk about it. Doing it is only half of it; bragging's the other half."

"That's weird."

"We're hard-wired to tell. So I'd be doomed, one way or the other."

"Suppose I said it didn't happen? Whom would they believe?"

Now, he considered. "Normally, they'd believe the white over the black. But they might figure you're trying to cover your shame."

"What is shameful about voluntary sexual expression?"

"Nothing, honey. Except when the races mix. Then the Klan gets on it."

"The Ku Klux Klan. I read about it. A disgraceful manifestation of racism."

"It's still there, honey, down under. Maybe you don't see it, but I do."

"Maybe this: we do it, we get rescued, we don't

say a word. Until we both get home. Then you talk about it, I don't, and nobody believes you."

He nodded in the darkness. "That might work. They'd figure I day-dreamed it."

"A fond hallucination."

"Yeah. Thinking about what might have happened. 'Cause no white gal'd want to make out with a man who stinks of garbage."

"Then we are covered, dead or alive. How do we proceed?"

"You really want to do it?"

"I'm serious, yes. But I have no experience. No boy wants to date me, let alone get fresh with me. I'm chopped liver. You're going to have to show me how."

"Honey, you got me hot. But with you being scared of dying, it's like you're out of your mind, and that's rape. You'd never do it if you weren't so scared."

"Not entirely true. I have dreamed of sex with a big black man, as I mentioned."

"Why? I mean, why not with a white prince or something?"

"Because the white prince would take half a look at me and laugh at the notion. A black man might really find me desirable. As you say is the case with you."

"Got me there, honey. I'm not lying to you; I got a king-sized hard-on."

"An erection, yes. So you're ready. So am I. I'm wet where it counts."

"I'd really like to fuck you. But I don't want to hurt you, and I don't want to get hung by the balls for screwing a white chick."

"We have already covered this ground. If we do it and die, it doesn't matter. If we do it and are rescued, we won't admit it until we're safely separated, never to meet again."

"And what if you tell right away? I'm dead."

"I ask you to take my word, as I accept yours. I have no reason to implicate you. This was my idea."

"Honey, you got me so hot I can't tell you no no more. But if you change your mind, tell me to stop, and I'll stop. I ain't going to rape you if I can help it. Okay?"

"That's fine. Tell me what to do."

"Okay, now, we'll take off our clothes. It's getting hot in here anyway, with the air conditioning off. Start with that."

"Agreed." She lifted herself off him and set about it in the darkness. He did the same.

"You bare yet?"

"I am naked, yes."

"So am I. Now usually the man, he gets on top of her. But I must weigh twice what you do, so we'll reverse it. I'll lie on the floor, and you get on me."

"Do I simply lie down on top of you?"

"Yeah, to start."

She felt for him, her small hands finding first his knee. She slid her hand up his thigh. It collided with his solid erection. "Oh!"

"That's my rod," he said. "Stiff as a bone. You sure you want it in you?"

"It's so big!"

"It's normal sized, honey. We ain't really hung like horses."

She straddled him on hands and knees. "It seems impossible for that stake to fit in me."

He hoped she was not changing her mind, now that he had committed. "It can't hurt you, honey. But you decide. If it's too tight, you stop. I won't move."

She lay on him, her body safely above his member. Her breasts came down on his chest, exciting him further. "I will try. Should we kiss?"

"You want to kiss a black man?"

"Well, if we're going to have intercourse, it seems appropriate."

"Some gals will fuck for pay, but won't kiss. Kissing's too personal."

"A remarkable inversion. But I want it personal." She slid up along him, her breasts caressing his chest, and found his face. She kissed him, delicately. "Thank you."

He laughed. "Thank *you*, honey. You're doing me the favor, you know. I never dreamed I'd ever get to fuck a white bitch."

"It's very different, but nice to hear it phrased that way. You really do desire me."

"Honey, I'm about to spout into space. Let's get on with it, if we're going to."

"Of course. What is my next step?"

"Slide back down to my cock. Lift your ass a little. Take my cock and set it in your cunt. Then let yourself down, slowly, sliding it in, so it don't hurt. When it's all in, hang on, because I'll be coming like thunder."

She slid down. "Lift my bottom," she said to herself. "Take penis, set it in vagina. Allow it to penetrate slowly." She did it, step by step. When she put her small hand on his hard member and lifted it, he almost went into orgasm.

"Put it to your gash," he said. "Get the angle right."

She did so. Her cleft was wet, as she had said; she was sexually excited. That meant there would be no trouble about dryness. "This way?" she asked uncertainly. "I've never done this before."

"You got it right. Hurry," he said urgently. "I can't hold back much more."

She settled down on it. The fit was tight. "It's too big, or I'm too small. It will never get in."

"It'll fit, honey, it'll fit! Cunts stretch. Just relax and take it in. Please! I'm coming!"

"I'll try." She pushed down. His member wedged into the taut channel with excruciating deliberation. First the head found lodging, then the shaft, like a barge pushing into a narrow harbor. "It's getting there!"

"It sure is, honey! You're not hurting?"

"It—it's firm to the point of discomfort, but also rather exhilarating. As though this is meant to be. I feel your member pulsing inside me. That is strange but nice."

"You said it, honey! Cock and cunt are made for each other. One more nudge to get it full depth, if you can take it. Try coughing."

"Like this?" She coughed, and her channel shoved down hard, taking him in the rest of the way. "Oh! I think I'm impaled!"

His orgasm was upon him. "Hang on!" He wrapped his arms around her body, put his hands on her buttocks, and held her close in to him. He thrust, withdrew, and thrust again, spurting copiously, pressuring his thick fluid into the snug confinement. "Glorious!" he gasped as he jetted. "Jesus Christ Almighty!"

"I feel your emission!" she said, excited. "Like hot balm in my core."

He had to laugh as the pulses ebbed. "It's cum in your cunt, girl. God, but it's great."

Then he was done. The girl remained as she was, lying on him as his member softened within her. "Is that it?"

"You didn't come?"

"I did not climax. Did I do it wrong?"

"Oh, honey," he said, chagrined. "I forgot. It doesn't just happen with a gal. It takes extra work. I should've remembered."

"What should I have done differently?"

"Not your fault! I was so hot for it I couldn't wait. I should've worked you up first. I'm sorry. Let me recover a while, and I'll do it again, and take you with me. I guess I'm too used to gals faking it."

"Faking it?"

"Pretending. They sigh and groan as if they're in ecstasy, fooling the man to make him feel good. Then they get theirs in their own time. Of course you don't know about that. I just wasn't thinking."

"I want to learn how to climax in the course of intercourse. It's not complete until then."

"It sure ain't, honey. My bad. I'll get you there next time. I promise."

"But for you—it was satisfactory?"

"Honey, it was great! You've got the tightest little ass I ever got into. Best fuck I've had in years."

She made a silent laugh that he felt on his belly and chest, as her own belly and breasts moved against him. "Thank you. It's good to be tight?"

"It sure is. Experienced gals, had some babies, they get loose. Man might as well hang it out over a cliff, for all the feeling he gets. But a really tight cunt is a wonder, and you've got the tightest."

"I was afraid that close fit was a disaster."

"You got that backward, honey. I didn't do right for you, but you did great for me. Your ass is perfect."

"Maybe if you take the initiative next time, instead of having me do it, I'll get there."

"Maybe. Mainly, I need to be looking out for you instead of me."

They lay in place for a while. "I like being close to you like this. I think I received a fair amount even without climaxing."

"I like holding you. Taking time. You're not trying to get on to some other appointment. And you got nice boobs."

"You like my breasts, even after your orgasm?"

"Honey, I like everything about you, before and after."

"I once heard it said that a man desires a woman, while the woman desires the desire of the man. Is that true?"

He thought about that. "I sure desire you, honey. But I guess you have to say about the other."

"I do desire your desire. I like the fact that you find my body appealing. No one ever did, before. They date me only because I'm rich, and I pay for everything. They pretend they are being gentlemen, but I know they keep their hands off me because I don't turn them on."

"Those boys you knew, they're all fools. If they'd ever got close to you like this, they'd have been as hot for your ass as I am. The way you're touching me now, it's gonna get me hot again soon."

"You may fondle my breasts, then, if you wish."

"Oh, yeah, I wish!" He let go of her buttocks and turned her to the side. Then he put his hands on her breasts. They were not large, but were well shaped. He stroked them. "Damn, they're nice!"

"Maybe in darkness. They're nothing special in daylight, and my abdomen shows."

"They're plenty good enough, honey. I bet they'd be knockouts in a push-up bra."

"I will consider it."

He continued squeezing her breasts, feeling his urgency slowly returning. "I just wish it could've been like this without us having to die."

"I agree. You don't mind talking?"

"I love talking to you, gal, as well as feeling you. It keeps my mind off the other thing."

"Death," she said. "Yes, that is the case for me too."

"When I'm thinking about sex, I'm not thinking about death."

"Me too. So we can justify this interaction on the basis of psychological need."

But then their dialogue lapsed. He continued caressing her breasts, but the novelty was fading. He needed something else. "You want to hold my cock?"

"Is that part of sex?"

"Yeah. Gal gets to know what she's putting in

her. Some gals like to suck on it."

She stiffened. "I don't think I could do that."

"I didn't mean *you* honey," he said quickly. "Don't do nothing you don't want to. We're just passing time."

She reached down to find his penis, which was now moderately solid. "What you described is oral sex, isn't it? Is that as good as genital sex?"

"Depends on your mood. When you fuck a lot, after a while it gets stale. Then the other stuff is fun. But nobody *has* to do it."

"Maybe some day I'll be able. As you know, I lack experience."

Joe thought of something. "You got a few extra pounds, and some pimples, right? That's what makes you plain."

"I suppose," she said uncomfortably.

"In the dark I can't see your face, and all I'm feeling are your boobs. You're sexy as hell this way."

"Thank you. But I can't live in darkness all my life."

"What I'm saying is, you don't have to be the way you say. I knew a gal once, she was like that, getting fat and pimply. Then she got a job with the forest service, and spent all her time out in the wind and sun, hiking around the parks. And you know, in a few months she was lean and clean. Something about the air and exercise took the weight off and cleaned up her face. You been living indoors, right?"

"Yes. An interim office job while I try to decide my future."

"I'll bet if you change your job, get outside—you don't have to do my kind of work, on a dozer shoving piles of garbage around, but you could make yourself look by day the way you feel to me right now. If you want to."

"Oh, my," she breathed. "I'll try it." Then she kissed the tip of his member. "Thank you."

"Honey, you don't have to—"

"I'm discovering something. I always thought sex was dirty, despite what I said, and it had to be only missionary position."

"That's a damn lie."

"Yes. When you start getting aroused, there is no dirty part of the body, is there? I'm not ready to—to do oral sex, but it no longer repulses me. Maybe you can show me how to do that, in due course."

"Anytime, honey. When you want to."

"Right now I'd prefer to talk. I have an idea. Suppose we compare our most secret shames? Get them off our chests before we die."

She kept coming back to death. That unnerved him.

"Sure. I'll start. When I was a teen, I stole a little electric motor from a store. I wanted it real bad, and I didn't have no money, and I saw my chance and I took it. But then I thought about it, and I didn't much like myself. I threw it away, but that didn't get rid of the guilt. I wish I hadn't done it. I've tried to be honest ever since."

"I broke a rare vase by accident," she confessed. "My parents thought my little sister had done it and blamed her. I let them. I remain ashamed today, but I lack the nerve to confess."

"Say, that's like mine! The guilt."

"That seems to be true. We are both imperfect

people."

"Yeah."

"I have an idea. I've got money. I'll give you enough to pay for that motor."

"Fat chance if I'm dead!"

"Let's make a deal: if we survive, let's set our liabilities to rights. You'll pay for that motor, and I'll confess to my parents."

"Honey, it's been fifteen years. Way too late to make it good."

"You could still tell the store manager and offer recompense. The point is to clear your shame."

"Deal. Only I won't take your money. I'll pay for it myself, so much a week."

"As you wish." She squeezed his penis, which was surprisingly becoming hard again. "Now let's exchange favorite dreams."

"You mean, about fucking a nice white gal? I just had that."

She laughed. "I have heard that every person deserves fifteen minutes of fame. What would yours be, if you could have it?"

He pondered a moment. "What you gave me, honey, it's a dream, and I really appreciate it. But for fame—I guess I'd like to have this glamorous white doll on my arm, fawning all over me, and everyone would see and be jealous. I know it'll never happen, but you asked for my dream."

"I hope to do some good deed that will benefit the world," she said. "Or at least some person. To make the world a better place than it was, if only marginally."

"You're a better person than I am," he said

ruefully. "I never thought of that. I like your dream better."

"We are of different cultures. I don't have to worry about earning my living, so I'm free to think noble thoughts. But I have no idea how to do it."

The dialogue lapsed. Time had passed, and he was ready to have sex again, but something else got in the way. "It's been too long," he said. "They're not going to find us."

"That is my concern."

Emotion welled up. "Oh shit."

"Is something wrong?"

"It's getting to me. The claustrophobia. The darkness. The hopelessness. Damn, I'm crying. I don't want to die!"

Agitated, disturbed, frightened, comforting, she got up, then sat beside him, her back propped against the elevator wall. "Come here, Joe."

"No. I don't want you to see me like this. I'm thirty five years old, damn it. A man don't cry."

"Come here, Joe," she repeated, reaching for him. "I know about depression."

He yielded, turning into her. She clasped his head to her bare breasts and held him tight. He sobbed into her marvelously soft bosom, hating himself, but unable to stop. "Damn, damn, damn!"

She rocked a bit, carrying him with her. "It's all right, Joe. You've been great. You comforted me. Now it's my turn. It will pass. I have been there many times."

And after a time she proved her point. His hopelessness faded somewhat.

"You know something, honey? You're more of a

woman to me now than you were before. Don't get me wrong; you were one great fuck. But now—"

"I understand." And obviously she did. Their roles had reversed.

Then, gazing up, he suddenly noticed something. A faint sliver of light. "Damn!"

"It will pass," she repeated.

"Naw, it's not that. There's a seam in the ceiling."

"That's nice, I suppose."

"Honey, it means there's an access panel! We can open it and get out of this box. I was a fool not to think of it before. We're going to live!"

"Oh!" She quivered, her breasts jogging his cheek. "I was set on dying, but now I want to live. Can we really get out?"

"Come on," he said, scrambling up. "I can't reach it, but I can boost you up to it."

She joined him, and he caught her by her thighs and heaved her up to his shoulder, setting her bare bottom there. She braced her feet against his chest and put one arm around his head to steady herself. This brought her left breast up against his head, and gave him a renewed erection. Because it was an accidental contact, not one she intended.

She reached up, slid the panel aside, and in a moment light poured down into the elevator. "Escape!" she cried, and reached up into the square hole with both hands. Soon she was scrambling up through it.

"Come on," she called. "There's a floor within reach."

But Joe was assessing the situation. "That panel didn't open the whole way."

"I know. It's jammed. I had to scrape off a bit of skin to squeeze through." Then she saw his point. "You won't fit!"

"That's what you said before," he said ruefully. "But unless you can jam that farther open, it's no good for me."

She tried, but could not. "Maybe I can get a tool or something."

"And maybe you'll dislodge the elevator, and the thing will plunge to the basement with me in it."

"Oh, Joe—what can I do?"

"You can go get help. But first get dressed. You don't want to be running around the building naked."

"That's right," she agreed. "I forgot."

"I'll pass up your clothes." He did so, holding them high so she could reach down to grab them. "But look, honey—don't tell them you were in here with me."

"Why not?"

"They might come to an evil conclusion. Such as that we were fucking."

She laughed. "I appreciate your point. Actually we haven't finished that business. Maybe I should come down again."

"Don't do that! We don't know how long this thing will hang here. Find help, tell them you heard a man caught in an elevator and tell them where. Then get the hell out of the building. That'll save your reputation, and my hide."

"Got it." She paused, then put her face down into the hole. "In case we don't see each other again, I love you, Joe. You have done so much for me."

He laughed. "Get outta here, gal."

Then she was gone, and he wondered what she had meant. Now that he was alone, it didn't seem like a joke. She had given him his best sex of the year, but he hadn't given her anything in return. She had also comforted him when the pressure got to him. He might love her, but she had no call to love him.

He got dressed, made sure there was no evidence of their activity, and waited. She wouldn't leave him here to die, would she? That would sure keep her secret!

Then there were sounds above. "Here it is! Hey, anybody in there?"

"Yo!" Joe called.

"Girl said she heard someone in the elevator, but she couldn't help him. How you doing?"

"Great, now!"

They pried the panel the rest of the way across and dropped a cable to haul him up and out. There was no sign of the girl. She had made her escape, leaving only the fantastic memory of her with him.

* * * *

Six months later, Joe was taking his break before the last haul of the day. There was a mound of garbage to be 'dozed into the pit. The other workers were joshing him as usual. "Maybe you'll uncover that elevator with that gal in it," one said. "The one who gave you your greatest fuck."

He should never have bragged about his two hours of scared bliss with the white girl. They didn't believe him and wouldn't let it rest. Yet he had had to brag; it was all he had left of her. He did love her in his fashion. He wished he had told her that, instead of trying to laugh it off. She had not said a word after that. Maybe he had hurt her feelings.

"Look at that car!" another worker exclaimed. "What a honey."

They all looked. "Ferrari," another said. "A bright red one. Must be worth two hundred G. What's it doing here?"

"He's sure not going to trash it," another said.

The car stopped at the foreman's station. A svelte young woman got out. They stared as she approached the foreman, talked with him, and passed something to him. Then he pointed toward Joe's group.

The woman nodded and set off on foot. "She's coming here!" a man exclaimed. They all stared, amazed.

She was a stunning blonde, sleek and slender, moving with the inherent feminine grace of her kind. She was wearing classy blouse, skirt, and makeup. Jewelry sparkled on her wrists. Her dainty dressy sandals made her feet look tiny as they navigated the packed earth of the temporary trail. Her perfectly formed breasts quivered slightly under her light blouse as she walked. She was even more out of place here than her fabulous car. What was going on?

She arrived, like an angel descending to a pit of hell. They did not even pretend to work; she compelled their attention just by her presence. They were a circle of stout black men gazing on a shining vision from heaven.

"There you are, Joe!" she exclaimed. "Did you forget our date? I had to come fetch you."

Joe's jaw dropped. Could it possibly be?

"Honey," he breathed.

She came up and took his arm. "Come on, Joe. The foreman says it's all right. I've got big plans for us today."

He remained dumbfounded. The pimples and extra pounds were gone. She looked like a movie starlet. Why had she come here?

"You sure?" he asked, unable to believe it.

"Don't play dumb with me, Joe." She turned to the others. "Joe's my man, the best lover I ever had. I met him in an elevator during the quake, and he took care of me. He taught me everything." She tugged on his arm. "Come on, my pad's waiting. I have food and wine and everything."

"But I'm filthy," he said stupidly.

"So I'll wash you in the shower. That'll be fun, won't it! That elevator didn't have a shower. Come on."

One of the staring men stirred himself. "But we need you for the 'dozer, Joe. You're the best man on it. We got a mountain to move."

Honey let go of his arm and approached the man. Now Joe saw her petite rear, outlined seductively under the close skirt as she walked. "I need Joe right now," she murmured to the man. "You don't mind, do you?"

"But the dozer— "

She kissed him on the cheek, her diamond earrings glinting. "*Do* you?"

That silenced him, as the others laughed appreciatively. What man could ever resist a blonde angel?

Honey returned to Joe and guided him

possessively toward the Ferrari.

Joe heard them talking excitedly as he departed. "The bastard was tellin' the truth!"

"Naw, he didn't do her credit. She's twice the doll he said"

"Billionaire bitch." It was a compliment.

Honey squeezed Joe's arm, smiling.

"They're right, you know," Joe said. "You're like the Star of Bethlehem shining over a dirty stable. What happened?"

"I followed your advice, Joe. I got outside, into the forest. I hiked everywhere. It changed me, just as you said. And not just outside."

"Outside?" He still could not quite take in the magnitude of her transformation.

"The outside of me. The inside of me changed more. I'm going to college, Joe. I'll major in forestry. Forests are our major threatened natural resource; they need to be preserved. That's the good I'm going to do for the world: saving the trees. 'In wildness is the preservation of the world'. You showed me how to realize my dream."

"I didn't even know it. But it's great for you."

"But first I made amends, as we agreed. I told my parents how I broke the vase. My sister cried, and so did I, but it was good. It was an incubus off my back."

"I did too. The store said they had no records that far back, but insurance would have covered it. Seems they allow for damage and thievery as part of normal loss. They wouldn't take the money. So I gave it to the United Negro College Fund, and they said I was a good man. Maybe it will help some black kid make good. It was a load off my mind."

"So we did each other some good, with that agreement."

"We sure did, honey."

They reached the car. "I rented this for the afternoon. I don't own it. Don't tell."

He laughed. "I can tell the world I fucked you, but not how you rented a car."

"Correct," she agreed, smiling. "I have an image to maintain. Now kiss me, so your friends can see." For of course his crew mates were still watching.

"You sure?" But she was already stepping into him. He enfolded her and kissed her. Her lips met his eagerly. "Oh, honey, you're a dream."

"I mean to be. Did I do it right?"

Then he caught on. "My fifteen minutes of fame! You remembered. Classy white gal clinging to me, with everyone seeing."

"Exactly. I owe you at least that much."

"You don't owe me nothing! You already gave me twice as much as I ever deserved."

"Did I change your life significantly?"

"Naw. I'll always be a dumpster. That's all I'm cut out for, and it's not bad. But the memory of your tight cunt—that'll be with me forever."

"You changed mine. You gave me my first passion, and told me how to improve my body and my outlook. I'm glad for our elevator encounter."

They got in the car. "Buckle up," she reminded him as she did so.

"You can drop me off anywhere. You gave me what you came for. I don't know how to thank you."

The engine surged into life. The Ferrari felt like a

panther on the prowl for something to consume. It picked its way out of the dump area, then leaped forward on the highway. "Joe, I'm not letting you go until we're done."

He hardly dared believe. "You really do want to fuck again?"

"I really do. This time you will take me to orgasm and show me how to pretend when I need to. That was our bargain, as I recall."

"When we thought we'd die. But now we're alive. Honey, if your folks see a black man go in your pad, he'd better be there to fix a clogged sink or something."

"I rented the room, too, for this purpose, using a nom de plume. Others will assume I'm a common prostitute."

"They'll think you're a whore!" he agreed, laughing. "And I'm your pimp."

"We are both anonymous. Only your friends at the dump will know the truth."

"The truth? Honey—"

"That I just had to have you." She glanced at him. "You have a problem with that?"

Then he caught on, again. "You already learned how to fake it! To make me feel good."

"I do feel I owe you," she agreed. "But it is more than that. You are the one man I can be candid with about sex. Teach me what I need to know, including how to fool any other man when I want to."

"I'll sure try, honey," he promised.

"When I told you I loved you, you did not take me seriously."

"I thought you were joshing me. Then I

wondered. You sure got to me, honey. But a classy white girl just don't love a poor black man."

"You are the first man to truly desire me. The first and only one to have sexual intercourse with me. It has to be love, because otherwise it's God's trial that I failed."

"What are you talking about?"

"People are given leeway to sin if they're going to. Sex without love is a sin."

"God don't work that way, honey! He loves the sinner too. Nobody knows His ways, is all."

"So I concluded. Because my encounter with you did change my life. I have a purpose now. I'm not depressive any more. God put us together for a reason, and now I understand it. But it's unfair to use you without giving something back."

"Honey — "

She steered the car to a side road, and thence to a secluded spot among trees. "I can't wait any more. Do it now."

"Do it?"

She ripped open her blouse, tore off her push-up bra, and showed her bare breasts. "Fuck me, in your vernacular. We'll still go to my apartment for a more leisurely series; we do have the afternoon and evening. But I need it at this moment."

"But I'll spout the moment I get in you! That won't give you what you want."

"Yes it will. Instant passion." She hauled up her skirt, lifted her legs wide apart, and drew aside her panties. Her thighs were marvelously fleshed and conducive, and the blond hair lightly furring her cleft made it the prettiest he had seen. "Get in me, now!"

"You got it, honey! I never saw a sexier snatch."

"All that hiking developed my legs."

"It sure did!" He lunged for her, ripping open his fly and bringing out his rigid member. The position was awkward, as they were half straddling the seat, but possible. He guided the head to the tight opening, thrusting hard into the paradise of her slick channel while she clung to him and kissed his neck.

His climax came almost instantly. To his amazement, so did hers. "Oh! Oh!" she cried as her vagina squeezed him rhythmically. "Glorious! Jesus Christ Almighty!"

That was when he knew she was faking her orgasm; she was copying his exclamation. He would compliment her on her demonstration, in due course. He would be the first and last man to know when she was pretending. That was part of what he owed her.

But he also owed her the truth. "Honey, I got to tell you. You're still depressive. It makes you do crazy things."

"Oh? How?"

"Like in the elevator. You came on to me to fuck you, and I did. Sure, you thought we were going to die, but then you came out to the dump to fetch me. That was a crazy risk, dressed like that out here with these roughnecks. Any one of them could have grabbed you and screwed you silly and thrown you into the pit to be buried in garbage. Don't get me wrong; you did great, and I loved it. But it was crazy. You gotta see that."

"Perhaps," she said guardedly.

"Then you fuck me right here in the car, when

anybody could come see, without even a rubber. You're riding the thin edge, daring fate to wipe you out. You ain't really changed. I loved the fuck, and even that you faked it for me, but you're crazy."

She did not deny it. "You may be partially right. There remains that element in me, and I don't mean just your ejaculate. But I do owe you, and I did want to see you again and finish our business. Consider this my final crazy fling, my last venture beyond the pale, before I get serious with my life. I changed because of you, and it is fitting that you be the one to participate."

She was making some sense. But there was one other thing. "You know we'll never see each other again after today," he said as they relaxed and started to put themselves back together. "You'll go away to college, and I'll return to the dump. We'll be quits. This is just for now."

She nodded. "I did not want to put it that way. We do not have a future together. Some relationships are temporary by their very nature, but not necessarily invalid simply because of that. I will never forget you. I just wanted to—to give you a really nice parting gift. Because of what you did for me."

"Honey, you're doing that. I really like it. My—my dream is just not as big as yours. You made it, for me. It'll be the talk of the dump for months. I'll be a big man."

"Thank you, but you're already a big man. Very." She looked relieved. He was sure she did want to learn about sex, and trusted him to teach her, but the rest of it was make-believe.

"Now we got that clear, I can say it. Honey, I love you too, you crazy hot-panted little bitch."

She froze for an instant. Then she laughed, and kissed him. "Turnabout—fair play," she said as she started the car moving. "We understand each other. We have one hot farewell afternoon coming. I expect to enjoy it almost as much as you will."

"Yeah." He was already getting hard again.

* * * *

The idea for this story occurred to me when there was news of people getting stuck in elevators at the time of the Hurricane Katrina New Orleans crisis, and I summarized it September 12, 2005. I am subject to constant chains of thought, which can form into stories, like flowers blooming from dull vines, and I save them if they seem worthy. I changed the locale so that the crisis could occur without warning; it's probably in California. I try not to specify any more than I have to, so that people anywhere in the world can more readily relate, but there are only so many cities built on earthquake zones.

The dump site derives from a more local experience. My wife and I drove out to the county dump to donate old computer monitors and printers, and I was struck by the scale of the operation. It's not just a pit where you toss things in; there is restricted access with a line of cars being directed to the correct sections. The complex is like a major construction zone, which I suppose it is. Anything I experience is grist for my creative mill, even a dump.

You may have noticed that Honey (who is never actually named) and Joe speak different dialects. One criticism of an uncertain writer is that his characters all talk the same. Mine don't. But what I know of black worker dialogue is limited. I had to hark back to my two year stint in the US Army over 45 years ago for that, and it's quite possible that things have changed in the interim. My memory is hardly perfect, also. So probably I got it wrong in various respects, but I hope I have the essence right. Joe is a good guy, regardless how he talks, performing a necessary job.

Or you could simply say that when it came to dialogue, I faked it.

Downtime

He glanced at the chore board, verifying that today was downtime for him. He remained on ready reserve, but had no assignment at this time. He was a robustly handsome young man, muscular and alert. It came with the territory.

A young woman approached. She was a starlet-quality redhead. She glanced at the board and nodded, satisfied.

"Downtime?" he asked.

"Yes."

"Care to break together?"

She shrugged. "Why not?"

"I am Lance."

"Gloria." Both were their stage names, of course.

They walked together to the fitness complex. There, they stripped naked and dived into the pool, hitting the water together. They paced each other for two laps, then paused, breathing solidly.

"I don't recognize you," Lance said. "Have we interacted?"

"I doubt it. I transferred from Chicago two weeks ago and haven't had too many assignments here yet."

"I worked Chicago for two months last year. Then, on to Seattle, LA, and here."

"New York, Miami, Chicago. So we didn't overlap. Not that we'd likely remember."

"True. Assignments blur after a while."

They got out of the water and went to the communal lavatory, where they showered together, rinsed off, and dried. He used the urinal while she sat on the adjacent toilet. "They do blur," she agreed as she wiped herself. "Fortunately."

"Parasites," he said. "I can't wait until I retire."

"Which is the one thing about this business: you can retire at 30, rich enough to coast for sixty more years."

"If you invest it well," he agreed.

"What else? Waste it on riotous living?"

They both laughed.

They washed their hands, dressed, and moved in leisurely fashion to the game room. "Ping?" he asked.

"Pong," she agreed.

They picked up paddles and rallied, taking turns setting each other up for nice points, not keeping score. Then they moved on to the small golf course, played three holes without scoring them, and set the clubs aside. They took the exercise trail though the exotic garden, moving at an even four miles an hour.

"Do you plan on a retirement family?" he inquired.

"Yes, if I can find the right man."

"Would you marry a former host?"

"I don't think so. He'd know too much."

"That's my sentiment. I'll look for some halfway homely sweet-natured girl who believes sex is only for procreation and that a woman's place is in the home."

"Actually, I'd settle for that role."

They laughed again, understanding perfectly.

They came to an amusement park where tourists congregated. "Oh, a roller coaster," she said. "I didn't realize there was one here."

"Everything is here," he said. "We have free passes as long as we tag and mix with the tourists."

"No more anonymity," she said.

They went to the entry booth and got matching name tags: LANCE—HOST and GLORIA—HOSTESS. Each was paired, to be worn front and back. Now they attracted attention, which they ignored.

They got on the roller coaster, smiling as it made its scary dips and turns. Then they got on a boat and floated through the Tunnel of Love. They did not embrace or kiss, just continued their dialogue. "What's your worst hitch?" he asked.

"I was rented by a biker moll. She took me to their hangout. Fifteen males, fifteen fucks, each timed for three minutes so they wouldn't have to pay for extra time. The worst was the kisses and feels: whiskey and chewing tobacco breath, and their calloused hands were rough on my breasts. I had a sore vagina after those hard fucks, and a sore rectum too. But it paid quintuple the normal."

"And your best?"

"Rented by a prospective bride to see if her fiancé would stray with a lovely sex 'friend' on the make for him. He didn't, and I'm satisfied that he had no idea of the trap. He was a really nice guy, absolutely loyal to his girl. The kind I hope to marry some day."

"My worst was being rented by a woman, a butch, who wanted to experience a real man's sex with her girlfriend. The sex itself was fine—the girlfriend was choice—but the butch had weird emotions that nearly made me freak. I couldn't clear it after the hitch; it was making me impotent. So I contacted the girlfriend when she was alone. She recognized me, of course. I leveled with her, explaining that now I was speaking for myself. I begged her to have normal sex with me, so I could clear the contamination. She hesitated; she was a straight lesbian, not a bisexual, and the idea was a turnoff for her. 'Name your price,' I said. 'I'll give you anything in my power.' And she was such a nice person that she gave it to me free, pretending to like it. That cleared the contamination, but left me with guilt. I left her my card, owing her one at such time as she needs it."

"A lesbian," Gloria said. "I don't think I could stomach being rented by one of them."

"It may happen some day."

"It may," she agreed.

"My best was being rented by a gawky boy for his high school prom. His girlfriend helped pay for it. She didn't want sex or anything, just to have a snazzy date. I got to dance with all the pretty girls, who were thrilled for my attention. They were all well behaved and chaperoned. Except for a couple who got me alone for a moment behind a pillar. One kissed me ardently, then dissolved into giggles at her boldness. The other took my hand and slid it into her gown to feel her young breast. That was their idea of naughtiness."

"Quaint," Gloria agreed. "There's something refreshing about inexperience."

"And you know, that chaste kiss was the best I had all that month, and that nascent breast turned me on like a passion pill. Much of that was my client's feeling, but not all."

They were about to emerge from the Tunnel of Love. "We'll be viewed," she murmured.

"Oh. Right." He put his arms about her, faking passion, and withdrew as if guilty when they came into the light. She blushed becomingly, playing along.

They got on a ferris wheel, and several others came to fill it up. They were attracting attention, as they were supposed to. They were halted at the top while others were loaded.

"Damn," she said. "I itch. I think there's a wrinkle."

"You aren't that old yet."

"I mean in my condom. Can you check?" She lifted her skirt to her waist, exposing her crotch.

"I can." He put his head down, drew aside her panty, and ran his fingers over her vulva. "Yes." He hooked a finger into the edge of the transparent material of the female condom where it overlapped her pubic hair, and pulled it tight, eliminating the crease. "Got it."

"Thanks." She dropped her skirt back as the wheel started moving. "The new design is one-way, passing moisture out while letting none in. It's almost invisible, so the clients don't know it's there. But it can get kinked."

"Still, you wouldn't want to be without it. There's no telling what infections some of those freaks have."

"Especially the anal freaks," she offered wryly.

"That's the problem with being a host," he said. "You can't choose who rents you, or control what he does with your body. You're just along for the ride, and it can be some ride."

"Some ride," she agreed. "That's the main thing I don't like about this business. That feeling of losing control. It's like being in someone else's dream."

"Yet where else can you get pay like this?"

"Nowhere else. We put the high class call girls to shame."

"Because we do everything they do, and more," he said. "When the connection is made, the clients are actually in our minds, running our bodies as if they were their own. So they become instant super he-men, or female bombshells, with no effort on their part."

"No dieting, no exercise, no training in the latest sexual fads," she said. "They get it all, for a while, for a price."

"A formidable price. But at the end they have to return to their paunchy, flabby, unappealing bodies, coming out of suspended animation, and resume their pitiful little lives."

"With only the memory of being splendid for a few hours. They're parasites, and I hardly envy them."

"It's all so unnecessary. If they just took care of themselves, not only would they be more appealing, they'd live longer."

"And they wouldn't be our clients," she concluded.

The ferris wheel had stopped. They got off, carefully oblivious to the admiring glances they got from the paunchy, flabby, unappealing tourists.

Then both their earphones buzzed. They had to report immediately to the transfer office. They didn't even have to guess why.

"A couple," he said as they made for the office. "A couple saw us, and wants to rent us as a pair."

"That's why we have to go public. It's good for business. We're walking ads."

"We'll be fucking each other within the hour."

"Repeatedly," she agreed.

"But our downtime was nice while it lasted."

She took his hand and kissed the backs of his fingers lightly. "It was, Lance. Maybe we can do it again some time."

He gently squeezed her fingers. "Let's."

"It's so nice with no flirting, no sex, no hang-ups, and no expectations."

"And complete understanding."

She smiled in agreement. Then they were at the office. Business was business.

* * * *

When I checked my Idea File, this was the very first entry, undated. The following notions date from 1992, when I started the computer file. Before that, I typed them manually, and before that, I wrote them in pencil on bits of paper and stored them in old oatmeal boxes. Eventually I transferred the oatmeal box ideas to this file, but couldn't date the dateless ones. So I don't know how far back this story idea goes. Probably some time in the 1980s, possibly earlier.

So what is the point of this narrative? It's really just a slice of life, which is not normally the type of story I write. Well, the point is that for the folk who indulge the appetites of the masses, their idea of fun is not having to have more sex, score points, or impress their peers. They have no sexual or competitive interest in each other, though both are spectacular physical specimens. Their bodies are their business. Their pleasure is in being at ease with others who understand. In doing nothing at all.

Chessmaid

Pawna walked into the empty arena, as she thought of it. There were twenty tables with chessboards, the pieces set up ready for play. There was a camera over every board, to record the moves, and a hooded timing clock. There were also three remote-controlled cameras and lights focused on the center, where she stood. She was, of course, the center of attention. This was her big play, and not merely in chess.

She faced the main camera and nodded. The action light came on; she was now on closed-circuit television. The show was beginning.

She smiled. She had a good smile and knew it.

"My greeting to all. I am Pawna, mistress of chess. The game is my life, but I would like to have a suitable man in it too. One who shares my passion. Therefore I will marry the man who defeats me in chess, sight unseen. The clocks are covered, as there is a different deadline. Should more than one man beat me, the first one wins me. I trust no one will dawdle unduly." She smiled again, knowing there would be laughter elsewhere in the circuit.

She removed her shirt and bra, and stood bare breasted except for the descending strands of her long hair that outlined rather than concealed her curves. She knew she was a fine looking young woman of 25; that was part of the point of this exercise. She drew off her shoes, socks, skirt, and panties. Now she was completely nude. The pilotless cameras were taking it in from three angles, orienting on her motions. Pirated copies would quickly make their way from the private circuit into the worldwide web, attracting larger attention to this event. That, too, was part of the point. The World Chess Federation had been advised and made no objection; that was its way of granting tacit approval. This would have impact on global awareness of the game of chess, especially female participation. The Federation liked that.

Pawna produced a competent blindfold and fitted it over her face. "Admit the men," she said. "The floor is yours."

The voice of a male announcer came on. "Thank you, Pawna. It is a pleasure to see you." He paused briefly for the background appreciation of his pun, then grew serious. "The chess mistress has stripped nude and donned the blindfold, as you can see. She will now play simultaneous chess against twenty men. She is ranked number fifteen among female players, and number nine on the WCBC list. That is, she is the ninth most beautiful chess player in the world, according to the World Chess Beauty Contest site."

He paused again, giving the closed circuit audience time to appreciate the validity of the ranking. Pawna smiled and turned around in place, candidly showing off her body. It was after all her selling point. There were thousands of male players better than she in chess, but no prettier woman who could defeat her. She was depending on that rare combination to win a suitable man. Her beauty, after all, would not long survive the slow ravages of advancing age. Now was the time.

"There has been no problem filling the roster of opponents," the announcer continued after a suitable interval. "The only requirement is that they be single heterosexual males. It should help if they can play the game." He paused for audience laughter. It had not been necessary to screen in favor of high ranking players, or even to specify chess playing ability, as it would be pointless for a duffer to enter the tournament. However, the places had been allocated to the highest ranking players applying. Pawna had not inquired about their identity, but understood that no grandmasters were present. She was not sure whether to be annoyed or relieved. Most grandmasters were either married or uninterested, and not the type to sweep a girl off her feet romantically. In any event, they were too savvy to commit to a woman because of her appearance. Her opponents would be drawn from the lesser ranks, which meant she could readily take them. Even blindfolded in a simultaneous, multiple game tournament.

So the chances were that no man would defeat her today. Yet there was hope. Some excellent players were unranked, preferring to avoid the rigors of competition. They were in it solely for love of the game. She might have to stage another tournament, or a third, until she attracted the interest of a real player. Meanwhile, the events should do their part for the status of chess in the popular awareness.

She heard the shuffle of men entering the chamber and silently taking their places at the numbered chess boards. "Gentlemen," the announcer continued. "You will not speak unless Pawna addresses you as she comes to your board, and then you will confine yourselves to the subject she broaches. Violators will be summarily ejected. The tournament will now proceed."

"Board One, where are you?" Pawna asked, though she knew exactly where it was. Public events had to be clarified in more than one manner, because there were always viewers tuning in late, and some who could not necessarily see well.

"Here," a deep voice responded.

"Thank you." She went to that board. This would be the ranking chess player of this group, surely a master in his home locale. "Announce your move."

"Pawn to E4." All the challengers were White, with the first move. Pawna privately liked playing Black, being of mixed ancestry herself. Had that affected the turnout? She doubted it; more likely the better players were watching via the closed circuit, assessing the prospects should there be a second tournament.

"Pawn to E5," she replied immediately, and moved on, knowing that he would move it for her, in the special rules of this event. She could have found the place herself, as the chess board was like the back of her hand, but the verbal announcement made it easier to record.

"Move?" she inquired of the player as she came to Board Two.

"Knight to F3." An unconventional opening, though not unknown. He was trying to get her attention.

She smiled, made her response, and moved on.

The first round of moves was rapid, as most were standard. There was good reason for standard openings; they were the most effective. A player deviated at his own risk. It would probably not take her long to put F3 away. Getting her attention was worthless if he did not play a strong game.

The second and third rounds were similarly swift. Only when they got beyond the standards did individuality begin to show, and not much of that. Some players who might have developed promising lines of attack could have been distracted by her bare body and spoiled their chances; that was their misfortune. She had scant sympathy. Only the man who conquered her mind would have a chance at her body.

Soon opponents were resigning, and most who remained lacked the wit to resign; she mated them quickly and moved on. It was already apparent that none of the players were of high competition grade. They were simply not in her league. Barring some foolish mistake on her part, there would be no winner today. She was disappointed. But there would probably be stronger competition in the second tournament, as the real players came out of the woodwork.

Meanwhile, the announcer had news: "It has just been announced that Pawna, ranked number nine on the beauty scale, having shown her assets (as it were), has been advanced to number three."

There were stifled sounds in the room. "You may laugh," she said, smiling. They did, and some applauded. Actually, she had thought that her beauty ranking had been too low; that was one reason she had elected to perform nude. This way she showed that none of her "assets" owed anything to supportive clothing. That ploy had just paid off.

It came down to five, then three, then one, Board Number 20, supposedly the least qualified challenger. His position was abysmal, but he hung on doggedly.

"The end seems near," the announcer said. "We are going to open circuit for the finale."

So they could use the conclusion of the tournament as a pretext to show her nude to a global audience, with spot outtakes for the evening news programs. That would lead to much interest augmented by some conservative outrage. She did not object. She held her posture erect and breathed slightly more deeply for the cameras. The second tournament would have a wider audience from the start.

Still, she no longer needed to move around the circle of tables, and she had shown the cameras enough. "May I sit?" she inquired.

"Welcome, Pawna," he replied.

She got a chair from one of the other sets and sat opposite him. She heard the cameras dollying around to get better angles. One was almost under the table, orienting on her legs and lower torso. She did not put her knees together; let it see what it could see. She focused on the game.

She had two rooks and four pawns. Her

opponent was down to one knight, one bishop, and four pawns. She set about cutting him down, but somehow he managed to escape her ploys, playing with uncanny insight. Every time she took one of his pawns, he took one of hers. When she had a chance to trap his bishop, he countered with a position that would cost her a rook in exchange. She had to abandon that ploy. But her victory was inevitable; her two rooks were too strong a force.

They got down to two pawns apiece, then one. Then none. She was sorry to lose her last, as she was a strong pawn player, as her chosen name suggested. More than one opponent had lost his contempt for the power of the pawn, along with the game. But she retained the clear advantage.

Except that he continued to maneuver his pieces in nearly miraculous ways, repeatedly countering her initiatives almost before she developed them. She had never seen such clever use of the knight and bishop combination. It made them nearly the equal of her two rooks. That was remarkable, because she was no duffer; she could use her rooks as efficiently as anyone in chess.

"What is this?" she asked at last. "How can you play so well now, yet so poorly before?"

"It would not have been fair to play with full competence while you were distracted by nineteen other players."

"I took them all," she retorted. "Readily."

"Readily," he agreed as he countered yet another thrust.

It was clear that this was one of the unranked but thoroughly competent players. His defensive plays were verging on genius. "You might well have defeated me, had you played like this at the outset."

"I would not have cared for that victory."

Now she was really curious. What was his larger game? It seemed to be something other than either chess or victory. Yet what else was there, in this situation?

Then she recognized the pattern. She had never before played against it, but she had studied the masters. "Segmoy is dead!" she exclaimed.

"But not his son."

She ripped off her blindfold, which had become pointless at this stage, and gazed at him. There was a favor; he did resemble the picture of the late grandmaster. He was young, within three years of her own age, and halfway handsome.

"My father played your father, and lost," she said. "He had underestimated the potency of the interacting knight and bishop in the late game. He said it was his worst mistake as a grandmaster, and he never made it again. He said he should have had the hint when Segmoy named his son Knight Bishop."

"Perhaps," Knight agreed.

"But Segmoy died before they could rematch."

"And then your father died also," he agreed. "I appreciate your grief. Both went before their times."

"I need another man in my life, since I lost him," she agreed. "A chess man."

"Of course."

They continued to play, but she could not pursue her advantage to checkmate. She needed to eliminate one of his pieces, but could do it only at the cost of one of her rooks. A single rook would not be enough against this opponent.

Finally she gave it up. "Draw?" she offered, expecting him to decline.

"Agreed."

"Wait. You know that only your victory will require me to marry you."

"Yes."

"So you have nothing to lose by fighting on. A draw is the same as a loss, for this purpose. Perhaps I will make a mistake."

"I doubt it."

"Then why did you enter this tournament? I am the only prize."

"And a valuable one. I fear I love you already, and not entirely for your beauty. I have been aware of you since our fathers played."

"And I of you, to a lesser degree. I did not know you played chess, let alone at this level."

"I learned well from my father, but have never sought notoriety. I merely live for the game."

"You could have taken me had you played well throughout, instead of crippling yourself. I withdraw my offer of a draw."

"I have already accepted it."

She glanced at the overhead camera. "Do I have to accept it?"

There was a pause. Then the announcer responded. "By the rules of this tournament, which you approved, you proffered a draw. He accepted it. The chess game is a draw."

She sighed. "Then close your circuit. The game has been decided."

"Not yet," the announcer said.

She focused on Knight. "You knew you could not beat me with that handicap."

"True."

"Then why? I must know."

"I prefer to marry for choice, not necessity."

"So you brought yourself to my attention, but left me my choice."

"Yes."

"You think I will fall into your arms from gratitude?"

"No. You are an admirably independent woman."

She glanced again at the camera. "This is why you remain on open circuit? To witness the taming of the shrew?"

"To witness the completion of the game," the announcer said.

Pawna pondered briefly. She was accustomed to making decisions by the clock; she did not need much time. This was a good man who wanted more than a coup. He wanted a willing partner, rather than a captive woman. What were the chances that she would find a better one, with a better attitude, all things considered?

She made her decision quickly. "Then I shall do the sensible thing. Yes, I wall marry you, Knight Bishop Segmoy." Then she leaned across the table, one breast almost knocking over his king, and kissed him.

There was the sound of sustained applause and cheering from the television audience. They had seen the true game's conclusion, and were satisfied. So was she.

* * * *

I got the idea for this story on December 15, 2005, as I read a newspaper article about the beauty ratings of female chess players. There really is a World Chess Beauty Contest. is intended to promote women's chess, and I suspect it is succeeding. Some lovely players have web sites where they sell pictures of themselves, and some do pose nude. Why not take it the next step?

Could such a tournament happen in real life? A lovely woman playing on her beauty to win a suitable man? I hope so.

Doll

Belinda was fetching the mail for herself and her roommates when the boy approached her. She recognized him: Clive, one of three who shared a room down the hall. She had one class with him; he was dull in person but quite bright in class, a real nerd. He tended to stutter when excited.

"Pl-please, may I t-t-talk to you? I'm C—Cl—"

"Clive," she filled in helpfully. "You live down the hall from us."

"Y-Yes. S-something important. Can we—?"

"Talk?" The psychologists said it wasn't nice to fill in words for stutterers, but psychologists evidently had more time to spare than college students did. Clive never stuttered in class; evidently he felt more competent there than when talking to a girl. Even an unlovely girl like Belinda. He surely had no more social life than she did.

"Yes. P-please."

Now she was curious. She tucked the mail in her purse. "Five minutes? I've got a class."

"I'll m-make it fast."

They took seats in the common room. Belinda realized that he would never get his case made, whatever it was, if she didn't help him. "You have something important. What is it?"

"The d-d-d-doll."

She was surprised. "What would you ever want with a doll? Those are for little girls."

"A b-b-big doll. L-l— "

"Life sized?"

"Yes." And he was blushing.

Now she got it. "A life-sized anatomically correct model of a woman? One you can, shall we say, interact with?"

His blush became furious. That was answer enough.

Belinda was interested despite her aversion. "And this concerns me because?" She did not point out the obvious: that she might be an anatomically correct girl, but too plain to attract any male interest. The doll would be far more comely in face and feature than she was, and surely more sexually amenable. She understood that inflatable dolls were popular with college boys. They never said no.

He fumbled in a pocket and pulled out a folded piece of paper. He shoved it at her.

She looked at it. It was a printout from an Internet ad. Someone was selling an "android"—a full-sized androgynous model of a human being, with attachments to make it become male or female. It had been damaged in transit, so was being sold cut-rate without a warranty.

"The p-price," Clive said, pointing to the figure.

Belinda's jaw almost dropped. This was a two thousand dollar item, on sale for two hundred dollars: ten percent. As sales went, that was phenomenal.

She glanced up. "So you have a bargain. But

what has this to do with me?"

"We have only o-one hundred d-dollars between us. And the sale ends t-today."

She nodded. "And you want to borrow the rest from us."

"N-no. To go h-halves."

The five minutes was up, but this remained intriguing. "Why should we want any part of this?"

"C-call your r-roommates."

Belinda shrugged and dug out her cell phone. She touched the menu for her roommate Fern, whom she knew was home at the moment, and got her immediately. "Fern, do we want half of a life sized anatomically correct android doll at a bargain rate?"

"Is that Andy Android?"

"Andy?" Belinda repeated.

Clive nodded vigorously. "Andrew/Anna."

"Yes, it's Andy. Damaged, on sale for $200, and we can have half for $100."

"Take it!"

"But what use would we ever have for—"

"Don't argue, Linda! Take it! I saw the promo on that model months ago. It's a dreamboat. There'll never be another bargain like that."

"But the money—"

"We can make a hundred between us, can't we?"

"Yes, but—"

"Take it! Trust me. I'll tell Daisy."

Belinda shook her head, bemused. "She says we're in. Let me go to our apartment to fetch the money."

"That's great!" He looked pitifully relieved.

They went to the apartment she shared with

Fern and Daisy. It was in sight of the door for the three boys. They were all off-campus college kids, sharing lodgings for economy. She got the money and handed it to him. She didn't ask for any receipt or signed deal; kids who knew each other didn't. "You take care of the details, okay?"

"Okay!" He hurried to his own apartment.

Belinda sighed. What had they gotten into? Fern had some tall explaining to do.

* * * *

The three boys went to the local outlet and picked up the Doll, as they now thought of it, that night. It was boxed, but they could see that the lower portion of the box had been crushed and torn partly open. No parts had been lost, but the operating instructions were gone and one leg was cracked. Definitely damaged goods.

"But a bargain nevertheless," Edgar said. "We don't need that leg."

"Remember, we have to share with the girls," Clive reminded him.

"We'll break it in this weekend, and let the girls have it next weekend," Glenn said. "It'll work out.

"If *you* ask them," Clive said. Because Glenn was the handsome one. He could twist the average girl around his finger and was sexually experienced.

"I will. Now let's get it in operation."

There was a warning notice posted on the box. "ADVISORY: this unit has been damaged in transit and may malfunction. It is deemed safe to use but may provide less than optimal performance. Call 1-555-555-5555 for service."

"Less than optimal?" Edgar asked. "Is it going to

short out in the middle of a fuck?"

Clive winced. Edgar tended to be crude-tongued, which was why they had elected Clive to approach the girls, difficult as that had been for him. He rather liked Belinda, who was smart, which made it worse.

"It says 'safe to use,' Ed," Glenn reminded him. "Probably some commands have been lost, is all."

They got it out of the box, laid it on a bed, and considered the attachments. The main unit was sexless, possessing head, arms, legs, and a torso. But the face was a blank plate, and the midsection was a blank hollow metal column. Sexless? It wasn't even human.

Clive considered the packaged attachments. "Okay, this box is faces. One face on each side, male and female. It should plug in here." He put the male face side to the plate, so the female side faced outward and pushed it into place. There was a click as it connected. Now the android had a girl's features.

"Anna," Edgar said approvingly.

Clive opened the crotch box. This was much larger, and contained six attachments: three male and three female.

"Look at those!" Glenn said with admiration.

For the three male crotches had three different sizes of penis: a small, uncircumcised one under five inches long, a circumcised six-incher, and an uncircumcised seven-incher. All attachments were shaped to wrap around the torso and snap into place, the limp penises to the front.

"We'll leave those for the girls," Glenn said. "We

want the beavers."

These also wrapped around to snap on the torso. One was slender hipped with a small bottom; one was medium, being fuller in both hips and buttocks; the third was large in both respects. All had small internal drainage tubes attached to plastic bags that could be detached for cleaning, and apertures for oil reservoirs for lubrication. He found the oil and squeezed a dollop into her nether orifice.

"What an ass!" Edgar said admiringly as Clive held up the largest.

"Well, put it on, dolt," Glenn said.

Clive wrapped it around and found the connections. Then he wrestled with the chest units, which also came in three sizes: B-cup, C-cup, and D-cup. He didn't need to ask what the others wanted; he put on the largest, snapping it together behind like a bra strap.

Finally he sorted though the package of wigs: short-haired for the male, long-haired for the female, straight blonde, wavy brunette, and curly redhead. They tried all three, and decided on the blonde.

Anna was now complete in naked splendor, a generously endowed sleeping beauty with one bad leg.

"But she can't just sleep," Glenn said. "She's supposed to seem alive."

"This must be the power unit," Clive said, digging it out of the box. "Remote control, as I find no physical switches on her."

"No switches on that box, either," Edgar pointed out.

"Voice controlled," Glenn said. "That's what it

said in the ad."

"But we don't know the commands."

"So we'll find them. She's supposed to be intuitive, user friendly."

Clive plugged in the power unit. Nothing happened. The android just lay on the bed.

Then they noticed something: the android's chest was slowly expanding and contracting. Anna was breathing! Obviously she did not need to, being a machine, but for realism it was required. It enhanced her breasts, which quivered slightly with the motions. They watched for a while, fascinated. She certainly resembled a naked sleeping woman.

"Hey, wake up, Doll," Glenn said, shaking her shoulder. "Hey! She's warm!"

Anna opened her lovely sky-blue eyes and gazed at the ceiling. She had awakened on command.

"Well, now," Edgar said, satisfied. "She's warm. She breathes. What else does she do?"

"Kiss," Glenn said.

Anna's mouth moved in a pursing, kissing expression.

"So who wants to kiss her first?" Edgar asked. As he spoke, Anna kissed the air again.

"Would a malfunction make her bite?" Clive asked nervously.

"Hell no," Edgar said. "More likely it'd just make her mush-lipped."

"So you try her first," Clive said.

"Um." Edgar did not look eager.

"I will," Glenn said. He leaned down over the bed, put his face close, and repeated, "Kiss." Then he pressed his mouth to that of the android.

Clive and Edgar held their breaths. This was a breakthrough moment. Maybe.

Glenn lifted his head. "Wow! She's some kisser!" Then he put his head down again to catch the next kiss.

After him, the others took their turns. They had to agree; Anna was a great kisser. Clive was especially impressed because he had never been kissed by a girl, and this seemed real. The android had evidently been programmed to do it right.

"But we didn't get her just for that," Glenn said. "Now for the screwing."

"Who first?" Edgar asked nervously.

"You, if you want to."

"Not me!" Edgar protested. "I never had sex." His foul mouth had faded with the challenge of actually performing.

"Neither have I," Clive said.

"Well, you'll get it with Anna. But I guess I'll have to break her in." Glenn loosened his belt, dropped his trousers, and removed his briefs. He already had an erection. He was plainly eager for this. "Watch and learn."

They watched as Glenn bestrode the android. There was a drop of fluid at the tip of his penis. He used his hand to place it at Anna's crotch, which had light pubic hair and the start of a nether crease.

But her legs were together, closing off access. "This sucks," he complained, drawing himself up, his face passing hers.

Anna pursed her mouth and began sucking on his nose.

Clive and Edgar stared. Then they burst out laughing. "We've found another command!" Edgar said as Glenn jerked his head back, cursing. The sucking stopped.

"Suck? But what's it for?" Clive asked.

Edgar just looked at him. Clive blushed, catching on.

"Spread 'em," Glenn ordered. And her legs spread. "That's more like it." He guided his penis to the crevice, found the place, and pushed it in between the labia.

The other two watched closely. This looked exactly like sex with a real woman. Clive was getting an erection and was sure Edgar was too.

Glenn drove in all the way. The sight of his member disappearing into that crevice was phenomenally exciting. "Fuck," he said. "She's too big inside. I need more squeeze."

Anna's hips started bucking.

"Fuck!" Edgar exclaimed. "You said fuck! She's fucking you."

"And getting tighter," Glenn said. "Now I can make it." He thrust, and thrust again, and in moments was gasping as he climaxed. "She's—some—fucker!"

The android's pelvis motions had ceased. Now they resumed vigorously, because of the word. "Damn!" Glenn said as he pulled free of her to spare his fading member.

Clive and Edgar were laughing again. This was one literal-minded Doll, good for only one thing, but very good at that. Except for the possible malfunction. Clive wished they knew more about that. Yet he knew he would take his turn having sex with Anna; he was too worked up to do otherwise. She looked so much like a real woman, but she was not; that was what made it possible for him.

"My turn," Edgar said, getting out of his clothing. His penis was already standing tall.

Clive got to work on the Doll, changing her bosom and groin to the middle units. Glenn took the detached firmware and brought it to the sink for washing. Soon Anna was ready again, less generous of form but still every inch a naked woman.

Edgar gazed at her, now hanging back. "I don't know."

"You're getting a second thought," Glenn said. "That's normal. Ignore it."

"But she's so much, like, alive. She's even breathing."

"That's the point," Clive reminded him. "She's supposed to be just like a real girl."

"Now that scares me."

"Come off it," Glenn said. "I mean, get on it."

"I know what you mean," Clive said. "I want it something awful, but actually doing it—that's hard."

"What's hard needs to shove into what's soft," Glenn said impatiently. "Come on, flex your courage and—"

He broke off, for Anna was moving. She hoisted her two legs up and held them in a V over her body, her crotch fully exposed. The three of them stared.

"Flex!" Glenn said. "I said flex, and it's a position. We've got another command."

"Can it be done like that?" Edgar asked dubiously.

"Sure, it's a great position. Tightens up the ass. Just climb on."

Edgar climbed on, resting his hips against the raised thighs. "God, it feels great," he said.

"It ain't even in yet," Glenn said. "Get on with it. Dip your stick."

Edgar used one hand to guide his member. It slid down the crevice and lodged at the base. He pushed it on in and lay supported on Anna's thighs and torso. "Wow!"

Clive's thought echoed the expression. Wow! This was as good as a sex video. Better, really. The anatomy was so, well, real.

"Now pump it," Glenn said. "Make her feel your power."

"I want to kiss her first."

"You're stalling."

"Kissing is part of it," Clive said. "Like feeling her breasts."

"Say, yeah," Edgar agreed. He lifted his upper torso enough to free his hands, and closed them on the breasts. "Oh, great!"

This was exciting Clive more than the entry had. There was something about breasts.

"I'm coming!" Edgar exclaimed.

"You aren't even thrusting," Glenn said, disgusted.

Edgar dropped his head and fastened his mouth on Anna's mouth. "Kiss," Clive said helpfully.

Edgar's body shook with the force of his climax. He continued kissing Anna throughout. That, too, excited Clive. Straight in and out sex was one thing, but the associated fondling and kissing enhanced it immeasurably, making it seem more authentic. His penis was painfully stiff, caught in his pants.

Edgar lay there for some time, subsiding. "That's the best fuck I ever had," he said.

"That's the *only* fuck you ever had," Glenn retorted as Anna went into her hip-bucking routine.

"Still the best," Edgar said, hastily disengaging. "Thank you, Anna. My tongue can't express the joy you have given me." He returned to the kiss.

Then his head shot up. "What happened?" Clive asked, alarmed.

"She tongued me!"

"Another command," Glenn said and the android extended her tongue again. "I'll be damned."

"Don't say that word!" Edgar said. "It might be a command."

"It wasn't before." Still, Glenn was thoughtful. "But maybe we'd better watch our language around her, just in case."

Edgar got off, and Clive tackled the firmware again. In isolation it was just plastic and padding. Only when properly attached to the torso did it come to life as the sexual portion of a seemingly living Doll. He put on the smallest set, because that was all that remained clean and dry.

"You get stuck with the bitty titties," Edgar remarked. "Sorry about that."

"Actually, they look okay," Clive said. "I was never partial to the pregnant cow look." Indeed, the breasts were large enough, and nicely shaped, while there was a similar appeal to the slender but still quite feminine midsection.

However, there was a problem: Anna remained

in the flex position. Her midsection was flexible enough to be changed regardless, and he had done it. The open exposure of her cleft remained exciting, but Clive preferred to start normal.

"There should be a reverse command," Glenn said.

"Straight," Edgar said experimentally.

The legs came smoothly down to rest again on the bed. Good enough. "Just don't say—that—when one of us is in the middle of a fu—function," Clive said.

"I don't know," Glenn said. "Might be quite an experience."

It was Clive's turn. Anna was ready and loaded. He got out of his clothing, got on the bed with her—and his erection faded to nothing. "Shit," he muttered, then froze, afraid it might be a command. But Anna did not react.

"Stage fright," Edgar said. "I started to get it too, but got in her before it messed me up."

"She's just so much like a real woman," Clive said, frustrated. "I'm afraid she'll laugh at me, or something."

Now Glenn was atypically understanding. "It happens. Just lie on her a while, kiss her, feel her boobs, whatever, and it will pass. In fact, you can put it in limp, and maybe it will stiffen inside her. Whatever works."

Clive tried it. He kissed the mouth, and it kissed back deliciously on command. He kissed the breasts, and they were marvelously soft and evocative. His member began to recover. He got in position and fed it into the vagina, and that felt so good that it hardened further. But it still wasn't a full erection.

"Maybe you need more squeeze," Glenn suggested.

The vagina contracted around his penis. "Another command!" Clive said, gratified. "Squeeze. She's doing it."

He thrust, but his member still was not fully hard, and the motion seemed to lack force.

"I got it," Glenn said. "Put your legs outside hers, and have her close on you. That tightens it."

Anna's legs started to move, evidently responding to the command "close." Clive hastily got his legs outside. Now he was somewhat in the position of a woman, his crotch open, her thighs inside. But the connection remained, and Glenn was right; it was deliciously tight.

Clive thrust, and now he felt the slippery friction—no oxymoron!—of the channel. His member swelled to full erection. He thrust again, and then his orgasm was upon him. Jet after jet surged into that divine chamber, pressuring irresistibly. He felt as if he were a steam engine shoving the cylinder out with the sheer force of his ejaculation.

"God!" he breathed, collapsing on Anna. She had certainly delivered for him. He felt as if he loved her.

* * * *

The second weekend the girls got the Doll.

"R-remote control, v-voice activated," Clive told Belinda. "J-just plug in the power unit. She warms and breathes and kisses and—"

"Kisses?"

"Yes. And other things. You have to think of likely commands; we've figured out only a few."

"We'll work on it," Belinda said. "Thank you."

"Really, she's great! I mean—"

"I suspect I get the picture."

"But don't say f—f—"

"The F-word? What happens?"

"S-she does. She bucks. So don't—unless you w-want her to."

"We'll be careful," Belinda said, intrigued.

He departed, blushing. Obviously the boys had had a time with the living Doll. But could it possibly be worth it for the girls? The mere availability of a naked man was not necessarily a turn-on for a woman.

It was interesting exploring the parts. They put on the male face and short black hair. They fastened the masculine chest in place. Then they considered the groin.

"Three sizes!" Fern exclaimed. "We'd better start with the smallest."

"You speak as if we're actually going to—to use this thing," Belinda said, staring at the three sizes of penis with morbid fascination. She felt like a bird meeting the gaze of a hungry snake.

"Look, girls," Fern said reasonably. "We've sworn off boys for this semester. All they ever want is one thing, and if they don't get it, pffftt! and they're gone. And if they do get it, they think they own you, and want it twice a day. We don't need them."

"What has this to do with Andy Android?" Belinda asked, though she suspected the answer.

"With Andy we won't need any boys. He will take care of all our sexual needs. Once we get him humping."

"*What* sexual needs?" Belinda demanded. "I never had sex and never missed it."

"And I had it only once," Daisy said. "It was awkward, it hurt, and I was sore after. Then he dumped me. I don't need more of that."

"That's because you never had it right," Fern said. "Now with this tame android man, we can do it right. You'll like it. Trust me."

"You're going to get us both screwed," Daisy muttered.

"Precisely. I'll show you how. Now let's get his crotch set, and find out how to make it perform."

They discovered that the flexible scrotum was a reservoir for water or some similar fluid. A tube led from it into the depth of the unit, probably feeding into the penis. They filled it and closed it up.

"Ready?" Fern inquired. She was the prettiest one, and the most sexually experienced, therefore the leader in these proceedings.

"We'll watch," Daisy said.

"Right." Fern plugged in the power supply. "It's probably best that all three of us be present any time one of us uses Andy, because of that less-than-optimal performance business."

"Agreed," Belinda said fervently. Open sex with a Doll was bad enough, verging on deviant behavior, but the risk of malfunction made it worse. She did not trust this at all.

They had Andy lying face-up on the bed. He began to breathe. Fern touched his shoulder. "Yes, he's warming, just as they said he would." She faced the android. "Wake, Andy."

The brown eyes opened and focused on the ceiling. But the penis remained flaccid.

"We need the command," Daisy said.

"A real man would get stiff just from being alone with three girls," Fern said, frowning. "Maybe I should flash him with my breasts."

"Hard," Belinda suggested naughtily, touching the thing.

The android's member thickened and lengthened. It became stiff, standing against his taut belly. Belinda jerked her hand away.

Belinda was pleased. She had guessed correctly. She was also slightly appalled; how could she be seriously playing with such an organ? Yet it fascinated her, now more than ever.

"Okay," Fern said. "Now let's get it in." She got out of her clothing and climbed on the bed, straddling the figure. She was a shapely young woman and knew it. Her face was lovely, her breasts perky, and she was slender throughout. She took the hard penis with her hand and guided it to her cleft. "Got to get the angle right," she explained as she shifted position slightly. "Oops, I forgot. Get me some of that lubricant."

"This?" Belinda asked, bringing the tube. Her repulsion and fascination remained, warring with each other.

"Right. Spread some on his dick."

"Me?"

"Who the hell else? I don't have a hand free at the moment. It needs to be lubed so it doesn't scrape going in." Fern glanced at Daisy. "That's why you hurt, girl, when. It was dry. When you're wet and slippery it can't hurt. Much. Men don't pay attention to that detail; they're louts."

Belinda nerved herself to touch the member again. It was warm and slightly pulsing. She smeared oil on it somewhat messily.

"Get the glans too," Daisy said. "Pull back the foreskin."

"The prepuce," Belinda said. She gripped it distastefully and spread oil on the glans, then drew the foreskin back over it. She hated this, yet it was also turning her on something fierce. She could never have done this with a real man.

"Okay," Fern said. "Now you lower yourself slowly onto it." She let herself down, keeping the penis centered with her hand until it was fairly lodged. "It feels good, but it's only the start. It's not really sex until it's all the way in." She kept descending until she was sitting on the android's hips, the member fully embedded. "I could have used the larger one," she said, frowning. "I just wanted to be sure, this first time."

Daisy and Belinda were watching closely, studying the situation. "It does seem to fit," Daisy said. Her hands were shaking; this demonstration was bothering her the same as it bothered Belinda. That gave Belinda comfort.

"Sure it fits," Fern said. "And it's really in there, see." She raised her bottom enough to show the member filling it, then plumped down again. "Men think that a big penis is everything a woman wants. Just as they think big tits make the ideal woman. They're such fools. Too big a pecker in you can get uncomfortable. But of course more is needed."

"More?" Daisy asked.

"I need the thing to vibrate. To get clitoral stimulation by convection or whatever. Mere penetration doesn't do it for a woman. That's another myth: that she comes when she's plumbed." Then Fern's eyes went round. "Oh! It's doing it!"

Indeed, they could see the slight shaking of her body and rippling of her breasts as the member vibrated within her. She lifted her bottom, letting the piece affect different sections of her vagina. "Oooo!"

"Swell," Daisy said sarcastically. "The world's most versatile penis."

Belinda knew how she felt. This display was disgusting. But she could not take her eyes off it and was disconcertingly conscious of her own vagina. How would it feel to have a rod like that massaging her from the inside? She had literally never even dreamed of such a thing, but now she was intensely curious.

"Oh!" Fern exclaimed again, louder. "It's expanding!"

Daisy's mouth fell open. "Because I said 'swell,' and it heard me," she said. "Another command."

"Don't tell it to spout," Belinda said, smiling.

And of course the member did exactly that. The water they had put into the scrotum coursed into Fern's vagina, flooding it and dribbling out around the shaft. It was the android's emission.

"Oh! Oh! Oooooh!" Fern cried, jogging with the pulses. "What a plumbing!"

"It really brought on your orgasm?" Daisy asked.

Fern flopped on the body. "Oh, I came, I came! Andy's some man! Better than any dildo."

That made Belinda wince again. Of course Fern knew all about sex toys, but Belinda had preferred to tune them out.

"And no malfunction," Daisy said.

"None I know of. Andy's the perfect man."

Belinda hated to admit it, even to herself, but the show had really excited her sexually. One part of her wanted to try it too, despite the repulsion she felt.

Fern got off. "Okay, your turn, Daisy," she said. "You have to experience this. Get your clothes off."

"I'm not sure," Daisy said. She was a black girl of average complexion and shape. She had reason to be wary of sex. Belinda suspected her one experience had been virtual rape.

"Meanwhile we'll change the hardware," Fern said. "Linda, how do we get the prick off and the balls refilled?"

"You have to take off the whole unit," Belinda said, glad for the diversion of a spot task. She got to work on it, and soon had it unfastened.

"Put on the middle one," Fern said. "It's clean."

Belinda put the spent unit in the sink and set up the middle one, filling the scrotum and oiling the penis. At least now they knew it worked.

It took considerable coaxing, but Fern got Daisy stripped and onto the refurbished android. "Hard," Fern said, and its penis filled out and stiffened, larger than the other but without the foreskin. "Now put it in there." Fern put her fingers on the member and moved it to the place.

"Hey!" Daisy protested. "This is my fuck, not yours."

The torso lifted, thrusting the member hard into

her. Daisy screamed, but stayed on, perhaps unable to raise herself fast enough to get off. The android relaxed, then thrust again, repeatedly. It was fucking her. They had learned a new command. Rather, Belinda had forgotten to relay Clive's warning.

"I'm riding a bucking bronco," Daisy said. "And you know, it's sort of fun." She glanced down. "That thing in me—it's hot and smooth and urgent. Feels good, actually."

Belinda felt her pants getting wet. This was teasing her to no end. She knew she would have to do it too.

"Swell," Fern said. "Vibrate."

"Hey!" Daisy protested. But she remained on. "Oh, that's something. It's filling my whole inside and rocking everything. It's going to make me come!"

"Spout," Fern said.

It did, and Daisy felt the surging fluid. "God, what a feeling! It's making me—making me—ooooh!" She was achieving her orgasm.

When Daisy was done, she and Fern insisted it was Belinda's turn, who didn't really protest, despite having to use the only clean unit: the big one.

"But I've got rules," she said firmly. "The two of you can watch, but you must keep silence. No yelling out commands the way you did before. It has to be all my own show, and I can quit any time I want. Got it?"

"You're taking all the fun out of it," Fern protested. "We want to help you get your ass in gear."

"It's my ass, and I'll gear it exactly the way I want. I never had sex before, and I don't want to get screwed this time." Oops. She saw their smirks. "You know what I mean."

"We do," Fern said.

"We promise," Daisy agreed.

"If you mess in, I'll not only get off, I'll look for new roommates."

"We got it," Fern said meekly.

That was not to be trusted. "I'm not fooling."

"She's not," Daisy said to Fern. "Stifle it, girl."

That seemed to be sufficient. Belinda removed her clothing, feeling awkward though of course her roommates had seen her nude many times before. She was heavyset, with too much tummy, belly, bottom, and hips. She hated that, but couldn't seem to get the pounds off. Even if a man had been interested in her, how could she ever get naked before him? She would expire of shame.

But by similar token, a man-emulation like Andy Android would be the only kind of male she could afford to get close to. Andy would never gaze at her flab and be turned off. So she pretty well *had* to make it here; it was her only chance. It wasn't sex she wanted, so much as appreciation. Fern could provide a peek down her décolletage or a flirt of her hip and have a man drooling. Belinda could never do that. So the artificial appreciation of the man-Doll was all she was ever likely to garner. Even though it was only at her specific behest.

She girded her loins, literally, and mounted the android. She straddled his thighs, gazing at the flaccid penis. She gulped, took a breath, and spoke. "Hard."

The member lengthened and thickened

impressively. It heaved itself up to stand tall before her. It looked monstrously huge, gleaming with the oil they had applied. How could she ever get all that meat into her virgin vagina? She should have started with the smallest one.

She put her fingers on the head of it and drew back the foreskin. There was the glans glistening in purple splendor. Weird, the way a man was constructed.

She moved up to get her cleft over the implement. She took the glans and put it to her vulva. She stroked it back and forth along the crease. It felt surprisingly good.

She set it at her vagina, letting herself down just enough to bring the glans up against her aperture. Its rounded surface pushed at her slick tissue as it nudged in. She felt her vagina opening to receive it, but the fit was close. She was not at all sure the breadth of it would find room, let alone the full depth of the huge member. Only the upper half of the glans was in, really only denting her flesh instead of getting all the way into it. Like pressing a marble into clay to make a concave pattern. Still, this was farther than she had ever been sexually and was sinfully exciting.

She glanced at her roommates. Both were watching intently, not at all bored. She realized that they had missed something by performing the act quickly. Her effort was more like slow motion, every detail visible. So instead of dawdling she was making a better show, serendipitously.

Then she got a wicked notion. "Spout," she said, holding the glans in place.

The member pulsed. Jets of water squirted out of its slit and shot into her vagina like a douche. Two, three, four, five—a total of eight separate jets before it ended, washing her channel before dripping down and out. She had received the emission! Only technically, as only the surface of the glans was in contact, but the fluid had indeed pumped into her.

Then the member subsided, having finished its act. She was left hovering above it, dripping.

"Wow," Fern breathed. "I wish I'd thought of that."

Thrilled by her innovative success, Belinda tried for more. She lifted the limp penis and carefully stuffed it into her vagina. It retained just enough solidity to make it possible, without putting any painful pressure against her. When it seemed to be all the way in, she sat firmly on it and issued her next command: "Hard."

The android was of course indefatigable. The member responded immediately to the order, lengthening and thickening within her. "Oh! It's weird!" she exclaimed, holding her position. "Like a snake wriggling in there, or maybe a balloon being blown up. What a sensation!" Indeed, her internal pleasure was increasing. Could this be the start of her orgasm?

"Honey, you got more imagination than I do," Fern breathed. "You sure you never did this before?"

"Never," Belinda said, pleased. The fit had become tight, but the penis was unable to expand beyond the confines of her vagina. She was actually containing the monster!

So why not go for it all? "Swell," she said boldly.

Now the member pushed larger, distending her vagina into her belly. She remained sitting tight against it so that none of it could squeeze out of her. The effect was becoming almost painful, but it was a sexy pain. There was pressure against her clitoris. She jogged a bit, getting some rubbing. But the main thing was her mind: her awareness that this huge thing was vibrating inside her. That made her squeeze it back, milking it of its awesome power. Her pleasure intensified.

"I'm coming!" she cried, and hung on as her vagina squeezed against the thick member. The pleasure was so intense as to be almost unbearable. "Oh! Oh! Oh!"

Then, before her climax could ebb, she called out the finale. "Spout!"

The member tried again. This time it had only a small amount of fluid, having expended most of it the first time. Still, she felt it squeezing into her and rejoiced. It was a fitting complement to her own joy of orgasm.

"She had the best one," Daisy said enviously. "Who would have thought it?"

"Who, indeed," Fern agreed. "How good was it, Linda?"

"The best," Belinda said proudly.

"Good going, girl. You win the trophy. I nearly came again, just watching."

"Me too," Daisy said. "I've got to change my pants."

Belinda was completely satisfied, in more than one manner. She had been so afraid of it, and expected so little, yet it had worked out so well. She already knew she would be doing it again, seeking new variants. Andy was the man for her.

* * * *

The boys were more ambitious the second time they got Anna. They had tried straight, flex, and closed before; now they sought other positions. "Turn her over," Glenn said.

Clive was shocked. "Glenn, you're not going to—to—?"

"To cornhole her? No. I just want to try the rear position." Seeing Clive's continuing doubt, he clarified it. "Same hole, just getting in from behind. It's a nice variant; her ass cheeks feel great against your crotch."

Oh. Clive watched as Glenn performed, parting Anna's generous buttocks and wedging his member in. Now that he saw the position in action, Clive found it wickedly exciting.

Edgar tried the side position, with Anna lying with her knees brought up before her, her bottom nicely displayed. It was a variant of the rear position, with the cleft readily exposed, and it too was exciting. It had the additional advantage that Edgar could reach around to put one hand on her shapely breast while he remained connected. It was all Clive could do to appear to be a passive observer; he was phenomenally turned on. When Edgar thrust and came, Clive almost did, too.

Clive got to try what Glenn called "doggie fashion," with Anna on hands and knees. They had discovered that she could be locked into position so as not to be pushed down. This provided the best view yet of her vulva, which now showed as an actual round hole, and the best access yet to her hanging breasts. The only liability was that it was almost impossible to kiss her while in this position.

Clive kneeled behind her, set his member at the hole, and slid in. Glenn was right; when his groin came into contact with her buttocks, his sensation was enhanced. He put his hands on her breasts, gently squeezing. Both buttocks and breasts had evocative powers of their own, apart from the cleft. He thrust, and came immediately, jetting copiously. It was as if all the world, nay, the universe, was centered on his flaming penis as it radiated its sheer joy.

He wanted to kiss her, after, but was afraid the others would tease him about falling in love with the Doll. There could be some truth to that; his attraction was becoming more than sexual. He wanted to hold her, kiss her, talk to her, get to know her and have her get to know him. He was personifying her; he knew it was a recognized psychological phenomenon. So be it; he still felt that way, but did not want to embarrass himself.

Then he got an idea. It was hard to perform again soon after the first ejaculation. They normally took a break, then returned in an hour for another session. If he tried it immediately, he could conceal his real purpose.

"I want to see how fast I can come again," he said. "Maybe a different position will do it."

Glenn shook his head. "Only another woman can help a man do it again immediately. The batteries need to recharge."

"Let me try."

The others shrugged. If he wanted to discover the futility of it for himself, that was his problem, not theirs. They went to the kitchen for a snack.

Clive put Anna on her back, got over her, and kissed her. She was just so feminine! "I love you, Anna," he whispered, so the others would not overhear.

Anna smiled. Her arms came up to embrace him. Her mouth started kissing. Her eyes closed.

Astonished, Clive kissed her. She had reacted! She seemed more alive than ever, though he knew it was merely programming in response to another command. A suite of actions, emulating a woman in love.

Such was his gratification, Clive found himself responding. His spent member recovered enough to make entry, and he thrust and thrust, met by her internal squeezing. It took time, but he did have a second climax, slow, extended, but very sweet.

"Oh, Anna!" he said, his emotion overflowing.

"Hey, he came again!" Edgar said, coming back to get a closer view.

"How'd you do it?" Glenn asked.

He might as well confess. "I said 'I L-O-V-E you,'" he said, spelling it out so as not to invoke the command again. "She—it's a complex of reactions. She responded so well it got me there."

"I'll be damned," Glenn said. "A composite command."

After that, both others tried it, and got the love suite. It was a significant discovery.

Fortunately, Glenn and Edgar did not realize that Clive had not just said it, but meant it. He was smitten with Anna, android though she might be. He wished he could have a day alone with her, not even bothering with the sex. But the other two would never understand.

* * * *

Belinda was interested. "She has suites of expression? I wonder whether Andy has them too."

"He p-probably does," Clive said. "And she can lock into position, like hands and knees. And there's the flex. But I guess you wouldn't be using that."

"Flex? Flex what?"

Blushing, stuttering, he managed to get the concept across.

"Oh. You're right; we wouldn't need that. But I'll tell the others, just in case. Thanks."

"W-welcome." His blushing renewed. "B-B-Belinda, could w-we—that is—talk?"

What was on his mind? "Of course, Clive."

"S-somewhere p-private?"

His stuttering was bad. That meant it was important." An isolated corner?" She led the way there, and they sat facing each other cornerwise.

"I n-need a w-woman's advice."

"I am a woman. I can't speak for the validity of my advice."

"P-p-p-privately."

Really serious. "What you tell me here, stays here," she said. "No sharing with friends."

"Th-th-thank you. B-B— "

"Try just Linda. Less blockage."

"Linda," he said. "We—I—have sex with Anna."

"And we have sex with Andrew. This is a private matter known only to the six of us, but perhaps suspected elsewhere. It's a sex doll, after all."

"It's great. She—I'm falling for her. Am I crazy?"

Belinda gazed at him. "If I could have any boyfriend I wanted, I think I would choose one like Andrew. One who is unfailingly attentive to my needs and who never tries to impose his will on me. Is this what you mean about Anna?"

"F-falling in love."

"As though she were real? Alive?"

He nodded, blushing again.

"Let me ask you a question, Clive. Do you get jealous when your roommates have sex with her?"

"No. We share."

"Then I think it is not love as conventionally understood. You know she is an android. A machine. It's like becoming smitten with the picture of a movie star. You know it's just a picture, but you can't approach the star, so you imbue the picture with the qualities you require. It's not crazy; it's a coping mechanism."

He nodded. "Coping."

"You may be smitten with some living girl you can't approach, such as a married woman. So you think of her on some level as you embrace Anna. Because you *can* possess Anna. That may not be ideal, but neither is it crazy. We all have our little personal illusions. I would call it harmless, especially if it keeps you out of mischief."

He looked at her, the light seeming slowly to dawn. "Yes. I think that's it. Thank you."

"Welcome, Clive. But I think you will be better off not telling the others. They might not understand."

"Yes."

That was it. They separated. Belinda was puzzled and flattered that Clive had chosen her to tell his secret to. But probably it was because he had so much trouble approaching any girl, and the two of them met to compare notes every week. He spoke for the boys and she for the girls. It was a viable system, and it attracted no awkward attention.

The Doll was transferred, and the girls had Andrew Android again. Belinda told the others about the new discoveries the boys had made.

"Andy can love?" Fern asked, interested.

"Maybe not the same way Anna does," Belinda cautioned her.

"Let's try it." Fern was always the boldest about sex.

"What could he do, flat on his back?" Daisy asked. "We should get him in an action position first, or it won't work."

They found that Andrew could assume the man-above position, locking his knees and elbows partway lowered and holding his body six to nine inches off the bed. They set him up that way, unaroused.

Fern slid under him, arranging herself just so, with their groins almost touching. "Andy, I love you," she said.

The android moved. His face came down, kissing. Then he pushed himself down some and put his mouth to her left breast. He kissed it and licked the nipple. His penis came erect. Then he moved up again, his groin pushing up against hers so that his member lodged in her cleft. The aim wasn't quite right, so she used her hand to steer it correctly. He pushed in, slowly. Then he thrust and thrust, two, three, four, five times.

"He's locked in a loop," Daisy said.

"Maybe not," Belinda said. "It takes a woman time to get there, so he has to give her that time."

"Oh, Andy!" Fern cried, faking it. She put her arms around him and pulled him down on her. "Oh! Ooooh!"

That was the signal: her climax. Andrew thrust twice more and jetted, kissing her all the while.

"Damn, I should have waited longer," Fern said. "I'm only halfway there."

"Turn him on again," Belinda suggested.

"I need more than that. I'll never come this way."

"Oral!" Daisy said.

The android reacted. He moved down until his face was at Fern's groin. He put it to her cleft and started licking.

"Say, now," Fern said. "He's good." She wriggled to get it just right.

Andrew continued licking indefatigably, and in due course Fern writhed and groaned, achieving a fine orgasm. The new form of sex was working out.

Daisy tried the hands and knees position, assuming it herself and having the others set the android up behind her. "I love you."

He went at it with a will, wrapping his arms around her, taking both breasts in his hands, and kissing the back of her neck. His touch was evocative; Belinda saw Daisy reacting as her breasts and neck were stroked and kissed. He thrust while she touched her own clitoris, bringing herself off.

When she started her climax she sounded off, and Andrew went into his, jetting into her.

It was said that men were visually stimulated, while women reacted more to emotional stimuli, but Belinda was amazed by the extent to which watching this turned her on. Oh, to have a man paying such attention to her! A man who thought her neck, breasts, and cleft were the most wonderful things on Earth. Who could revel in them indefinitely, not finishing until she was finished.

"It's not perfect," Daisy concluded. "But it's good enough, considering."

"A real man would shoot off in three thrusts," Fern said. "You'd be left cold. At least Andy has the courtesy to take the time you need."

That was, of course, the key; Andrew took all the time a girl needed, letting her choose the mode. Sex was one thing: sex exactly as she wanted it was another. Men wanted it *their* way, and that was the problem.

"Too bad we can't have a real man programmed like that," Daisy said.

"They don't program well," Fern said. "They have to be carefully managed, and then it still often goes wrong. The ideal lover would be tractable and teachable."

Belinda tried the side position, with the android behind her. "Andrew, I love you," she said, and he proceeded to enter her and squeeze her breast with his hand while kissing her neck. She was conscious of his groin against her bottom; that added to her reaction. She imagined him being turned on by his contact with her flesh, and that turned her on.

But she didn't stop there. "Clit," she said.

It worked. He moved his arm down and found her cleft with his hand. His finger oriented on her clitoris and gently massaged it. His technique was good; his programming was apt.

"Swell," she said as she felt herself rising toward the climax. "Vibrate."

The penis expanded, and both it and the finger vibrated. Suddenly she was being catapulted into orgasm. "Ooooh!" she cried, and it was no fake.

He thrust urgently, his groin smacking into her bottom, and jetted, then lay quiet, still holding her. She liked that lingering touch, as though he valued contact for more than just the sex. Closeness—with an android, but pleasant nevertheless. She also liked the way his penis slowly faded and slipped out of her, as if she had fulfilled it. It had been a wholly satisfactory experience.

"So you can pile on commands," Fern said. "You got it figured, Linda, again. Who needs a real man?"

"If only a real man could act like Andrew," Daisy said wistfully. "The only thing wrong with Andrew is he's not alive."

"A living Andrew," Fern agreed. "The perfect date."

"Irony," Belinda agreed.

* * * *

Clive had been wary approaching the first session with the android, and cautious with the second, but now he was eager. He really appreciated the way Belinda had explained his crush on Anna. He had thought about that, and come to the conclusion she was right; Anna was a substitute for another woman. And that woman was Belinda herself. She was always polite to him, and never ridiculed him, and understood him better than any woman did. That understanding and acceptance was a major factor. Yes, she was no beauty—but neither was he any hunk. She was the kind of person he could get along with.

And the kind he would like to have sex with. Now he saw that Anna, lovely and obliging as she was, lacked the special quality of a live girl. He wished he could speak his heart directly to Belinda, but of course he couldn't; it was likely either to generate her pity, or to entirely alienate her. So he had to settle for Anna, pretending in his secret mind that she was Belinda.

And, really, would Belinda respond to commands? Kiss, spread, fuck? If she didn't laugh at the notion, she would be angry. He didn't know how to do it otherwise; the moment he left the android programming he would be helpless, stuttering and impotent. That was part of the hell of it.

This time they got into alternate sex. Glenn lay on the bed with his legs spread. "Anna, suck."

She did. She took Glenn's member into her mouth and worked it with such efficiency that it soon jetted. "Oh, that's something! She's really got the touch."

Edgar was interested in another variant. "Spread," he said, then put his face into Anna's cleft. He licked her vulva and ran his tongue into her vagina. Clive, watching, was amazed. Edgar seemed to be getting almost as aroused himself as his licking was doing to the theoretical woman. His penis was hard and dripping.

And Anna responded. She quivered, and her breathing accelerated. Finally she writhed and pressed her thighs against Edgar's head as if suffering her orgasm.

Clive's own member was throbbing. Watching the female climax was sexy as hell.

Edgar, satisfied, mounted her and thrust into that wet orifice, rapidly completing his own climax. Anna, of course, welcomed his effort.

But Clive did not want to suck or be sucked. Seeing it done made him react, but he was ashamed of reacting. He preferred normal sex: penis and vagina. How could he have that without incurring the irritation of his roommates?

He came up with a solution. "I want to do it standing," he said. That made it different without requiring oral-genital contact.

They stood her up against the wall and locked her in place, legs moderately spread. Then Clive approached her. He kissed her mouth, then her breasts, which were interesting in this position. They tended to fade back into her chest when she lay on the bed, but now they were fully breast shaped. Then he bent his knees, angled his stiff penis, and brought it up into her groin. Entry turned out not to be automatic; the angle was wrong, and he slipped aside. He ducked and tried again, then a third time. Finally her got it in and pushed up. It still felt not quite right. He wasn't sure how good a climax he could get, and was afraid he might not get it at all. He realized that this was a limitation of the android; a live woman would subtly accommodate his efforts, facilitating entry. Anna was not that sophisticated.

"Maybe the other side," he said, withdrawing.

They turned her around, but entry from behind wasn't any more convenient. "Maybe if she bends over."

Anna obeyed orders to bend, but had to be steadied. They got her balanced on hands and feet, her rear elevated, her breasts descending. He tried to enter, but now his effort tended to push her over. Edgar had to grab her upper section and hold her in place. That made it look like rape, but he was stuck for it.

Finally he got into her, and actually the position worked this time. He put his hands on her hips and held her in place as he thrust. He liked the feel of her buttocks as he connected; they were resilient. He also liked the way her breasts quivered each time his groin came up against her posterior, making a muted collision. It still took him some time to climax, but he did get there.

He did not mean to do this again. Hereafter, she would be on the bed.

But, oddly, his effort turned on the other two, and they proceeded to upright sex thereafter.

* * * *

"Next is oral," Fern decided.

"You did that, remember?" Daisy said. "You made him lap you, and you said it was great."

"The other way. Us on him."

"Fellatio?" Belinda asked, repulsed.

"Giving head. Some men expect it. You have to be prepared for when you go out into the real world. Also, if you got your period, you can bring him off that way. No fuss, no muss, you don't have to wash out your crack, after. Can't get pregnant, either. It's convenient, when you need it. Learn it with Andy."

"What about when he comes?" Daisy asked. "Andrew's just water, but a real man's got jism."

"You swallow it. It's nutritious, and the taste is neutral. As I said, there's no mess. You don't have to get undressed, and neither does he. Just his pecker. You can do it in a car, fast, and not only does it save you trouble, he's grateful. Double value."

"But why go to all this trouble to learn obscure variants?" Belinda asked. "The average man will settle just for missionary position, won't he?"

"Two things," Fern said seriously. "First, when you get into a serious relationship, he soon wants variety. You have to know what else there is, so as not to be unpleasantly surprised, such as if he wants to do it standing, fully clothed, in a public place."

"Clothed!" Belinda exclaimed, halfway shocked. She had appreciated the convenience of oral sex in this respect, but straight sex was another matter.

"Public!" Daisy said, appalled.

"You don't always have time or a bed or privacy. He can get so hot in a hurry that you just have to do it or risk a fight. Men aren't necessarily reasonable about sex; never forget that. We can generally take it or leave it; they can't. Ninety seconds against a wall in a dark hallway can work wonders. It's best to be prepared."

"So you won't get raped?" Daisy asked distastefully.

"So you won't lose him to some floozy who hoists her skirt the moment he looks at her. If you want him, you have to be prepared to do what it takes to keep him. It's a sexual jungle out there."

Belinda exchanged a glance with Daisy. Fern's mind seemed to be too much on sex. But she did have experience they lacked. She just might be right.

"You said two things," Daisy said. "What's the second?"

"Control. You have to keep the upper hand, or there can be real trouble. Never let him take control."

"You make it sound like a war," Belinda said.

"It *is* a war, Linda. Not one with blood and teeth flying around, but war nevertheless. We women have the assets; the men want them. They will lie or cheat or rape to get them. We have to be ahead of the game to avoid becoming victims. Knowledge is power. We have to know what they want before they even know they want it, so we can steer them our way. We need to understand every little nuance of sex, as much to avoid it as to solicit it. So we can be in control. Sex is the ring in the bull's nose; chances are he can't see beyond it. Use it correctly and you can govern the monster. Not only is that much safer, it's more convenient, and its own kind of turn-on. We can make men be like Andy, to a degree, if we know what we're doing and they don't catch on. Now's our chance to perfect the techniques."

She was making sense. "Show us how," Belinda said, still not turned on, but neither was she completely turned off. She had become considerably more interested in sex since encountering Andrew. She saw now that she had not properly appreciated its power over men.

Fern demonstrated. "Hard," she said, and the

android's penis came erect. "First lesson," she told the others. "Teeth do not exist. It's all lips and tongue. Start by licking." She touched the tip of the penis with her tongue. "Work your way down and around. Or vice versa, whatever works best." She licked the hard stem. "Don't ignore the balls."

"The testicles!" Belinda exclaimed, astonished.

"They connect," Fern said patiently. She licked the android's scrotum, then put her mouth around one half of it, taking in a testicle. She gently spat it out and did the other. "Turns on some men something awful."

"Suppose it turns him off?" Daisy asked.

"Then you return to the flagstaff." She did so. This time she put her mouth around the head. Then she slid her face down, slowly taking in the whole member.

Both Belinda and Daisy stared. "I didn't know that was possible," Daisy said. "What are you—a sword swallower?"

"She's—she *is* swallowing it," Belinda said. "Literally." For there was simply nowhere for the member to go but down the throat.

Fern made a signal with one hand, remaining with the member fully inside her mouth.

"Spout," Daisy said, catching on.

They saw the base of the member quiver as the emission came. They saw Fern swallowing. After a few seconds she drew her mouth off the slackening rod, still sucking. There was no leakage. It was completely dry in its fashion. She had made her point.

After that Daisy tried it on a new groin,

following Fern's directions. Then so did Belinda. She had expected it to be distasteful in more than one sense, but found that it wasn't; in fact she had gotten so worked up watching the others that she was, if not eager, at least quite satisfied to do it herself.

"So have we graduated, sex mistress?" Daisy asked when Belinda was done. "Do we know all about sex now?"

Fern smiled. "Hardly. Now we tackle anal."

"We tackle what?" Belinda asked, shocked.

"Ass fucking. That comes in two types: hers and his."

"His?"

"I'll show you. Let me fetch my dildo."

She showed them. The dildo was a plastic rod in the shape of an erect penis with a scrotum at the base. Belinda had never seen one before, but she recognized the form instantly. They put the android on his hands and knees, then worked the oiled dildo into his rectum. Fern assured them that some men liked it.

"But isn't that homosexual?" Daisy asked.

"Not necessarily. Actually, for straight men, it's probably better to have one that's just a polished rod. But this is all I have, and it will do. The point is, they like to have something up their ass."

"Weird," Daisy said, and Belinda agreed.

They watched Fern push the dildo in up to its base, pull it out, and push it in again in a plainly sexual manner. Belinda found this fascinating in its repulsiveness.

"He's getting a hard-on," Daisy said.

Belinda looked. So he was; the penis was full

and firm. This must be another programmed response. The man, having been plumbed, wanted to plumb somebody else. "Weird," she said, echoing Daisy.

Then it was Andrew's turn to do them. On command he insinuated his hard oiled penis into Fern's rectum, she holding it in place so it couldn't slide into the adjacent hole. "It's really similar to the vagina," she explained as Belinda tried to mask her horror. "Feels much the same, and you can't get pregnant. Easier to hold the jism in, too." She glanced back at the android. "Spurt."

Nothing was visible, but soon the penis softened, and Fern drew her bottom off it. There was no sign of fluid. This was another "clean" way to handle it.

"But suppose you have a turd in there?" Daisy asked.

Fern shrugged. "Better poop it out first. Be prepared. Do an enema if you have to. You have to be clean for him."

Both Belinda and Daisy laughed, embarrassed.

The others did it, afraid to back down. Daisy winced as Andrew's member nudged her rectum, but held firm, and it slid in readily enough. Belinda couldn't admit it, but seeing the thing push in past the oil-glistening sphincter was another turn-on. It did look a lot like straight sex.

When Belinda's turn came, she found the penetration uncomfortable at first. But she reached back and wiggled the head with her hand, setting it just right as she pushed against it. She felt it lodge and slowly sink in as her tight anus relaxed to accept it. Once the member was all the way in it was all right. Fern was right; it didn't feel much different from vaginal penetration. Except that she kept thinking she was having a bowel movement. She had expected to be disgusted, but discovered it was after all just part of the process. It didn't give her any orgasm, but neither did it appall her. It was another variant that could be handled if necessary. Right through to the jet of water at the conclusion. That made her jump; it was cold. The heating coil must have malfunctioned.

She mentioned that, and the others checked by having Andrew harden and spurt into the air. The water was definitely cold.

"He's starting to break down," Daisy said. "Maybe it's the first glitch. But we can fix that by putting in warm water and not taking too long."

Belinda didn't say anything, but seeing that spurt into space turned her on more than the anal penetration had, because it was so visible. The emission was certainly part of the sex act, and she wanted it to happen. In her vagina, mouth, anus, or the air as she watched, holding the member in her hand. The proof of the man's passion.

But she wouldn't have wanted to try it with anyone but Andrew. He was known, and clean.

* * * *

"Oh my god!" Clive exclaimed, reading the notice the landlady had posted on their door. "This is awful."

For they had forgotten that the landlady had access to their apartment during the day when they were in school. She had entered on a routine fire inspection and seen Anna spread out on a bed, gloriously naked. They had forgotten to put her away after a hot session.

"We're doomed," Edgar said. "She'll have us crucified as sexual perverts."

Clive hastily arranged a meeting with Belinda. "We left Anna out," he said. "The landlady saw her. She wants to know how we explain it." He noticed with part of his mind that he wasn't stuttering; this was too urgent for that.

Belinda nodded. "Simple. You have an anatomy class. This is a home exercise, studying all the parts of a woman. You need to get them exactly right, or you'll flunk the course."

"Perfect!" he said, leaning toward her. Then he caught himself.

"What were you about to do?" she asked sharply.

He blushed. "K-k-k—" Naturally he was stuttering now; this had become personal.

"Kiss me?"

"Yes. I was s-so happy for your solution. I—I'm s-sorry."

"Why would you want to kiss me?"

He answered before he could marshal an evasion. "I have a c-c-crush on you."

"But you have Anna Android."

"S-She's a s-s-substitute for y-you. Y-you're alive."

She nodded, evidently not entirely surprised. "So I'm your anonymous woman."

He wished he could turn off his burning blush. "Y-yes."

"I'm not beautiful."

"You are to me," he said without hesitation. It was, in its perverse way, good to have it out in the open at last, regardless of her reaction. "You're smart, and you treat me right, and I love you."

"Complete your action."

"M-my what?"

"Kiss me."

"B-But— "

She pursed her lips, waiting.

He leaned forward and touched her mouth with his. She put her hand around the back of his head and pressed it toward her, making the kiss twice as firm. It was a slice of heaven.

Then he was back with his roommates, telling them how to handle the landlady. He didn't quite remember anything with Belinda after the kiss, but things were in his mind. "The girls will confirm. We have an anatomy class."

It worked. "But at least make that mannequin decent," the landlady said grudgingly. "Put some clothing on her."

That set off a small flurry of activity. They arranged to borrow skirts, panties, bras, and blouses from the girls for Anna, and loaned them trousers, underpants, and shirts for Andrew. The android was now decent.

This had a remarkable effect. They discovered that the clothed figure was in certain respects more appealing than the naked one. When they set her up in a chair with her legs crossed she looked eerily alive. The partial view of her thighs under the skirt could be electrifying. A hand threaded into her blouse to cup a breast was almost unbearably exciting. Kissing her clothed had a special quality.

And the sex was something else. Glenn led the way, as usual, bending her forward, braced against the wall. He hoisted her skirt, drew aside her panty, and worked his member in from behind. "It's great!" he gasped as he climaxed.

Indeed it was. Edgar set her in a chair with her legs spread wide, put his head under her skirt, and did oral sex on her in that position. All the others could see was the skirt bobbing over his head. It was a remarkable turn-on.

When Clive's turn came, he fondled her breasts under the blouse, then fondled her buttocks under the skirt, and finally pressed her back on the bed, her skirt bunched around her waist. He felt her covered breasts against his chest, so real. He got in around her panty, then kissed her mouth as he thrust and climaxed. His orgasm was intense. "Oh, Linda!" he gasped, collapsing. It was, by no coincidence, Linda's clothing he had dressed the android in.

If the others heard, they had the wit to keep silent.

* * * *

Belinda was intrigued by Clive's confession of love for her. More than intrigued; the knowledge buoyed her spirits. She had supposed that no boy would find her interesting, let alone crush-worthy. But there had been certain hints, and on occasion she had closed her eyes and imagined it was Clive she was having sex with. Now she had confirmation, and she liked it. True, he wasn't handsome, muscular, or socially gifted. But she was no prize damsel either. What they had in common, apart from the secret of the android, was their intelligence. That, in her considered judgment, was more important than all the rest combined.

But Daisy had started dating a boy, despite their joint resolution to avoid such activity, only to get abruptly dropped. Again. It had never gotten to the point of sex, and hardly beyond a kiss and a feel. He had simply found someone else he like better, and pffft! he was gone. She cried quietly for two hours, then turned to Andrew for savage sex. Fern and Belinda kept quiet, letting her work it out her own way. "Boys can't be trusted," Fern murmured to Belinda. "They'll break your heart, if you let them."

That was one thing Andrew would never do. But the incident made Belinda especially cautious. Maybe Clive really was smitten with her—but suppose she let herself respond in kind—and he dropped her? She really would like to have a real relationship with a real boy, and the prospect of sex no longer turned her off. In fact, she would like to discover how well what she had learned with Andrew applied to a real boy. But she knew this was treacherous ground.

Then she dreamed of having sex with Andrew, and he faced her and said "I l-love you, Linda." That woke her immediately. She was responding to Clive's interest despite her caution.

The sexercizes continued another month, as they explored every facet of sexuality with the obliging Doll. It was fun dressing him in the boys' clothing, and sometimes a turn-on. Fern had him fully clothed once with only his hard penis sticking out, and had sex with him that way. Daisy had dressed him above, leaving his nether section bare, then pretended to catch him in the middle of changing, and seduced him that way. Belinda simply sat beside him and had him reach inside her blouse to fondle her breasts while she reached inside his trouser fly and massaged his penis. It was naughty fun. But secretly she wished she could do the same with Clive. Andrew was perfect, but he wasn't real.

They also, at Fern's instigation, went bare with him and tried group sex. He licked Fern's vulva while Daisy sucked on his penis and Belinda fed the dildo into his anus. It was fun, but not as satisfying as straight regular sex. They agreed that one on one worked best, regardless what the boys might think.

Clive, stuttering, reported on another thing the boys were doing: taking turns with Anna sharing their beds at night. They would wake in darkness, kiss her, stroke her breasts, and have sex with her, alone. That had a specially potent effect. It took him several tries to get that word "potent" out.

Intrigued, the girls tried it, too. When it was Belinda's night, she woke in the wee hours, found him there, remembered, and started kissing him. She handled his penis under the covers, made him erect, and got on him for satisfying sex. Would it be like this with a real man? Her curiosity was increasing.

And how would it be to have Clive in bed with her like that? The idea of fondling him into desperate passion turned her on so thoroughly that she had to have sex with the android a second time in succession. She was becoming a sexual creature. It was the control that really got to her: making a man do her sexual will.

They discovered a new command: "Watch." Fern stood before naked Andrew propped in the chair, and did a slow striptease. Sure enough, his member swelled. She came to sit astride his lap, put his hands on her breasts, kissed him, and set her vagina on his hard penis. She jogged, and succeeded in making him jet into her—without ever giving another command. The Watch command enabled it all.

But Daisy had less success, and had to augment her performance with commands. Belinda had no success at all. She pretended it didn't bother her, but that night she cried herself to sleep. She was not an attractive woman; even the android knew it. Her dreams about sexually enticing and tormenting Clive crashed; she did not have the equipment. If she tried it, she would only embarrass herself and him.

Next day she started a determined diet and exercise program. The pounds started coming off and she felt better about herself. In a month she knew she was looking nicer. She proved it by doing the striptease before Andrew, and getting his member to react. It didn't get to full mast, but it was firm enough to get inside her when she sat on him, and she knew that in time she would be able to make him spurt.

They told the boys, but there did not seem to be an equivalent reaction in Anna. She did not find a disrobing man all that exciting. However, they could make her climax with sufficient kissing, stroking, and licking in the right places.

Belinda thought of Clive doing that to her. Damn, she'd like to have him try!

The boys reported a glitch: Edgar gave the Kiss command, and Anna started licking his face. Then

Belinda, having her vulva licked, got it sucked instead. That was not dangerous, but did turn her off. The Doll was wearing out.

Then the android became inoperative. Something had broken down, probably in the command and response mechanism, and he became a completely passive Doll. This was a crisis, because they had come to depend on his dependable attentions.

They checked with the boys, who were similarly disgruntled. Clive checked online and learned that it would cost $300 to have the Doll overhauled to make it function again. They simply did not have that kind of money to spare.

Then the girls hatched an especially wicked notion. They hashed it out, concluded it was viable, and sent Belinda to negotiate with Clive. They had found a way to eliminate the risk of getting emotionally involved and getting dumped. They hoped.

She began their private interview with a kiss. They were not openly dating, but she had confessed to being taken with him too, so they were working up to a more open commitment in their own time. It was weird that each of them was having semi-public sex with the Doll, yet found it bold to merely touch their lips together. But they were two living people, and that made things enormously more complicated.

"Here is the situation," she said. "Andrew Android—Anna to you—is lost, unless you want to have sex with her inanimate. That is, unplugged."

"Glenn tried it," he said. "He said it's not worth it. She's cold—literally—and doesn't breathe, and her v-vagina is just a stiff tube. He said he'd get more fun f-fucking a corpse."

Belinda smiled sympathetically. "We can't go even that far, as he can no longer make an erection. Anyway, the Doll is gone, but the six of us remain. We have all become accustomed to regular sex."

He nodded, starting a blush. She was doing most of the talking because it was easier for her. It also helped her to stifle her own threatening blush. She was acting as if this was purely a practical notion, but some fierce subterranean emotional currents were there.

"Here's our idea: why don't we eliminate the middleman, as it were?"

"I—I don't understand."

"I think you do. We've all been having frequent sex. We're used to it, we like it." An understatement. Andrew had made them almost wanton.

"But real people are complicated."

"Exactly. It surely wouldn't work well if we just tried to have sex with each other. We'd each expect to dominate. The android has hopelessly spoiled us."

"Y-Yes."

"So what about this: we take turns playing android. Say it's your turn, then I get to command you what to do. Kiss, hold, get hard, thrust, whatever. You do only what you are told to do, to the best of your ability, except if the command is 'I love you.' Then you can improvise some."

"I—I could do that, I think," he agreed.

"When it's my turn, you will command me. Spread my legs, kiss, whatever. You do what you choose to do."

"Yes!" he breathed. That was encouraging. She did not want him to see her naked and change his mind.

"We can't allow free choice of partners, because all of you would want Fern, and be hopelessly spoiled for the other two of us. So we can choose by lots. Only when all three of us—and all three of you—have had sex to climax, can any repeats be considered. That seems fair."

"No."

She lifted an eyebrow. "No?"

"If I got Fern, I—she—she's beautiful. I'd get all shy and im-im—"

"Impotent? I see the problem."

"I want to do it with you."

Victory! "Well, how about this: when you're androids, we get to choose you. You stand up there first. One of us must choose you before either of the others get chosen. I will choose you. I don't think anyone will object."

"Yes!"

"Then it will be Edgar's turn, and one of the others will choose him. The last one gets Glenn. And vice versa, when we girls are the Dolls."

"Yes," he agreed again.

"One thing: we want the sex public. That is, we all will watch the active couple, the same as we do with Andrew. If something goes wrong, the others will serve as a jury to decide what's okay. So there will be no defaulting."

"Yes," he said again. "We watch with Anna. In case there's a glitch. And we learn things. We're used to doing it that way, with the Doll."

"Good enough. I'll tell my people; you tell yours. This coming weekend?" Was that a pun? The weekend when there would be plenty of "coming."

"Yes." He hesitated, then got it out. "But a-aside from th-that, can we d-date? Openly? I mean, the sex—no one outside will know, but we, in public, the real public—oh, Linda, I'd sure like to be with you!"

It was harder for him to agree to chaste dating than to having sex. That was an inversion! But she understood. The Doll had made a phenomenal difference, thoroughly educating them all about sex, making them competent. It had become almost a laboratory exercise. But the Doll wasn't much for the nuances of interpersonal interaction. "We can date," she agreed. "Like any well-behaved couple. We can hold hands and look at each other fully clothed, whisper sweet nothings, and sometimes even kiss."

"That's great, Linda!" He was puppy-dog appreciative. She liked that; no boy had ever cared for her company before. Not socially. Only for help with homework.

She looked around. They were alone in the common room. She made a bold decision. "Here's how it will work. A demonstration run. You be Andrew. The Doll. Obey my command."

"I don't— "

"Lift your arm."

He lifted his right arm, still puzzled.

"Slide your hand into my shirt." She unbuttoned it.

His mouth dropped open. "I c-c-couldn't!"

"Clive," she said patiently. "This is role-playing. There are no complicated interpersonal interactions.

When you are the Doll you are not in control. You make no decisions. You merely obey. Now do it."

Still he hesitated. His hand shook.

"That's why we'll have roommate witnesses. So I can call a balk, and they'll make you do it even if you don't want to. You don't have to *like* it." She was pushing him.

"Oh, no, Linda, I want to, so much. But—"

"Is it that my body is unappealing to you?"

"No! I just c-can't."

She gave him a level gaze. "But you can do it with Anna. What am I to think?"

"You—you're *real*!"

"Precisely. My body can't compare to what you have become accustomed to. So on your own you may not be inclined, but as the Doll you have no choice. That's why we want to do it this way."

"Linda, it's not like that at all! You're so much more than Anna! I have s-stage fright."

"Not allowed. The Doll doesn't have feelings."

"But I do!"

"And so do I, and you are hurting them."

"Oh, Linda, please!"

She held his gaze, unyielding. She was actually enjoying this, in a manner.

"I—" Then, evidently thinking of the android, who always obeyed, he did it. He pushed his hand clumsily into her shirt, his fingers colliding with her bra. She felt the shiver of it; he was frightened or excited or both. She hardly blamed him; so was she.

"Unhook it."

He fumbled with the catch, not getting anywhere. She had to help him. Then her bra parted, falling away to either side, exposing her bosom. It was a good one; her problem had been too much flesh, rather than too little.

"Fondle my breast," she said.

He took her left breast awkwardly in his hand, gently squeezing. He lacked the touch Andrew had, but that was not the point of this exercise. In time she would teach him how to do it effectively. "Oh, Linda! I'm ready to come in my pants!"

Oops. She hadn't thought of that complication, but he surely wasn't fooling. "Then we had better stop. Remove your hand."

Reluctantly, he did so.

"You were the Doll," she said as she re-hooked her bra and buttoned her shirt. "But you may enjoy it, both ways."

"Yes!"

"But I won't do that on a date," she said. "Only when we're having prescribed sex."

He started laughing uncontrollably. "Linda, you're so great!"

"Thank you." But it wasn't enough. She wanted to really make the point. "Now your turn. I am Anna. Command me."

His blush renewed. "I c-c-couldn't."

He was balking again. That, oddly, gave her courage. She was the mistress here, completely controlling the situation, regardless of who did what physically. She liked that empowerment. "Then let me help you. We'll pretend that you just have given me the command to fondle your penis."

"B-b-b-but—"

"So this is what I would do in response. I am

Anna, the obliging Doll, doing your will." She reached to his crotch, under the table, and worked to unzip his fly. He sat seemingly stunned, neither moving nor protesting further, his gaze fixed on her face.

She reached in, felt his undershorts, and found their front opening. His rigid member came into her grasp, slick with the early leakage of his excitement. Yes! His hesitancy was not because of any lack of interest, but natural shyness. She was turning him on with a vengeance. She was thrilled by this unfakeable confirmation of his desire for her. She had been emotionally cautious, but now was assured of his commitment. She could safely let herself go. That was a relief.

She moved her fingers down the hard shaft to find the scrotum, with its two precious testicles. They were like smooth wren's eggs in that warm living bag. Handling that turned her on. Then she brought the member out of his trousers so she could see it clearly. It was not aesthetic, but it *really* turned her on. It was the font of a man's power, the thing that enabled the ultimate connection. The penetrator that sought a woman's most hidden secret orifice, thrust inside to make its imperative way, and filled it to capacity. Not pretty, but essential. And now under her complete control.

She studied the details. His penis was not circumcised, but the foreskin was starting to draw back, stretching like a glove coming off a finger to expose the pulsing purple head with its little terminal slit. From that tiny orifice would come the semen, the substance of life, the origin of babies.

Already there was a clear drop of sap in it, sliding down the underside of the head, like a kitchen tap with a slow drip. Yes, he was excited; he was near ejaculation. She realized that this could get messy. It wasn't just water supplying that instrument.

She paused to fetch a cloth handkerchief from her purse. She deployed it around the area. Then she put her thumb and forefinger around the shaft of his member, just below the head, as she had practiced with Andrew. She grasped it lightly and drew down the foreskin so that the head emerged complete, the slit widening like a tiny open mouth.

Just like that the penis was bucking in her grasp and spouting from that slit. He had a hair trigger compared to Andrew! Quickly she surrounded it with the handkerchief, as jet after jet of whitish fluid shot up like a tiny intermittent fountain and landed on the cloth. She felt the shaft quivering, expanding slightly with each rush of ejaculate. Soon the spurts diminished, hardly clearing the head, and the last one merely oozed out. It looked like egg white. Maybe wren's egg white. She stifled a smile.

She made sure the geysering was finished, then folded in the dry section of the cloth and gently mopped up the spillage. Now she saw that it was not thin like water, but thick like hand lotion. Already the rod was softening and shrinking, just as Andrew's did after the emission. She was so glad she had gotten that practice, so knew what to do. Then she took her finger and thumb and stripped the penis in the manner of milking a cow, drawing out what remained inside the tube and wiping that up too. She was fascinated by the way it came up to the little slit and dribbled out, as though she had conjured it on her own. One day she would have that happen in her mouth, and would suck out the remnant, a cleaner process. One part of her mind was amazed; six months ago she would have been horrified by the thought of even touching a man's penis, let alone taking it into her mouth for its culmination. The Doll had truly changed her perspective.

Finally she folded the handkerchief with the moisture inside and returned it carefully to her purse. She put the limp penis back inside his undershorts, and zipped the fly back up. He was done.

Clive remained frozen, his mouth open. "See what you made me do?" she said. "Anna had to obey your command."

"Oh, Linda!" he breathed. "I love you."

She rather thought he did. "I may love you too, Clive. Women are slower about these things, but I have dreamed of you." She smiled. "So we'll do it this weekend," she repeated. "All six of us together. To take turns playing Doll. Don't forget."

He had to smile back. Obviously he would not forget. None of them would.

Then she kissed him, chastely, and they separated. She was wet herself, and would have to clean up and change her panties. Theoretically, only Clive had been the one sexually turned on by their interaction, but her participation as tacit dominatrix had reached right into her core. Bending Clive to her sexual will was a new and rare stimulation. Actually she might after all do some things on a date. Even up against a wall in a dark alcove. Maybe she would surprise herself—and him. She had developed potentials he had not dreamed of, and she meant to explore them in this "safe" context.

The near future promised to be interesting. Too bad about the Doll. She considered Andrew to be her worthy "ex."

* * * *

I started writing this story in January, 2006, but it got interrupted by novels I had to read for blurbing and galley proofing, and by another tale suggested by an inset story in the galleys, and by my bimonthly updating of my ongoing Survey of Internet Publishers and related Services, and my bimonthly Hipiers.com column. My life seems to be largely composed of interruptions. So I completed and edited it in February. I am of retirement age, 71 at this writing, but the supposed relaxation and spare time of the senior generation have not caught up with me. I'm not sure they ever will; I'm a workaholic, and I love writing. And of course, I still try to imagine what young sex is like, half a century after the fact, though I'll never experience it again in real life. So "Doll" had to be shunted aside for a time, but it was not about to leave itself unfinished.

Most stories in this volume came from ideas I had recorded and saved for years. This one occurred to me the morning of December 28, 2005, as I was working on another project, and never made it to the Idea File. Suddenly I had a page of notes for "Android" and added it to my list of stories to write at this time. I found a more relevant title and it was on its way. So it really has no pedigree; it just came out of the ether as a walk-on player.

Sometimes writing is like that.

Friends of Bolivia

Columbia "Sugar" Bunn gazed for a moment at the pathetic little bundle of letters her sister had saved. Obviously Bolivia had treasured the correspondence. Now what was to be done with it?

She untied the ribbon and read the return address on the most recent envelope. She recognized it: the island military stockade unpopularly known as Nothing Atoll, where Bolivia had been confined three years before her release and discharge from the army. She had been sent up for shoplifting. It had been a bum rap, but the one who had done it was a white woman with connections.

Columbia had known better than to protest; as a plain black woman, Bolivia had been presumed guilty from the outset. She had stoically served her time. She must have a friend there, a fellow prisoner, Columbia thought.

Maybe that correspondent should be notified. The name wasn't on the envelope, which was unusual; normally prisons refused to let letters out that were not fully identified with name and prisoner number. Columbia hoped there was a full name on the letter itself.

She opened it, and was surprised again. This was from a man, and it was a love letter! "My darling, I must see you again soon. I think of you constantly. I want to hold you and kiss you and have beatific sex with you, over and over."

Columbia paused. How could this be? Not only had Bolivia been a prisoner without access to men, she was by her own description as homely as a broken board, and not much smarter. How could she have encountered a man there, let alone evoked his passionate love? An educated man who wrote, "Have beatific sex", instead of, "Let's fuck"? A white man of some means, by the quality of the envelope and paper. This seemed impossible. Yet here were the letters.

She checked the other envelopes. They were all of the same type. There was definitely a man there, one who was not confined to the prison, because a prisoner could not make visits to his girlfriend. A guard, perhaps.

She went to the bottom of the pile to take the oldest letter. She brought it out and read it. And was utterly amazed. Her sister had had much more of a secret life than anyone had known. It came to life for her as she read the letters.

* * * *

Bolivia did not know what the prison commander wanted, but she went willingly with him to his office. She had used her points to buy a twenty-four hour date with him, and he had delivered, though now she knew that it had been only a facade. He had done everything correctly, "by the book", though there was no book for the hidden system of points. She had wanted the illusion of his love, and in the end that illusion had been futile.

Now it was over; they were, as he put it, off the clock. He owed her nothing more.

She halted before his desk and turned back to face him as he closed the door. She waited for whatever was to come. Was he angry because she had bought him with her points?

"I never saw a prettier liar," he said.

She was taken aback. She had lied to cover up the nature of their date; it was no business of the hound dog investigator. She thought the commander understood. "Thank you, sir."

"You saved my ass."

It was odd to hear him speak like that, though what he said was true. "Well, I love you, sir." Which had been the whole point of the exercise.

"What is your name?"

This confused her. "You know who I am, sir. Honey Bunn, lowest of the low."

"Your given name."

"I don't use that, sir."

He merely looked at her.

"Bolivia, sir. Bolivia Bunn."

"Tell me again why you love me."

"You know that too, sir. I was always so sloppy, couldn't keep my prison uniform straight, and then during your inspection I almost fainted on my feet. I thought you were going to put me in solitary, or at least chew me out. But you took me to the infirmary, where they put me to bed, tested my blood, and my sugar was low. They got me medicine, and after that I was okay. You came to see me the day I got out, and said 'Good show, Honey.' Nobody ever said that to me before, or even cared whether I lived or died.

And it was like a storm took me, just blew me away, and I loved you. Ever since."

He nodded. "So much, for so little."

"Yes sir. I know it's stupid, but I ain't the brightest bulb on the chandelier. I didn't mean to embarrass you."

"Perhaps you do not understand how a military officer values his career."

"I guess not, sir. If I'd known it would make trouble for you, I never would have done it."

"You know I am a hard man."

"Yes sir. That don't make no difference to me. I'm sorry."

"Nobody ever loved me enough to lie for me."

"I had to, sir. I already made enough trouble for you; I couldn't let it get even worse."

"And now I love you too, Bolivia, in my fashion."

"Sir?"

He strode forward, swept her into his arms, and kissed her forcefully. She kissed him back, loving the sheer passion of it that he had never shown before. This was real!

He half-carried her to the couch at the side of the office. He threw her down on it. His mouth left hers and traveled down her neck, kissing all the way. He ripped the blouse of her borrowed dress open, exposing her bra, then ripped that off too. He kissed her modest brown right breast and sucked on the hardening nipple.

"Oh, sir," she breathed. Could this really be happening?

"Shut up." He grabbed the hem of her dress and hoisted it up so hard it tore. He hooked his fingers into her panties and tore them too as she spread her legs to accommodate the action. Then he ripped open his fly and brought out his hard member. He pressed her down and jammed it into her willing crevice like a pylon, ramming full depth without pause. His mouth found hers again, kissing savagely as he thrust and thrust and jetted in her center.

Then he collapsed on her, panting. "Oh, sir!" she repeated. "That was great!"

"That's only the beginning. Kiss me." His mouth sought hers.

She cooperated, meeting him halfway. Now his tongue thrust into her mouth, demanding, and she let it probe her, staying close. Nobody had wanted to do this with her before, not face to face. Only the other, and she had learned that well. An ugly face didn't matter down there, only its skill in evoking pleasure, male or female.

"I will have you again," he said. "And bring you with me. But I need time to recover. Have patience."

He wanted more? This was utter heaven! But of course he couldn't do it right away. No man could. She had developed a fine perception of male capacity.

"Let me do you, sir," she gasped after a moment. "I know how."

"You don't have to, Bolivia. I have no intention of demeaning you."

"I want to, sir. I want to give you pleasure."

"No, I want to give *you* pleasure. I owe you."

"Sir, I love you. I get my pleasure giving you pleasure. Let me, please."

"Bolivia, you know I'll be using those points you

gave me to have my will of the prettiest female prisoners. You have set up my pleasure for months to come."

"I know, sir. That's what they're for. But I got you right now. Let me."

He paused, gazing into her face, fathoming the sincerity there. "If you're sure."

"I'm sure." She worked her way out from under him as he twisted on the couch. It was awkward, as the couch was not made for this, but soon he was lying on his back and she was kneeling on the floor beside him.

She lifted his limp penis and licked it off.

"Bolivia! I should at least wash it first."

"No, sir. There ain't any part of you I don't love." She took the head of it into her mouth, sucked gently, and caressed it with her tongue.

"You *do* know how," he said, half in wonder. "You have an exquisite touch."

She couldn't answer, because she was taking his member further in. She had learned long ago to suppress the choke reflex as the tip brushed the back of her throat. She moved her head up and down, drawing almost completely off it, then slowly swallowing it again. The suction was making it swell.

Since she couldn't talk, he did. "My point being that the incidental kindness I did you, treating you like a human being, making sure you were well, was a narrow avenue for the emotion it evidently stirred in you. I did not properly understand that, until you did me an incidental kindness in return. Then my own emotion suffered a perhaps similar evocation, and I saw you for the dedicated creature you are.

Bolivia, I don't want to end it here. I want you to send me your address when you get settled outside. Write me a letter, and I will write to you."

Now she had to respond. "Sir, you don't want no written contact with me! I'm just a no-count black bitch."

"You are someone who knows me for what I am, and still loves me. You proved it. I value that."

"I love you, sir," she agreed, and took his thickening member in again.

"We will have a correspondence, and I will visit you when I can. I would prefer that this not be advertised, for reasons you surely understand."

She gave an extra suck, indicating her agreement. Nobody outside knew about points, and officers did not mix openly with prisoners. Part of the code was to keep the secret.

"I apologize for not giving you passion before. That was unkind of me."

She lifted her head. "No need, sir."

"But you have my passion now, and not merely because of your skill with oral sex. You truly love me, and I love that love, and I think I love you too."

Then he was silent as she got serious about his sensation. The penis was hard now, ready to deliver. She could feel the well of passion rising, and knew that she could soon bring him off. Never before had she truly wanted to do it. Her cleft was wet with her own desire as well as his spume. She had not gotten her orgasm before; it had been too fast, and she had been too distracted by the wonder of his passion. But now she was getting there.

She felt the first shudder, like the rumble of the

deep pipe of a volcano. She sucked and licked and thrust, carefully triggering the reaction. She focused on the section just under the head, the man's parallel to the woman's clitoris, tickling it just so.

There was another shudder. She sucked harder, taking it as deeply into her as it would go, closing her throat about its head as she pursed her lips around its base. It was coming, coming, COMING!

It got larger and harder, and spewed out its hot fluid, a geyser down her throat. And her vagina clenched and quivered, getting its own orgasm at last. She sucked and swallowed, taking in everything, while her climax shook her similarly. What a feeling! It was as though his emission was coursing right down inside her to her vulva, setting it off simultaneously.

They basked in it together. He put his hand on her head, gently stroking her hair. "You are some woman."

"You are some man, sir."

"Remember: write to me."

"I will, sir."

That was about it. She changed back to her own clothes, returning the torn and soiled dress to the commander's savvy secretary, who merely smiled. A few days later Bolivia was released, from the stockade, and the army. She was a civilian again.

She was determined to go straight, now that she had a reason to live. She had not been a model citizen before; she was now. But making an honest living was hard, and there was no help. She had to do a few men to get money to eat; her sister Columbia lived in another town and was barely getting by herself.

A yarn company sent her a pitch, and she took it seriously. She wanted to do it, to run her own mini-business. To show customers the different types and colors of yarn the company offered, and order the hanks they wanted. She wrote about it to the commander, because she needed something to say to him, and her life was dull compared to his. He wrote to her in detail about the pretty women he was having now, with her points; she insisted on it. "It's like I'm doing it with you, when you get it from my points," she told him. "I get so hot when you tell me how you plumb them." And she did. Some of those gals knew tricks she didn't, and she practiced them in her mind. It made such a difference to have a man who treated her like a sex object and meant it.

He visited her, and there in her dingy one room apartment they had sex so hot she managed to get her orgasm the first time. She was so thrilled to be in his arms, to feel his desire, to get his hard penis as deep into her as she could, to feel it pulsing while he kissed her. She loved it that he kissed her, during; it meant he really did desire her, and not just her vulva. And this time she let him do her, licking her crack and her clit till she clamped her thighs on his ears and moaned and writhed in ecstasy. It was just so great to be doing it with *him*. And he told her that it was just as good with her as with those pretty girls. She knew he was lying, but she loved the lie.

And he gave her a thousand dollars to start her business. That floored her; she hadn't asked for it or even thought of it. But he was right; she needed it to rent the shop and set up her window.

So it continued for most of a year, and the shop

was almost breaking even. She was determined to make money, so she could repay the commander; she never meant to keep his money, only to borrow it.

Then the gang called. It had no name; it was just a local clot of tough young punks getting into drugs, whores, and the protection racket. They told her how much she would pay them, every week, to start. She told them no. She was trying to go straight, and if she paid them, she would never make a profit and be able to repay the commander.

They warned her, once, by bashing in her window. That hurt; she could not afford to replace it. She had to board it up and put her sign on it, saying that she was still open for business. Somehow she intended to manage. Fuck them.

Then they killed her. They came by day, dragged her out, and beat her to death on the street. They wanted the whole neighborhood to hear her screams; it was an object lesson for any others who might try to stand their ground.

* * * *

That was yesterday. Today Columbia was here to see to her sister's meager estate, half blinded by tears. She knew it was no good reporting the crime; the police had already collected the body, just one of a number that the gang left lying around. The police didn't like the gang, and neither did the people, but anybody who snitched got brutally killed. There was nothing they could do.

This packet of letters: it was dynamite. Not relating to the gang, but to the prison commander. It could get him fired. That business about points—she wasn't sure how they were earned, but it was clear that they could buy anything in the prison, including especially the favors of lovely women. Including a public date with the post commander. It was a secret whose revelation could destroy the careers of everyone associated with the prison. Columbia could not bring herself to destroy the packet, so she did the next best thing; she took it to where it would do no harm.

They let her into the island prison on a visitor's pass. All she said was that she was a friend of Bolivia Bunn's, and she was in. She came to the commander's secretary and repeated the magic words. Then she was standing before the commander himself.

"Sir, I am Columbia Bunn, Bolivia's sister."

"Welcome, Columbia," he said. "I see the family resemblance. What is your concern?"

Suddenly she realized that he didn't know. It was hardly national news, not even state news; it was just one more local incident, and the prison was elsewhere. It had happened only two days ago. The word had not gotten around.

"Sir, I hate to tell you, but my sister is dead."

He stared at her, his face congealing.

"She—she was trying to run a little yarn business, as you know, and this gang had this protection racket, and she told them no, and they killed her. She wanted to save the money so she could repay you. She loved you, sir. There's an informal wake next week, just her friends. I thought you might want to—I'm sorry."

He remained silent, staring at her. She had to stumble on. "She saved your letters. I read them.

That's how I knew to come here. We don't want these getting around. So I brought them to you." Jerkily she pushed the packet toward him, setting it on the big desk.

Now he spoke. "I loved her."

"Yes, sir. So did I. It's a shame what happened. But there ain't nothing to be done about it."

He made an expression that reminded her of nothing so much as the baring of the fangs of an injured but still savage wolf. "We shall see. Thank you for bringing me this." He took the letters and put them in a drawer in the desk.

"I'll go now," she said, feeling awkward.

"An officer will take you home. We shall meet again."

"There's no need, sir. I can make my own way."

"I depend on that."

What did he mean? Then an officer entered the office. He took her arm, guiding her out. To her amazement, she got a helicopter ride to the mainland, then to the closest empty lot near her home. She could walk from there, saving the bus fare.

"Thank you, sir," she told the man. He was white, like the commander, so she treated him with respect. Black ghetto women learned that at birth. Then, "If you don't mind my asking, sir, can you tell me what the commander meant when he said he depended on my making my own way?"

"That you will do what you need to do, without involving others whose business it is not. There are things that should not be bruited about."

She took a wild flyer. "Like points, sir?"

"Exactly." He shut the cabin, and she had to scurry back before the whirling blades threatened to blow her away.

So others did know about the points, and kept them secret. Well, she could handle it; she was good at secrets.

Two days later, back home, she received a message, delivered by the officer, who appeared at her door. "The commander will attend the wake with friends of Bolivia. See that only those you trust participate. Go to the lot the hour before. We will convey you there. Questions?"

"No, sir," she said. "I got it."

He departed without further word. Military folk were like that.

The day of the wake she dressed in her best and walked to the empty lot an hour and a half before the wake. In fifteen minutes the helicopter arrived. It contained the officer, the commander, and four black people: a man and three women in civilian clothing. What was going on?

"We are friends of Bolivia, in prison," one woman told her as the helicopter took off. "We have a deal; we will speak at her wake, and talk with those who want to. Then we have two hour passes, off the record. Please do not tell; it would be awkward."

"Points," Columbia said.

"Similar. We're glad to do it. We really are her friends. She was a good woman, and we hate that she got murdered. There will be consequences." Her gaze flicked to the commander, who sat impassively. "Off the record."

"Got it."

They flew to Bolivia's city, and to an empty lot near the house where the wake was to be. They got out and formed an irregular column led by the commander, with Columbia beside him, showing the route.

It was a bad section of town and two local toughs spied the women, one of whom was quite pretty, and cut them off. The party halted.

The male prisoner stepped forward. "We're going to a wake," he said gruffly. "We don't want no trouble." Then before the toughs could react, a seven-inch blade appeared in his hand as if by magic. "You understand."

The toughs hesitated. Two against one seemed easy enough. They had knives too.

The prisoner moved so fast that a blink would have hidden it. A spot of blood appeared on one tough's forearm where the knife had cut. "Try me," the prisoner said softly.

The toughs got the message. That slash could have been on a throat, and deeper. This was an experienced knife artist. They faded back. The knife disappeared. The commander's mouth quirked. The column moved on.

"That saved them from getting gutted by Silvie," the commander murmured, and there was an understanding chuckle behind. Silvie was evidently the pretty one, but obviously no patsy.

No one seemed to find it odd that a prisoner carried a deadly hidden weapon. The commander clearly knew his people.

They reached the wake without further event. Columbia introduced them to the man in charge, who looked surprised to see the white man here. "These are five friends of Bolivia, from prison. They just want to pay their respects."

They took their seats. There was no body; that had been hauled away, and of course this was an unofficial service.

One by one the local folk rose and spoke, telling of their respect for Bolivia and their horror at her brutal death. They agreed she was a good person who didn't deserve her fate. Columbia spoke too, but half of what she tried to say was drowned out by her tears and she was unable to finish. The commander, sitting beside her, put his hand on hers and squeezed it reassuringly. He, more than any, understood her grief.

Then the prisoners took their turns. First was Silvie. "I was new, two years ago, and I didn't know prison life. I was lost. Then Honey, as we called her there, took me in hand and showed me the ropes. She knew what I was in for—I cut the balls off my cheating man and let him bleed to death—and didn't hold it against me. I had my looks, and she told me how to make the most of them, in the game. Soon enough I had points—I mean, I did well, and my life was easier. Because of her. She never would take anything back; she had done it from friendship. Well, she got mine." She too was overcome by tears, and had to sit down.

The man spoke. "I was in for murder too, and I had attitude. No friends, money, or points. I hated everybody. Honey, she came to me, and said she knew how it was, though she was just a petty thief. I guess she did; she—she wasn't exactly a pretty woman, and maybe folk were hard on her for that. And she did me for free, and talked to me, and helped me catch on how to get along. It really helped, and I learned how to make it in prison. I owe her."

He paused, then spoke with a harder tone. "I'm sorry I can't take out the bastards who killed her; I still got years to serve. But if any of them should wind up in my prison, I guarantee they'll never get out alive. And Silvie—she couldn't finish, so I'll say it for her: the man who kills any one of those thugs, let him come visit the prison, and Silvie'll make him so happy he'll float out. It will happen, off the record. I guarantee she will not cut your balls off." He sat, to a murmur of mirth. Silvie, beside him, nodded.

Another woman stood. "Call me Les; I'm lesbian. Hon—Bolivia wasn't, so there could be nothing more than friendship between us. But she was a damn good friend. She didn't shy away from me, and stood up for me when there was trouble. Not everybody does that."

The last woman stood. "I'm an old-timer. I was the one who showed Bolivia the ropes. She wasn't pretty, and she was a bit slow, but her heart was good and her love, when she gave it, was true. She was a good woman."

Then the commander stood. "I am the commander of the army prison post known colloquially as Nothing Atoll. Bolivia was my friend. In fact, she was my lover. She loved me and I loved her. I mention this so you will understand that I am serious when I say I mean to have vengeance for her murder. I am a hard man; I do not forgive trespasses against me. I understand it was an anonymous local gang that killed her because she would not pay protection money. I mean to see every member of that gang dead and in hell. Toward that end I have made contact with the local authorities. They will act when they have sufficient information."

He paused, gazing around the room. "Let any person with information approach any police officer, meter maid, groundskeeper—anyone who works for the city. Say 'I am a friend of Bolivia,' and you will be granted anonymity and immunity from self-incrimination. Identify any gang members you know of. That's all. If you care to give your name, it will be forwarded to the prison, where you may visit and be compatibly received by Silvie or one like her. If you have a friend in that prison, you may obtain for that friend a twenty-four hour pass to visit you, off the record. All of this is off the record. Do not talk to the media. I trust your discretion; you mourn Bolivia, as do I. I will depart now, but the four will remain to satisfy your concerns. Thank you."

He made his way to the exit. Columbia hesitated only briefly, then followed him out.

"Where are you going?" she asked as he stood outside.

"I was going to go to a restaurant. Rendezvous for return is not for two and a half hours yet."

"Are you hungry?"

"No. Not for food."

"Wait for me." She went back inside, approached the man who had challenged them, and took him aside. "Is there a private room where we can wait a while? The commander wants them to be free to talk without being restrained by his presence."

He led her through the house. "There."

"Thank you."

She went back out to fetch the commander. He accompanied her to the room. It was nicely appointed, for a ghetto chamber, with a bed, table, two chairs, and an adjoining lavatory. Probably it was rented by prostitutes for their business.

"This is more convenient," the commander said. "I appreciate it."

"I had a weird idea. Hear me out and kick me out if you wish." Suddenly she was nervous.

He sat on the bed. "I am attentive."

"You loved her. So did I. We are in grief together."

"Agreed."

"I thought we could—" But she couldn't get the preposterous words out.

"Honor her together?" he asked.

She nodded.

"I am not a nice man."

"Good thing all I've seen of you is nice, and I want vengeance too."

"You could never be other than a surrogate for Bolivia. I would not value you for yourself."

"Yes. That's the way I want it. We can bring each other some piece of her that no one else can share."

"I would call you by her name."

"I would answer to it."

"Then it appears we understand each other. How would you have it?"

"Like the first time, the first real time, with her."

He shook his head. "I would not care to damage

your outfit."

She stripped away her clothing efficiently, and stood naked before him. She knew she was better looking than her sister, but still no beauty.

"Oh, yes," he said. He removed his own clothing and stood with a rampant member. "Ready?"

"Eager," she said.

He came to her, wrapped his arms about her, and half threw her to the bed. He kissed her face, then her neck, then her breasts. He lifted himself as she spread her legs, positioned his member, and drove it urgently into her. There was no resistance or discomfort, because she was more than ready, almost dripping wet. He ejaculated in a moment. It was much like a rape.

"Thank you, Bolivia!" he gasped.

"Welcome, sir."

"You *are* like her."

"Thank you."

"You have given me the single thing I could not ask for. I don't mean only sex."

"Sex with Bolivia."

"Yes. I still desire her. I feared alienating you by such a notion. Our love started with sex, really. It was what she wanted from me. That is, true passion. For a man that means sex."

"I understand."

"I did love her. But sex was always the center of it."

"She loved having you feel that way. Nobody wanted straight sex with her before, and certainly nobody loved her romantically."

"When I first saw you, resembling her, I desired

you. Because of that similarity. Even before I learned she was dead. I felt guilty."

"I read about you before I met you, sir. Your letters. The way you cared for her. I think I wanted to be with you then. But I was afraid it could never be."

He smiled. "It seems it could be. I would never touch you if she lived."

"Nor would I touch you."

"There will be ugliness on the street."

"That gang's been harassing this neighborhood for years. It's past time to handle it."

"It will be handled."

They proceeded to more sex, following the script defined by the letters. Then, seemingly suddenly, their time was up, and they had to reassemble and return to the site of the wake to collect the others.

"We already have two names," Silvie said with satisfaction. "I took care of the man. They have rooms here."

"And I was with the woman," the knife artist said. "She wasn't much to look at, but she was passionate as hell."

"I know the type," the commander said with the hint of a smile. "Leave the knife in the copter."

"You bet. But thanks, sir. It was good to have it for a while."

"Fair exchange. We have a common mission."

"Yes sir," all four said together.

Columbia marveled again. Four prisoners and the commander, with no trouble. Whatever this point system was, it could enable miracles.

They dropped her off near her house. "May I write?" the commander inquired, stepping out with her.

"Yes sir."

"To Bolivia."

"Of course. She will answer."

He embraced her and kissed her. Then he climbed back into the machine.

The helicopter departed. Columbia stood and watched until it cleared the horizon. She knew she would be seeing it again.

Nothing happened for a week. Nothing visible. Then, abruptly, hell broke loose. All thirteen members of the gang were slaughtered on the street, "resisting arrest." Their bodies lay there for hours for all to see. Some seemed to have been hacked apart with machetes. There was no news report. The neighborhood was free at last.

They probably had resisted, Columbia realized, but it wouldn't have mattered. They had been doomed the moment they killed Bolivia. Bolivia had friends.

* * * *

I wrote this in the middle of "Doll." I had to break off "Doll" because of a glut of three manuscripts to read, one of which was the galley proof of the first Relationships collection. When I read "Hot Game," which includes the inset story of Honey Bunn and the post commander, I wondered what happened in the commander's office. Yes, I wrote it; I still wondered. Too bad I couldn't return to explore it further.

I couldn't? The notion percolated in my cranium, and soon frothed into its own story, a sort of continuation. If you thought it seemed familiar, without quite fathoming where you saw it before, that was where. Thus it became a story in its own right, sequel to the inset. Then I returned to resume writing "Doll." Again, writing can be like that.

Siren

The Prince woke refreshed. Someone had evidently been taking good care of him during his convalescence. The drug they had given him to abate the pain and promote healing had done its job, but it also had the side effect of stifling his recollection of the occasion. The last thing he remembered was the arrow piercing his shoulder, not far from his heart.

He sat up, and winced. He was not yet entirely healed.

A woman was there immediately, a nurse. "Prince!" she said. "You must not stir, lest you re-injure yourself before being wholly well."

"I am well enough," he said, drawing off the covers to swing his legs off the bed.

He paused. He was naked under the sheet.

She drew the sheet back over him, unconcerned. Nurses were like that. "Stay, please, Prince."

He yielded for the moment. "How goes the battle?"

"I can't tell you, Prince. I have not left this room these several days."

"Then I will find out for myself. My armor must be nearby." He threw off the sheet again, heedless of the nether exposure.

"Prince, no! I will be punished if I let you injure

yourself. I must hold you here, and I will do so. Please do not make me force you."

He paused to gaze at her. She was a well featured young woman, hardly outstanding, but not unappealing. There was something odd about her hair, as though it was partly formed of feathers.

Feathers? He reached forward to touch her shirt just above her bosom. He unbuttoned it. She did not resist as he bared her front.

There, hanging between her full bare breasts, was a lustrous green gem. He knew its nature: it was magic, enabling a person to talk as an animal, and vice versa.

"You're a siren!" he said, surprised. "How can you be nursing me?"

"They are short of nurses."

This did not quite add up. If only one nurse remained in the city, that one would be assigned to him. "Where are the others?" He continued unbuttoning her shirt, and drew it out from the band of her skirt.

"Tending the troops."

It still did not align. "Has the city been evacuated?" He pushed the open shirt back around her body and off her shoulders.

She could not avoid a direct question. "Yes." She removed the shirt from her arms, which were now revealed to be feathered along the back sides. He knew that her back would also be feathered; from behind she would look like a large sea bird. The clothing enabled her to mask that aspect, and the gem made it possible for her to speak and understand the human tongue. Without it she might chirp like the bird she half-was.

"Then the situation is critical. I must join the battle."

"Prince, you must not," she protested. "You are not ready."

"Ready or not, I serve my country." He swung his legs off the bed, suppressing the wince as pain flared in his shoulder.

She was there immediately, her arms about him, supporting him—and restraining him. Her bared breasts were pressed against his bare chest, turning him on. "You will do your country no good if you die. You need two more days healing."

"Better to die defending it, than let it perish without me." He struggled to get past her. This only caused him to slide across her breasts, giving him an erection.

"Do not make me force you," she repeated.

He looked into her face, so close to his. Her eyes were moist. "You're crying!"

"I am, Prince."

"Sirens don't cry! They seduce." Indeed, his hardened member now pressed against her belly.

"I cry because I do not want to seduce you."

This was truly curious. He compromised. "I will rest while you explain this to me. But do not dawdle; my patience is limited." In more than one respect.

She guided him back onto the bed, lifted his legs, and covered them again. She ignored his erection; surely her kind seldom saw a man without one. Then she sat on the bed, facing him. "I care for you, Prince. That is why I wish not to seduce you. It would cripple you for the future, and that would not be right."

"Nonsense! Your kind has no conscience." His eyes remained fixed on her human upper section. "You tempt men to their destruction in the sea."

"That is false. We do have feelings and concern for right and wrong. We mind our own business, but sailors sometimes will not leave us alone. Regardless, it is not merely conscience. It is love. I want only what is best for you. That is why your father knew I could be trusted to take care of you, in the absence of qualified nurses."

He was intrigued. Sirens were notorious, and hardly limited to the water. They used sex appeal to lure men into sex with them, and that doomed the men. He had heard they were absolutely cynical creatures. But he was inclined to believe this one. "How?"

"Three years ago, by a rocky shore," she said. "A ship was anchored for the evening, and the men were spearing fish. One took aim at a big bird perched on a projecting stone, just above the water, facing away. You stayed his hand. 'That's a siren,' you said. 'Let her be.' So she survived."

"I remember," Prince said. "I have nothing against halflings."

"She was me. I turned, realizing that I had been in danger, and saw you. I knew I owed you my life. I loved you in that instant. I waved to you, and plunged into the sea."

"I remember," Prince repeated. "You were a child. It would have been a shame to hurt you."

"I was a child," she agreed. "But in two years I matured. Then I came ashore to seek you, that I might repay the debt."

"There was no need."

"It was perhaps a minor thing, to you," she said. "It was my life, to me. I wore the stone, so I could go among your people and communicate, asking after you. They directed me to the palace, and your father the King interviewed me." She paused reminiscently. "There was something almost familiar about him. I liked him. But I love you."

"There may be a certain family resemblance between us." He shrugged. "I spared you because I see no reason to hurt those who are no threat to us. Sirens are scenic, especially when viewed from the front. I did not realize you were immature until you turned. It was nothing personal."

"Not to you," she said. "The King told me to wait, and would take me to you when the occasion required. So I waited a year, training as a nurse, trusting him. Then when the battle turned bad, and you were injured—" She shrugged. "I am here."

"How bad is it?"

"Very bad. I think we are almost the only ones left in the city, as the enemy cannot be stopped."

"Now I know my father did not leave me to be killed or taken hostage."

"He did not," she agreed. "But you had to be kept immobile, for your injury was life-threatening. It would have required twelve good men to bear you on a litter in shifts. Those men could better be used to help evacuate the old folk, ill folk, women, and children who would otherwise be left to the brutality of the enemy front line. He made a decision to use them for that, saying you would understand."

"I do," the Prince said. "He enabled hundreds to get to safety, instead of one, knowing I could take care of myself once I recovered. Now I am ready, and I doubt much time remains."

"But you need two days more rest and healing. If the enemy comes before then, I will take you via water to safety."

"The river connects to the capital city," he said. "Thence to the sea. But the enemy will have all of it covered by archers. You have taken this into account?"

"Yes. I will swim with you, infusing my air into you, so that we can course along the bottom. They will not see us. But they may not come within two days, and by the third day you will be well enough to don your armor and ride your horse out, so escape will not be necessary."

"And it is your job to keep me here those two days."

"My duty," she agreed.

"And if I attempt to forge on out of here now, you will prevent me by seducing me."

"I will, Prince. I can't overcome you physically, but I can prevent you from departing."

"There are legends about sirens, but I do not credit many of them. They can lure fools to their deaths among the stormy shoals, but I am not a fool."

"You are not, Prince, and we do not seek mischief to your kind. Far from it! But I can stop you. I beg you not to make me do it."

"Let me verify: you do not want to seduce me, because you love me."

"True, Prince."

"This seems counterintuitive."

"I want what is best for you, Prince. If I seduce you, there will never be another woman who can give you satisfaction. You will not be able to fall in love with a normal human woman. This will cripple your social existence and perhaps interfere with your marriage. This would not be good. So I must leave you alone if I possibly can, enabling you to pursue your normal future life."

He nodded. "I have heard that legend. You are telling me it is true?"

"That one is true, Prince."

"I am inclined to doubt it. I have had women. None have spoiled me for my future. The woman I marry will likely be for political reason, to make a beneficial liaison with a neighboring kingdom, and to generate a male heir. Exactly as is the case with my father. For love, I will have a luscious mistress."

"You would be spoiled for that too, Prince."

He shook his head. "Perhaps you believe that. I am inclined to risk it. My country needs me."

"Please, I beg you no! You risk death on the field, being not fully recovered. Do not try to pass me."

He swept the sheet off again. "If you do not wish to seduce me, please stand clear."

Now her tears were flowing freely. "Prince! Allow me one demonstration that perhaps will not spoil you."

He paused. "You have one minute. Make your demonstration."

She leaned close and took his right hand in hers. She closed her hand around his index finger. "Just a little," she said.

Then there was a wash of sheer pleasure in his finger. It felt as though it was his masculine member, penetrating her encompassing cleft. The pleasure intensified almost unbearably. He thrust his finger harder into her grasp, and climaxed.

"Oh!" she exclaimed. "Too much! I'm sorry, Prince." The pleasure was fading as she let go of his finger.

He felt something, and glanced down at his groin. His member had spurted into the air, leaving goo on his legs.

"You were not fooling," he said, amazed.

"I'm so sorry! I am young and inexperienced, and you are virile. I misjudged the potency." She was busy mopping up the spillage with a sponge. "I hope I have not ruined you."

He laughed. "Perhaps to a naïve girl, sex is ruin. Not to an experienced man."

"I mean, spoiled you for human women."

"Oh, I doubt you have. I admit to being impressed. But the battle still needs me. You have made your demonstration, and I must be on my way."

"Prince! No!"

"You can't seduce me again so soon; I'm spent. Now do not force me to push you aside."

She paused. "You did it on purpose. To make me spend you harmlessly, so you could escape."

"You give me too much credit, Siren. I am merely taking advantage of an opportunity."

"I can still stop you. But so soon after the first, it *will* corrupt you."

"I doubt it."

"Please. I will do only a token, so you know."

"Then will you let me go?"

"No, Prince."

He sighed good-naturedly. "Token, then, if only to show you that you can't." He held up his finger.

She clasped it. In a moment he felt the divine pleasure, and saw his penis stiffening.

"Enough." She let his finger go. "It is effective because I do not depend on the restoration of your capacity. I can transmit pleasure to you, so that there is no limit for you. You can be in sexual ecstasy for as long as you choose, without suffering any physical damage. That is the real reason a siren spoils a man for any normal woman."

"Now I am really impressed," he said. "Suppose you take hold of my member directly?"

"It would spurt," she said. "And you might be committed. You must not." She was covering his legs again.

"What, then, is left for full vaginal sex?"

"Immediate, full commitment."

"Now I believe you," he said. "You will not relent?"

"I will not, Prince. I promised the King."

His father had always been a savvy man. He had known how to keep his son in line.

"So my choice is between remaining submissively here two more days, or being seduced and co-opted into passion with you that will ruin me for ordinary women."

"Yes, Prince. I apologize for such unkindness."

He considered a moment. "Siren, I like you. Can I safely kiss you?"

"I'm not sure."

"Why the uncertainty?"

"I can turn it off," she said. "Otherwise I would not be able to touch you for massages and necessary services. But I love you, and I fear I could not completely turn off a kiss. So it would be better not to risk it."

"You have been massaging me?"

"Yes, Prince, while you slept. Low powered massages, especially around your injured shoulder and your chest near your heart, to promote healing."

"Low powered? Similar to the sexual stimulation?"

"Yes. The King wants you mended soon."

"What other 'necessary services'?"

"You were unconscious, Prince, but you still needed to eat and relieve yourself of wastes."

"You have been spoon-feeding me, and helping me piss?"

"Yes."

"Help me piss now."

"There is no need, now that you are conscious."

"Humor me."

"As you wish, Prince." She fetched a bottle with a narrow neck, uncovered his nether torso, and took hold of his flaccid member. She set it into the neck. There was a brief urgent tickling; then his urine streamed forth, splashing into the bottle.

"How is it I am not stiffening?" he asked as it flowed. "You are handling me."

"I have turned it off, using only a trace to stimulate the flow."

"But normally having a woman handle me there

gives me an immediate erection, and I am unable to urinate."

"Yes. I am having to exert considerable suppression."

"Turn it off."

"As you wish."

The flow had been dwindling. Now it stopped, and his member swelled, filling the neck of the bottle. His reflex was normal.

"Suppress again."

His member diminished, and a weak residual flow resumed, emptying the last of his bladder. She removed the bottle, capped it, and set it under the bed. "Thank you, Prince."

"Could I have sex with you, in your neutral state, and not be compromised?"

"Yes, Prince, if I can suppress my natural inclination to capture you. I will give you that pleasure if you insist, but it is risky."

"If you did not love me, you could safely give me sex?"

"Yes, Prince. It would not be compelling for you, but would relieve your urgency somewhat."

"But if I attempt to escape, you will let yourself go, and make me yours."

"Yes, Prince. It is a threat I hope I do not have to implement."

He gazed at her cannily. "Or do you hope you *do* have to implement it?"

She blushed. Answer enough.

"I am inclined to take that risk. You have become appealing to me."

"Do not take it, Prince! It is because of the

demonstration. I used too much power, and it incites your desire for more. But if you do not touch me again, that should fade, and you will be safe in a day or so."

He nodded. "That may be so. But I can't say I want to be safe, as you put it. If I must remain here two more days, I would like to do it clasping you."

Her tears started to flow again. "Please do not, Prince. I am trying to guide you safely through this danger."

"Remove the rest of your clothing and join me here in bed."

"I must not, Prince."

"That was not a request," he said sternly.

Now the tears were streaming. "I cannot disobey you, Prince. But I beg you, do not command me thus."

"Because it would be rape?"

She nodded. "Not of me, Prince. Of you. I know I would be unable to remain neutral in your embrace. I would capture you."

"Then capture me."

"Please," she said, weeping. "I must not. I am an animal. You are the Prince. I must protect you to be best of my ability."

He merely waited.

Reluctantly, she drew down her skirt, exposing her feathered genital region and backside, and came to lie beside him. She closed her eyes as if expecting to be tortured.

"What is your given name?"

"I am Kiene, Prince."

"And I am James. You may call me that, since

you are about to capture me."

"Please, I fear you do not understand what you risk."

"Now listen to me," Prince James said. "Judge what I say, and if it does not make sense to you, I will let you go."

Her eyes opened. "I do not understand."

"You will in a moment, I trust. Consider my situation. I am the likely heir to my father's kingdom, in due course, if the enemy does not destroy it first. And even then, I would be subject to an arranged marriage of the enemy's choice, to lend legitimacy to its hegemony and pacify the people. My fate is unlikely to be completely my preference."

"I am sad for you, Prince."

"James."

"James," she said with difficulty.

"You surely are sad for me. You may be able to help."

"I am trying to. Let me get away from you. I am near the breaking point."

"In a moment. The women I will encounter are bound to be extremely cynical. Some will also be beautiful. They will do their best to play me sexually so as to bend me to their will, and I am too likely to yield to it."

"No, Prince!" Then she caught herself. "James."

"I know my liabilities, Kiene. When I am with a sexy woman my judgment clouds. I will yield on almost any other point, in order to have her sexual favor. In your judgment, is this not so?"

"I can't say."

"Answer," he said sternly. "You have played me

sexually without meaning to, and now I desire you despite my knowledge of the danger. If I am this way with you, how will I be with those who do not love me?"

"Yes, you will yield," she said reluctantly.

"If I could nullify that salient weakness of mine—my love of the ladies—I could be a much better ruler, in my time. My judgment would be superior, if unclouded by sexual distraction."

"Yes, James."

"If you capture me, as you put it, I will be bound to you. No other woman will command my passion. I will see through their artifices, unblinded. Does this not make sense?"

She stared at him, her mouth open.

"Answer."

"But—but you would be subject to *my* whim, and I'm not even human. That is not good."

"How smart are you?"

"I am less intelligent than I may seem. The gem facilitates my dialogue; without it I could not even speak your language. I have learned nursing; beyond that I know virtually nothing. I am an animal in the guise of a woman."

"An animal," he repeated musingly. "And I am an animal in the guise of a man. We are all animals."

"I mean, not human. Not enough to qualify."

"I think you are human with feathers, just as I am human with hair. But let's not quibble. Remove the gem."

"But if I do that—"

He waited.

She put her hand to it and lifted the necklace

over her head. She set it down and faced him.

"Speak."

She spoke. It was melodious, alluring, and indecipherable. Not twittering, but not intelligible either.

"Sing."

She understood him. She sang, and the allure became phenomenal. He wanted to clasp her immediately, to embrace her and kiss her. She had the siren song, without doubt.

He picked up the gem. "Speak," he repeated. And realized that his voice now sounded like hers. He was speaking her language, thanks to the stone.

She smiled. "You understand me again."

"Because the magic is converting me," he agreed. He handed back the gem. "Wear it; I have verified what I need to. You still appeal to me without it."

She took it back and put it on. "Thank you, James."

He returned to the subject. "So what devious political ploys would you be working on me?"

"None, James. I can't even advise you; I lack the mind."

"So your whim would be largely confined to repeatedly seducing me."

"Yes, James. I wish I could be more for you, but it is beyond my nature. All I can bring you is unfaltering love and loyalty."

"I think you have answered your concern."

She looked blank. "I have?"

"Kiene, I can't marry you; that would never be allowed. But you could make the perfect mistress. No other woman could seduce me, unless I chose to be seduced, and then I would do it with absolute cynicism. I would take what was offered, without being politically influenced, whatever she might think."

"I suppose that is true."

"I will have to marry elsewhere, and sire male children. I know my father did not marry for love, though he always treated my mother with the respect befitting her station. But for passion, pleasure, and love, I would always be yours."

"True, if you choose."

"So I believe it makes cynical sense to embrace you now. You will inoculate me against treacherous women of my own species. Does this make sense to you?"

"Yes, James. But I think I do not really understand your reasoning. Intrigue is beyond me."

"Precisely. Now I am going to clasp you, and I want you to let yourself go completely. Are you ready?"

"Oh, James, yes!"

He clasped her, his hands feeling the feathers on her back. She met him eagerly, and her kisses were divinely sweet. Her breasts pressed against him, twin mounds of pleasure radiating joy through his torso. When he penetrated her, he climaxed explosively, but this time as his emission ebbed, the pleasure continued unabated. She was sustaining it, wonderfully.

After a seeming eternity, the feeling faded. "Do you wish more, James?" she asked. "I can provide it."

"This is enough for now," he said. "Let me bask in your embrace. I think I am completely spoiled."

"So am I," she said. "All I want is to be allowed to love you."

"Granted. And I love you."

As he held her, reveling in the softness of the feathers on her back and her completely feminine front, it occurred to him that this could be his father the King's design. To give him time to heal, and to develop an immunity to the scheming women he would soon enough encounter. The King had always been canny, and had never been taken in by devious women. James's mother, the Queen, had remarked on it, with a certain frustrated respect. She had wiles aplenty, which worked on everyone except the King, who seemed mysteriously immune. Well, James would be too.

Did the King have a siren mistress of his own? That would explain a lot. The King had told James that there was special news for him, when he was ready for it. Could that be the news? Yet every man of importance or power had a mistress of some kind; it was expected. A siren would be a surprise, but not a really significant one.

He felt a warmness in his hurt shoulder. "What is that?"

"I am healing it," she said. "You must be mended in two days, for we can't risk a longer delay."

"Ah, yes. Your ability to send pleasure relates."

"Yes. At low power, maintained steadily, it mends. At high power, it transports. It is easy to do when we are close."

"How long would it take me to heal, without your help?"

"Weeks. Your injury was bad."

"So you may have saved my life."

"No, James. You would heal alone, just not as fast."

"There was surely reason my father left me here with you. I was too ill to be moved. True?"

"True," she murmured.

"Moving me might have killed me. But the city had to be evacuated. So I was left with a special nurse, and the hope that I would recover enough to follow in several more days, before the enemy arrived."

"Yes, you have fathomed it, James. The King said you would know where to find him."

He did. "So you did save my life."

"Not yet, James. You must still escape the city."

"And that may be a close call."

"It may be," she agreed.

"You will not let me go now?"

"You are not ready, James. If you leave my healing before it is done, it will unwind and you will collapse, worse than before."

He nodded. "I suspected as much. I can't say I mind. You are an utter pleasure to clasp. But I have one more question."

"Anything, James."

"This healing and pleasure you give me—what does it take from you?"

She was silent.

He put his hands on her shoulders and held her firmly before him. "Answer."

"There is an equivalent amount of pain and suffering I take, that must be dissipated."

"So you are hurting!"

"It is a willing pain."

"Because you love me. But this is not a price I care to pay. We must stop, and let you recover."

"No! You must be healed. The enemy is close."

He paused, assessing risks. "How close?"

"I believe they will be here in two more days. I must have you well so you can escape them."

"And you—in two days what will be your state?"

"It does not matter, James."

"Answer!"

And she had to. "I will be near death."

"You sacrifice yourself for me?"

"It is willing," she repeated.

"Not by me! You must survive too, to be my love-mistress."

"That is not fated."

"I do not accept fate blindly. I make it what I choose."

She did not reply.

"We have a problem," he said grimly. "I love you, Kiene. I know this is because of your power, which I asked you to exert. But I did not know that my pleasure came at the expense of your pain."

"Normally it would not," she said. "I would give you pleasure, then dissipate my pain elsewhere."

"And how do you do this?"

"A few hours radiates it away, if there is not too much."

"And if there is too much?"

"Then I must give it to someone else."

"Who? How?"

She closed her eyes. "Please."

"Answer."

She winced, and tears appeared. But she answered. "In the slum sections, on the street, there are always rough men."

He laughed. "They try to rape an unprotected woman! And you give them the pain."

"So I understand. I have never done it, because I have never given pleasure to anyone before you. But that is how it works."

"But the city has been evacuated. There are no rough men out there."

"True."

"So you are stuck with a huge burden of pain, and it is killing you."

"It is the way I want to die. Loving you."

"This vexes me. Give me no more pleasure."

"Prince, I must heal you!"

"But that causes you less pain, being low-power."

"Yes."

"Then heal me, but nothing else."

"But you will be frustrated. You will soon desire my body again."

He glanced at her cannily. "I can sate myself in you. Just do not send me any more pleasure. That way I will not be frustrated, and you will survive. Is that not correct?"

"It is correct," she agreed.

"And after this is done, and we are safely away from the city, you can recover, and give me what pleasure you choose, accepting my love."

"Yes, James."

She was humoring him. She had given him a lot of pleasure, so must have a serious backlog of pain.

He didn't like that, but saw no way to abate it.

Time passed, and his healing progressed. He did have sex with her, and took from it only the pleasure he generated on his own. That was actually quite sufficient, being as much as any ordinary woman could provide a man. She clearly liked giving him that, despite her internal suffering.

As the second day passed, his healing became virtually complete. He was ready to march and fight, as good as ever. He checked the empty palace, and found that only his war horse and the horse servant remained, loyally awaiting his need.

He also discovered that the enemy had circled the city and cut off the main exit route. There would be no escape that way.

"Lead my horse out of here, through the forest trails," he told the servant. "Try to avoid the enemy. We don't want such a fine steed to be captured."

The man nodded, and led the horse out. Prince James was actually giving the servant leave to save himself from capture. He might be able to escape notice in a way James could not. The enemy would not be looking for a mere servant.

He returned to the bedroom. It was time to attend to his own escape.

But the Siren could no longer stand. She lay on the bed, shuddering. She had given him everything she could.

"How can I help you?" he asked desperately.

"You can't, James. This is not a malady of the body, but of the feeling. There is no recourse."

He dressed and fetched his sword. "I am ready to go," he said. "I will carry you."

"No," she gasped. "I will slow you. You may have to fight. Leave me here."

"Hardly." He bent to pick her up.

A jolt of sheer agony stopped him. He fell back, half stunned. "You must not touch me," she said. "I can no longer contain the pain. You can't take me."

It was clear he could not. But he refused to leave her. "Then we remain," he said.

"Please," she begged. "They are coming. You must go."

Now he heard them: footfalls and voices within the palace, coming closer. "Too late anyway." He drew his sword and stood ready.

"Then I have failed," she said. "I deserve to die."

"First they must kill me," he said grimly.

"No! Hide! Maybe I will distract them while you sneak out."

"Never." But then he thought of something. "They will rape you."

"Yes."

"And you will give them your pain."

"Yes!" she said, realizing.

"Then I will hide, and leave them to you. And take them out after you stun them."

"But you will have to see them do it."

"Ordinarily that would put me into a fighting rage. But this is a special situation. I know what you will give them."

"Your pain," she said, smiling weakly.

"Actually you should not have to acquiesce to rape. Just take their fingers, as you did mine, and deliver that way."

"I can do that!" she agreed, seeing it.

He stepped into the nearest closet and closed the door most of the way. The siren lay on the bed naked. They waited.

They heard bootsteps on the floor outside. Then a soldier burst into the room—and paused, gazing at the displayed woman. "Well, now!"

"No," she cried helplessly.

But of course he was a brute front-rank soldier. She looked like a deserted concubine, invitingly laid out. He opened his trousers, hauled out his member, and fell on her. Before his member found the place and thrust in, she grasped one of his hands.

He cried out in agony. James emerged, hauled the man off her, and dispatched him with a thrust through the neck. He rolled the body under the bed and retreated to the closet.

Soon enough a second man entered. This one carried some of the loot he had found. He saw the woman and reacted as the first had, taking what was ? offered with hesitation. Looters had only brief chances before their commanders took over and confiscated the takings, but fast sex could not be undone.

Kiene took his hand. He stiffened more in agony than lust.

James clubbed him on the head and cut his throat, then shoved him under the bed with the other. This was working, so far.

"One more will do it," Kiene said. "I am much discharged."

A third man came, but this one was wary, perhaps aware that others had disappeared. "What's this?" he asked, staring at Kiene's naked body.

"Please don't rape me again," she pleaded.

"They raped you? That's no good. Get dressed, girl; hide." He turned and departed.

He had saved his own life, unknowingly.

Then three more came. "Well now!" They charged the bed. But they too were wary. "It may be a trap. Check the closet and under the bed."

Oops.

One man peered under the bed, and froze. Another strode to the closet and yanked open the door.

James charged out, swinging his sword. He cut into the man's neck, severing the jugular vein, and the man dropped, clutching his neck. But the other two, warned, were now on guard. Swords drawn, they faced the Prince.

James was skilled, but two swords against one was dangerous. In stories one man might hold off several, but in life the odds favored the numbers.

Kiene was getting off the bed, facing the men. "Stay away from them!" James cried. "They'll kill you!"

The men glanced at her, uncertain what she was up to. How could a naked woman harm an armed man? That gave James an idea. "Touch one," he murmured.

She nodded.

He launched himself at the two in their moment of distraction, surprising them; they knew about odds too. He swung at one while shoving the other toward the siren. She embraced that one while James tackled the other. In a moment her soldier cried out in agony—and the Prince lopped the distracted head off the other.

"Good enough," he said. "You are discharged, and we survive."

"Yes," she agreed faintly.

He looked at her. There was blood on her arm. The soldier must have cut her before he succumbed.

James quickly found a bandage and wrapped her arm. "I don't suppose you can heal yourself?"

"I am unable," she agreed with regret.

"But you have not lost very much blood. You should be all right." He hoped; he did not know what effect a physical injury would have on a siren.

Then they heard multiple footsteps running toward the room. They were about to be overwhelmed.

"The river," she said. "It is the only way."

He nodded. His bedroom overlooked the river, because he liked to watch the sailcraft. He was a competent mariner. The water below was deep. That was fortunate, because the room was on the third story.

The mob of men reached the door. There was no time to open the window. "Together!" James told her. "Feet first!"

"Cling to me," she said.

They charged the window and leaped, holding hands. His shod feet jammed through the glass and lattice as they hurtled out. Glass and pieces of frame exploded outward as they passed and dropped. Then they were falling, and she hauled him in to her. He wrapped his arms about her protectively.

They splashed into the water, feet first, and plunged below. Now the siren's stout swimming feathers spread, and she dived lower. He held on to her torso, slipping back, his clothing and sword dragging him.

Near the dark river bed she paused. She put her hands on his head and set his face firmly on her right breast, as if nursing him. Then he caught on, and sucked on her nipple. Oxygen came from it, infusing the stale air of his held breath, refreshing it so that he could breathe without breathing, as it were. It was practical, but he also found it rather sexy. She was a more versatile creature than he had known.

He clung to her, mouth locked in place, while she spread her arm-wings and stroked powerfully along the bottom. They could not surface, because the whole enemy artillery would be training their bows on the river, waiting for them. The archers did not know that their quarry was not going to surface at all soon.

The oxygen diminished. He switched to the left breast, and it was fresh again. Good enough. In the process he glanced down and saw that feathers had spread from her feet too, shaping them into flippers. And her hands: they were now feathered scoops, overlapping to catch the water when she stroked, and lying back when she drew her hands forward. Flying in air: she really was doing it.

But then Kiene angled upward. What was she up to?

Her head broke the surface. "It's not safe!" he whispered.

"I must breathe," she gasped. "My feathers take in oxygen from the water, but not enough for two. Not for long."

Oh. "I didn't know."

"Because of my injury. It weakens me. But I can still do it longer than you can hold your breath. I must find spots to surface every so often."

An arrow zinged into the water near them. "They've spotted us," he said.

"I am recharged. Down." She hugged him to her until he put his arms around her, then dived below, carrying him along. Again she flew under water, nursing him with oxygen. But now the enemy knew they had survived the fall, and would be more alert. They had to find better surfacing places.

The second time she came up amidst water weeds in the shallows. "There are piers along the bank," he said. "Come up under one of them. Or in the lee of a fishing boat."

She nodded. Then there was a hue and cry, and they had to dive again. He fastened to her breast, hoping his advice would help.

It did. She made it to a pier, and they dallied there some time, so she could recover fully. The bandage on her arm had become waterlogged; she removed it, and there was only minimal bleeding. So she had healed somewhat. There were boats all around, tacking their sails back and forth, watching the surface of the river. And no other close pier downriver.

"While we wait," he said, embracing her amorously.

She smiled. "Any time, James."

Which was of course the thing about a siren; she was always there for his interest. He held her close as they both treaded water, and penetrated her. "But don't send me any pleasure. Take what you can for yourself."

"It is only for you, never for me."

He paused, imbedded. "You don't get sexual pleasure yourself? An orgasm?"

"That is not my nature."

"*Can* you have it, if you allow yourself?"

"I do not know. I did not train for that."

"Let's find out. Let me do it fast, then I will do it slow, and see if I can bring you there."

"There is no need, James. I exist only to serve you."

"You will serve me better by sharing my pleasure." He thrust, and spurted within her. "Now I am slowed. If time can do it, I will take you there. But no faking; react only if it is real."

"As you wish, James."

He worked at it, stroking her body, kissing her, and thrusting within her as his member slowly recovered solidity. But she responded only slightly.

He was reluctant to give it up, but the water was chilling him and he knew he could not continue indefinitely. "Regardless, I love you, Kiene," he said.

Then her body responded, tightening around him. "Oh, James!" she gasped as she went into the throes of her climax.

So that was the secret! Not physical stimulation, not sex itself, so much as his expressed love for her. It made sense, in retrospect; she loved him, and wanted his love in return. She had it.

Then a boat sailed close to the pier, and they had to dive lest they be discovered.

They came up beside the boat, their two heads

hiding by its stern. It was a small sailboat with a stout ram's head carving for a figurehead. One of the battering ram type, not fleet of motion, but sturdy, and braced to collide with others and crush their hulls. In battle, properly supported by archers, they could be devastating.

That gave him an idea. "We'll take over this boat," he whispered.

"But there are no female mariners," she protested.

"I've got an idea. I'm climbing aboard. If I get taken out, you flee alone, so you don't get hurt. I love you." He kissed her, then clambered over the gunwale while she remained stunned, unable to protest or hinder him.

The boat tilted with his weight, attracting the attention of the mariner. "What the hell!"

"I fell in the water," James said. "Thanks for rescuing me."

"You're not one of us! You're the— "

The Prince's sword speared his neck, silencing him. He hoped no one in the other boats happened to be watching; chances were good, as they were focusing on the water, not each other. James heaved the body overboard, then took over the sail, angling the craft closer to the pier. "Wait for cover, then join me," he said to the Kiene.

When the pier concealed the boat from the other, he helped haul her aboard. "Prince— "

"Call me James," he reminded her sternly. "I'm no longer your liege, but your lover."

"You can't do this! The moment the boat goes out, I will be apparent, and they will know."

He was already working on the ram's head. It was attached to a frame projecting from the prow, tied in place by firm cords. "I want you to be a plain sight."

"Prince— "

"James." She tended to forget when excited or confused.

"Beloved. Have you lost your wits?"

"You will be the figurehead."

She stared at him. Then she giggled. "This is so absolutely crazy it might even work."

The ram's head dropped into the water. "Get up here. I'll have to rope you in place. Can you handle that?"

"Pad the ropes."

They found a battered blanket in the boat, and cut it into shreds. These cushioned the ropes about her waist and under her arms. She stood on the prow, her feet almost touching the water, and spread her arms to hold the crossbar. The ropes gave her the additional support she needed.

"But if they catch on— " she said nervously.

"Then slip the rope and drop into the water, escaping. It will be over for me, but I would not have you suffer." He kissed her again.

"If you die, I will suffer."

"Apart from that."

When she was secure, he angled the sail and tacked back out into the river. With luck they would be ignored.

"Hey, where'd that come from?" a mariner called. "That's not one of ours."

So much for luck. "Found it," James called back,

trying to mimic the enemy accent. "Figured it would bring me luck in the search."

The man peered across at him. "You're not Jud."

"He had to go on another errand. I'm competent."

The man looked dubious, but didn't challenge it. There were surely a good many strangers in the enemy force, as it would have been gathered from all around the enemy kingdom.

Kiene remained at the prow, attracting attention but no suspicion. She was an excellent replica of a siren, complete with realistic feathers and bare breasts. She stared straight ahead, in the manner of a wooden painted carving, yet looked almost alive. In short, a superior figurehead.

James tacked the boat back and forth, searching, and the other boats did the same. They were not having much luck. "They must have drowned long ago," one disgruntled mariner said as his craft happened close. "We're wasting our time."

"I don't believe it," James said. "One was a siren, like my figurehead. She could have escaped, but the Prince would have drowned. He should be floating somewhere."

They continued the futile search. The day was getting late. "They wouldn't be this far out," a man said.

"If they're not close in, they must be farther out," James retorted. "I'm not quitting until I'm sure."

"I am fatigued," Kiene murmured. "I can't hold this pose much longer."

"You won't have to," James assured her.

A foghorn blew. "Recall," a man said. "They're

giving up the search. About time."

The other craft angled back toward the castle/palace. James did not. He continued on downstream.

"Hey!" someone called. "Didn't you hear the horn? Come back in."

But James sailed the opposite way.

Then someone caught on. "He's one of them! A spy in our midst."

"Get yourself loose," James told her. "We'll have to make a break for it."

She worked her way free of the rope and got into the boat proper. She had rope burns on her torso despite the padding. "If they catch us, we can swim," she said, gazing back nervously. "For a while."

"At least there are fewer of them here," he said. "Most have returned."

Still, half a dozen boats pursued them. Fortunately they lacked archers, being one-man craft.

"Can you outsail them?" Kiene asked.

"Some. I can sail as well as any, but this is not a fast boat. Some will gain on us."

Sure enough, two enemy craft were keeping pace, and gaining during the tacking. It would take time, but they would inevitably catch up.

"What will they do?"

"If they're smart, they'll come up on either side and grapple, locking this boat between them. Then both men can board and tackle me. Even if I kill them both, the delay will allow the other boats to catch up, and I'll be overwhelmed. So we'll have to go to the water before then."

"Are we far enough along to escape by water?

We'll have to go to shore soon, as there are sea monsters farther along."

He considered. "They'll have archers pacing us on the banks. They'll take us out the moment we come within range."

"That was my fear."

"I have an idea. But it requires your help."

"Anything, Prince. But I can't fight a man effectively. I am not made for combat."

"That depends on how the combat is phrased. Remember how you took out three men in the palace?"

She nodded appreciatively. "Now I understand. The pain embrace."

"Yes. When they draw nigh, you will give me severe pleasure, then discharge it to one man while I tackle the other. If we do it efficiently, the other boats won't have time to catch up."

"You're so smart, James."

"Merely a matter of using what we have. But in this case my strategy and your nature may be our survival."

"If—if you have trouble with your man, jump into the water with him. I can help you much more there."

"Understood." He continued guiding the boat, working sail and rudder together.

While the slow chase proceeded, James gazed at Kiene. Now he could see all her feathers from head to toe, literally, where they lay back against her skin when not in use. It was as if she were outlined in white. But the front part of her was completely human woman. Her face, breasts, and hips were lovely. She was excellently crafted as both water bird and concubine.

"How came your species, Kiene?" he inquired.

She smiled. "It is a storybook beginning, perhaps untrue. We are of course a crossbreed between water fowl and human."

"Of course. But in real life, divergent species can't interbreed. How did it happen?"

"It is said that there was a very knowledgeable human man, a scientist or magician or both. He wanted to improve the human species, so he tried crossbreeding. This was illicit, as there were those among humans who felt it was improper to indulge in bestiality. So he experimented in secret. In the magic laboratory he merged the seeds of both species, one combination after another, and finally found a viable match. He grew manbirds and birdmen of many varieties, but most of his trials were not effective. Some had human legs and bird heads; others had human heads and bird tails. Some were ugly harpies, a number of which escaped by flying away. When he found the right formulation, he tinkered with it, establishing exactly the right combination of qualities, some of which did not exist independently in nature."

"Like feathers that take in oxygen," James said.

"Yes. And the ability to transfer pleasure. He was evidently a genius, considering how well he wrought. But there was one problem: all the crossbreeds were female."

"No male sirens? How does your species reproduce itself then?"

"No males," she agreed. "We are only half a

species. We must breed with human men, and then we have only siren daughters. No sons, no full humans. It is said that the magician scientist was so frustrated by this incompletion that he disappeared in an explosion of smoke and was never seen again. But we remain, strongly attracted to human men, perhaps by no coincidence."

"So you must have a human father," James said.

"And a siren mother. This is true. I think it is an ongoing affair; mother still slips away often to be with him. I do not know his identity, which frustrates me, since he is my human parent."

"And if you conceive by me, you will have a siren daughter who will someday seek another human male to love."

"Yes. It is our nature. We do try to make our men appreciate us."

"Yet you tried to hold back, because you loved me. I gather most sirens don't."

"Most don't," she agreed. "They spy a man they desire, and seduce him—it isn't difficult—and then he is their love captive. But I did not want to do that to you, Prince James."

"I appreciate the sentiment. So it seems that there will never be a siren King."

"Or a siren Queen. We are officially classified as beasts."

James frowned. "That may change in future."

"Do not risk your status on my account, Prince James. Just let me love you and please you."

"Speaking of which, they are drawing closer. Time to charge yourself with pain."

"It really is not pain to me, unless extreme. It is

my love offering to you, and I am thrilled to do it."

"I must continue to sail the boat. Can you address me as I sit here, my hands occupied?"

"Oh, yes, James!" She came to him, sat on his lap facing him, parted his wet clothing, wrapped her bare legs about him, pressed her breasts against his chest, and maneuvered to take his hardening member into her. She kissed him as her vagina squeezed, bringing him to an immediate climax. Then she sent her pleasure, sustaining his bliss for a seeming eternity.

"I'm hopelessly addicted," he said.

She eased off. "The boats are coming close."

So they were. "Try to act fearful and helpless."

"I am."

The two boats were coordinating nicely. They came up on either side, extending small grappling hooks. James did not contest this, and Kiene was looking wildly around as if terrified.

"Now," James said. He jumped up to intercept the man on his left, while the siren went to the one on his right.

The action was brief and brutal. James ran his sword through the sailor, who had expected to be one of two tackling him. Meanwhile there was a cry of agony from the other man. In a moment both were in the water, and the hooks were off.

They sailed forward, leaving the empty boats for the remaining pursuers to address. Instead of being fatally delayed, they had gained a new lead.

"Are you out of pain?" James asked her.

"Yes. Do you want more pleasure?"

"Just come sit on me again, passive; that's all the

pleasure I need now."

The pursuit faltered as dusk came. "I know a private retreat we can swim to," James said. It was the standing rendezvous where he would meet the King. "I'll tie the sail and rudder in place, so they can pursue the empty boat in the darkness. That way they won't know we're gone, or where to search for us. Take me below at first, to be sure of escaping their notice; then we can swim on the surface."

They did so, and in due course were approaching the retreat. A man was there by the waterside. "Come on in, son."

"Father!" James exclaimed, gratified.

"I figured you'd come here, per my message, so we came to meet you."

"We?"

"My mistress and I. I think it's time you met her."

Now a woman stepped forward, dimly illuminated by the spilling light from the house.

"Mother!" Kiene exclaimed, astonished.

"I think it is time for you to know, dear," the elder siren said. "Yes, my lover is the King, your father."

"She's your daughter?" James asked, stunned, seeing the feathers on the woman, and the green translation gem on her necklace. "But that means—"

"I'm your half-sister," Kiene said, horrified. "Our love is doomed."

"Not necessarily," the King said, unperturbed. "Come in, get comfortable, and we'll talk."

Talk? It would take more than that to untangle this. How could he give her up, now that he loved her?

They went inside the retreat, which was masked as a recycling collection center, the last thing the enemy would be interested in at the moment. They should be safe here until the loyal troops regrouped.

Settled, with new clothing, hot broth, and comfortable chairs, they listened as the King talked.

"Do you two remember how you met? Seemed like sheer coincidence, no? It wasn't. I directed your ship to that site at that time, James, and my beloved directed Kiene to the rock she perched on, looking for a surprise."

"But a man was about to spear her!" James protested.

"He was faking it, deliberately, when you were looking. That attracted your attention to the young siren, and you interceded, as I thought you would."

"It was staged?" Kiene asked, appalled. "You wanted me to see him? To owe him?"

"To love him, dear," the elder siren said. "He was your ideal match, when you came of age."

"My brother!"

"Now I need to clarify a somewhat private matter," the King said. "I trust you will not bruit it about, James, as it might embarrass your mother."

"Mother doesn't know about Kiene?"

"She knows and approves."

"Approves!"

"Here is the essence, son. I was not your mother's first husband. Her king was killed in battle. This made her suddenly available, and in need of support. And more, for she was pregnant."

James stared at his father, not trying to speak.

"So we made a political marriage of convenience,

not love or sex. She brought her kingdom into perfect alignment with mine, and supported me without question. This was valuable. I recognized her son as my own. You."

"I'm—not your son?" This was totally unexpected and unwelcome news.

"Not my genetic son. But you are my recognized legal son, and mine in all other respects. And I must say, you have proved worthy; I'm proud of you. I had not intended such a challenge to your ingenuity, when you recovered. The enemy cannily cut off your retreat. You prevailed regardless."

"But you should want your own lineage!"

"What I want is a worthy heir who will do right by the kingdom," the King said firmly. "You are it. You have heart, intelligence, skill, and conscience. You will be King after me, fulfilling my deal with your mother. But you have no blood relation to my daughter, Kiene."

"Then—then it's all right," James said, putting his arm around Kiene. "We can love each other."

"And that will please me, her mother, and your mother," the King said. "Our lineages will be united in your daughter. Who knows, she may the one to become a queen in her own right, instead of being someone's secret mistress."

"Legitimacy for our kind," the elder siren said.

"That would be nice," Kiene said dreamily.

Would it happen? Perhaps. But at the moment James was mainly pleased that his love would not have to be stifled. The rest he would assimilate in due course.

* * * *

I always thought a siren was a variety of mermaid: part woman, part fish. That's the way I have it in my Xanth series. But when I did spot research, refreshing my information for this story, I discovered that she is part woman, part bird, though still associated with the sea. Some pictures even make her look like a harpy, but I doubt that's the way mariners saw her. Who would be lured to destruction in the sea by a harpy? So I fleshed her out, as it were, my way, discovering how she must have come about, and what powers she might have. I think my version is more realistic and appealing than the classical one.

I wrote this story in February, 2006. I thought it would be short, merely displaying Kiene and the Prince's decision. But there kept being other aspects to explore, and the story expanded to novelette length. So be it; a story is as it must be. I like Kiene, and like the version of siren I have defined herein.

Exercise

Spence approached the newfangled contraption with caution. He had taken his exercise indoors with reluctance, but the city park really wasn't suitable for running, and he didn't like what he called sweat shops. So he was trying for the best of both worlds: home, yet seeming to be out in the country.

His brother Clinton had bought it and set it up for him in the garage, swearing that once he tried this, not only would he get plenty of exercise, he would never need or want any other equipment. "There have been advances in the past fifteen years you have to experience to believe. It's no chore any more. Trust me."

Well, actually, Spence did trust him. Clinton, two years older, had always been big brother, and remained so, even though Spence was now forty. Clint was more adventurous, discovered more things, and passed along the good ones. But Spence was dubious that anything existed that could make him actually *like* exercising. He simply wasn't the type, as his developing paunch attested. Clint, in contrast, was a robust figure of a man, the kind who seemed to grow more handsome with age. He said the secret was in his exercise. If so, Spence wanted part of it. But he knew that no matter how determinedly he started, his dedication would soon enough flag, and he'd be back being fat and fortyish. He was single, mostly eating out or getting a sandwich and pop from the machines at work, and that was not conducive to a trim figure.

Also, there was a continuing maintenance fee he would have to pay every month. Why should he have to pay that when he owned the unit? That would make it that much easier to drop the program. But he would give it a fair chance first.

It was supposed to work automatically, so he would not need to master complicated instructions. It was also supposed to represent a new frontier for home exercise. Certainly it was expensive, but he could return it after a thirty day trial period if not fully satisfied, and get his brother a refund. He rather expected to do that.

It was set up like a recumbent bicycle, with his feet extended to the front and the handlebars out to the sides. The "wheels"—actually a closed box—were geared for resistance; the faster he pedaled—actually pushed against the footboard so that his seat slid back—the stiffer it got, so he could have as heavy a workout as he chose. The handlebars were graded too, so that sharp turns took more strength than gradual ones, working his arms. Actually he had to pull on them as well as steer, to give his arms a workout along with his legs and torso. He understood that it could also be set up like a regular bicycle, or a rowboat, or a treadmill. Clint had selected this variant, for some unspecified reason.

It all made sense, in its dull fashion. It was after all an exercise mill. Still, the technology was sophisticated, because it seemed the cycle powered a holographic image that was responsive to his speed and steering. Would it really work? He liked the idea of seeing images as he "traveled", but did Clint really think that would satisfy him indefinitely?

He got on the comfortable seat and turned on the mechanism. He pedaled and pulled.

A scene formed around him: a farming countryside. He seemed to be on a highway crossing a corn field. The realism was amazing. The pavement moved backward under his wheels—he had wheels now—and the recumbent bicycle was fully apparent. He could see every individual stalk on the field, and the perspective changed as he moved. It was indeed as though he were there. He craned his neck to look to the sides and behind; the illusion was complete in every direction. Clint was right: there had been technological advances. Still, how long would he be diverted by a cornfield, no matter how realistic?

Then he felt a breeze of motion against his body.

Startled, he ceased pedaling—and the scene faded out.

Oh, that was the point of it. He could not enjoy the scenery unless he really did exercise. Good enough. Score one for the equipment. He did want to experience more of this phenomenon.

He resumed pedaling and hauling, and the scene returned. There was definitely a breeze. He wasn't sure how that happened; there must be some kind of force field that brushed by him. Touch illusion. Clint had not been fooling about amazing progress. Spence steered to the left, and his cycle seemed to veer left. But a car was coming toward him, so he veered back right away. And got dumped. There was a hard jolt.

What? He hadn't really fallen; he remained on the seat. But he realized he had not shifted his weight to maintain his balance; the seat had picked that up and put him where he would have been on a real bike. On the pavement.

The oncoming car blared its horn and swerved to miss him, blasting him with the wind of its passage. He flinched as the scene faded. This was realism!

But he realized that the first time he stopped pedaling, the scene had ceased immediately. This time it had continued for several seconds, allowing the car to have at him. Had he generated some reserve power, or had the system done that deliberately?

Ridiculous: he was personifying the system. So chances were that he could pedal a while, then coast a while, as was possible in real-life cycling.

Spence resumed pedaling, and the scene reappeared. This time he shifted his weight as he maneuvered. It was easy to believe he was really out in the country. It was an ordinary scene, but the sheer realism lent it fascination. For the time being. He exerted himself, pedaling harder, moving faster, feeling it as well as seeing it. This was actually fun!

Something else was coming toward him, but it was too small for a car. Nevertheless, he stayed well over on his side of the road. As they came together, he made out more detail. It was another cyclist, on a recumbent similar to his own. That was nice, but probably no coincidence, since the holo was programmed for that type. Make the exerciser feel at home, encountering his own kind.

In fact, it was a woman. A young, attractive one. He saw her hair flouncing out behind her helmet in the wind. She wore a white blouse and a long heavy riding skirt. That wasn't ideal for this kind of cycle, because her knees were as high as her head, and he could catch tantalizing glimpses of her legs beneath the hem.

She came almost parallel to him, glancing prettily his way and smiling. Then a gust of wind caught her skirt and whipped it up, exposing her pumping thighs just as she passed.

"Oh!" she exclaimed, embarrassed.

Then she was on beyond, leaving Spence bemused by the inadvertent flash. So he was forty, he still thrilled to such a glimpse. She had very nice legs. What an appealing coincidence, to get that gust just then.

Coincidence? This was a programmed holo! That had to have been set up.

He realized belatedly that she had spoken. So the holo was sight, feel, and sound. Some effects!

Clint had told him he would love this exercise. Clint must have known. Spence was a bachelor, not from preference but because somehow he hadn't connected with the right woman. Some were physically appealing, some were intellectually able, some were truly nice people. Perhaps it was too much to expect all three qualities in one person. They did exist in some—who were of course already married. Or looking for a man more impressive in all three respects than he was. Certainly he wasn't looking for any creature half his age. But that brief view inflamed his imagination. Would the program allow another glimpse?

He looped the bike around and pedaled back the way he had come, hoping the girl would do the same. This was of course utter foolishness, but it was his exercise; he could be foolish on his own private time. Who else would know?

And there she was, coming back toward him. "Hello!" he called as they came together.

"Hello," she replied.

The gust came, but this time she held her skirt down with one hand, and he got no glimpse as she went on by.

Just how responsive was this program? On impulse, he turned the bike again and pursued her. "Hello!" he called again as he pulled up beside her.

"Oh, are you going my way?" she asked.

"It's my way; I merely changed direction again. You—are you real?"

She laughed. "Yes and no. I am a real person, but this image is merely a recording. So you might say I am only partly real."

"Then how can you be having a responsive dialogue with me?"

"This image is keyed to respond to certain expressions, so as to simulate dialogue. You can readily get beyond it if you try, but that would spoil the illusion."

"I like the illusion."

"Thank you."

"You—how far does it go? I mean, I know it will all fade if I stop pedaling, and I'll have to do that soon, because I'm getting tired. But while the scene continues—do you know what I'm asking?"

"I think so. You want to know if you can touch me."

He hadn't formulated it that literally, but he was curious. "Yes."

"Yes."

"Yes, I can touch you?"

"As long as you continue pedaling, or rowing if you use the boat. The program is responsive to your direction: the way you steer the bike, where you look, and what you say. It is fairly intricate. Would you like to touch me?"

"Yes," he said before he thought.

"Steady your bike and take my hand." She extended her left hand.

"Won't that interfere with my steering? I don't want to get dumped again."

"The system makes allowances. Touching is permitted."

Spence took firm grip on the left handlebar, and extended his right hand. He caught her fingers with his own. They were firm and warm. "Wow!" It was all he could think of to say.

"It is good projection," she said.

He couldn't help wondering how far the touching could go. Was the rest of her body as fair and firm as her hand?

"Uh, who are you? I'm Spencer—Spence—Chowder." Then, embarrassed, he added, "Age forty."

"Welcome, Spence. I am Alia. That's my stage name, of course. Age twenty four."

"It's a nice name." What was he doing, flirting

with an image? This was ridiculous.

"What made you follow me?"

"Your skirt flared." That was out before he realized it. He was breathing hard from the unaccustomed exercise, and his legs were starting to hurt. Otherwise he knew he would be blushing.

"One glimpse of my legs turns you on?"

"They're good legs," he said defensively.

"Of course. So you are honest about it. I like that."

He felt foolishly flattered. What a program this was! "Thank you."

She glanced across at him. "Of course you realize that this was intentional. The program does it to ensure your interest."

"It is effective."

"The idea is to maintain your interest, so that you will return day after day. There are many lovely settings to traverse; the program will take you through them in turn. But statistically few folk stay with it indefinitely; they tire of scenery and find reasons to save the time and effort. So we spice it up. It is a calculated thing."

"I suppose there's no point in asking how you feel about it. Being gawked at, I mean."

"Because I am merely an image? The real person who made the recordings gets a small residual payment for every exercise-hour performed by clients in my company. So I am motivated to make it effective; I want her to know her effort is paying off. She had to do nine takes to get that skirt flare just right. So I can answer; I am pleased it worked. At least, she will be when she gets the royalty. It's nice to know my legs still have it."

He nodded. "And since it's just the recording, there's no embarrassment for you. For her. Whatever. It's like admiring a sexy scene in a movie."

"Yes, pretty much. But as you surely noticed, it doesn't work every time. If you want further glimpses, you will have to learn to play the game."

This was intriguing. "If I learn what I need, I can see more of you?"

"Yes. But you'll have to do a lot of exercising to accomplish that. Nothing comes easy."

"I admit it; this is motivation."

"Thank you.

"But I think I must break off now. My muscles are not used to this."

"I'll make you a deal. Next time you come here, if you ask me for more information, I will provide it."

He liked that. "Okay." So she was a mere recorded image, programmed to respond verbally; he was already into this game, as she put it. He wanted to play it right, if only to see more of her, literally, and to discover how much more he could feel.

She disengaged her hand. "See you then, Spence." She veered away from him.

He stopped pedaling before his legs cramped, and the scene slowly faded. He was back in his exercise room, alone. And sore. He had overdone it, the first day.

Clint had said he would like this exercise. Clint was right. Clint must have interacted with Alia himself. That made him vaguely jealous.

Spence went to take a shower, bemused. He

would be sore for days, but it was worth it. He had an erection. So Alia was only a figment; he remained fascinated by her. Would she really tell him more next time? Such as how to see more of her than just a flash of legs? Well, there was one way to find out.

Spence was sore the next day, but simply couldn't wait for that to pass before returning to the scene. It was ludicrous to look forward to interacting with a recorded image, but it was some image.

He started pedaling, and the scene formed. This time it was a path through a jungle. Huge trees spread their branches overhead, and exotic parrots perched on them. It was very nice, but it wasn't what he had come for.

A battered jungle car came barreling toward him. There was barely room for it to pass; he had to veer sharply to the right, almost scraping the trunk of a huge tree. The car had the audacity to honk, as if he were the intruder.

But then he saw the cycle. That would be Alia.

Sure enough, she came toward him, waved, smiled, and her skirt flared, showing her thighs right up to the white panties. Oh, yes, she had legs!

He continued the way he was going, slowly. Sure enough, she looped about and returned to ride beside him. "Nice to see you again, Spence."

"Thanks for showing—up."

She laughed. "All part of the program. I did promise to tell you more, didn't I?"

"Yes. But I wasn't sure you'd show." There it was again. He wasn't trying to be clever or crude; it just came out that way. Why was he being so foolish over an image? Even if she were real, she'd be twenty-four, hardly a serious romantic prospect for him. Was he that lonely?

The answer was unfortunately apparent; yes he was. Alia was compatible female company. He hadn't realized how much he missed that, until encountering her.

"I will be here whenever you summon me. I'm like the genie in the bottle."

An interesting analogy. "Are there other bottles?"

"Oh, yes. You can specify any age and type you like; the databank has a fair selection. They are all programmed much the same, however, it's just the image that changes."

"Much the same? What are the differences?"

"Teen girls giggle more and inadvertently show more. Older women play harder to get and show less. Foreign girls have accents and can be very open-minded. Body types vary from slender to buxom. Some are more approachable than others."

"Why would a programmed image be unapproachable?"

"We are called figments. Some men like the challenge."

"Figments," he repeated, assimilating it. "All aspects of the same general program."

"With superficial variations," she agreed. "Do you want to change figments?"

"No!" That was too emphatic. "I mean, I'm satisfied with you."

"That's nice. Let me give you the tour-guide spiel on the Amazon jungle; then we can talk."

"Good enough."

She described the jungle, and the manner it was being decimated by logging and mining interests, and the effect this had on the native tribes that depended on it for their very existence. He found it both interesting and unsettling; was she trying to recruit him to an environmentalist cause? No, apparently it was just spicing for the spiel. He was being educated as he exercised.

"Thank you," he said as she concluded. "I gather this is one way to keep me pedaling longer."

"True. We space out the presentations. Now we can talk. Why did you select me?"

"I didn't. My brother Clinton set it up. He—he knows what I like."

"And you like them young but mature."

"So it seems. I hadn't realized, until I saw you."

"That's so sweet. Now I am programmed to respond to your questions and statements; I'm not much for volunteering information. And there's only so much I can tell you in any one session."

"Why the limit?"

"If you knew it all, you might lose interest, and your exercise program would founder. Remember, that's the point of this. The program prides itself on a very high client repeat ratio."

"What sort of information can you give me?"

She glanced sidelong at him. "What sort do you want?"

He was intrigued. "Personal?"

"Such as how to get me out of my clothing?"

Hoo! This program was definitely for men. "How is that accomplished?"

She shook her head. "That's too direct. A girl

prefers some subtlety."

Subtle as that deliberate flash of her legs. She was playing him along. But she had already hooked him. "Sorry. But assuming I figure it out, I have two related questions. What would I be able to do with you, if I got you nude, and why would you tolerate it?"

Again that sidelong glance. "You are ignorant of what a man does with a woman?"

"No. It's that you're an illusion."

"I'm a figment: a tangible image. That's not the same. And that answers your second question. I literally don't care what you do with my image. I lack the scruples a real woman would have. So it's not a matter of toleration, but of facilitation."

More than intriguing! She was pretty well inviting him to try something. "But an image has no substance!"

"That depends."

"Depends? On what?"

"On how you see it, as it were. Don't you remember holding my hand last time?"

"I felt it!" he exclaimed. "Just as I feel the wind."

"You can feel any part of me. If I let you."

So there were limits. "But that's still illusion. You're not really there."

"I *am* here. Just not physically, exactly."

"So then what's the point?"

She shrugged. "That would be for you to decide."

His stiff muscles had loosened somewhat with the exercise, but Spence knew he was in danger of overdoing it. Not merely physically. "I'll think about it. Thanks. Now I have to get some rest. I haven't yet recovered from yesterday."

"It does take time to harden."

Was he reading more into it than intended, or was the program teasing him? "I hope to see you next time."

"I hope so too." She smiled. "When my original recorded these responses, she hoped they would be invoked some day. Thank you for invoking them."

"You're welcome," he said wryly.

He stopped pedaling, and after a moment the image faded. He was back in the exercise seat in his garage.

His legs felt the additional exertion. He knew he should wait a few days before resuming the exercise. The program would not care. But *he* cared. He wanted to see Alia again. She was to an extent a tease, yet he was developing a foolish crush on her. Exactly as the program intended.

"You're never too old," he muttered as he stripped for the shower. Indeed he wasn't; his erection was back. He wished he could have Alia here in the shower, wetly embraceable, her breasts pressing against him as he fondled her bottom and kissed her. She no longer seemed too young for him. So she was a figment; maybe that was what he needed.

So what was the point in trying to make out with a holographic image? That he could actually feel? That turned out to be no easy question to dismiss. If she looked, sounded, and felt real, what was the difference? What did a man really know of any woman, other than that?

"I have a right to be foolish on my own time," he concluded, not for the first or second time.

His leg muscles were easing on the third session, and they got into the routine. For one thing, he didn't have to pedal hard, just enough to maintain the power for the holo effects.

This time the scene was an arctic wasteland, but it didn't feel cold. He wasn't sure whether that was moderation on the part of the program, or simple lack of capacity. It was a charging dog-sled that almost sideswiped him. He waved to the soundly-swathed man guiding it as they zoomed by.

Alia was similarly bundled, but her heavy skirt still managed to flare. How he loved that fleeting glimpse of her thighs! Then she joined him, and they talked. She caught him up on the virtues of the arctic, and the danger that global warming meant to polar bears and cold-adapted fish. And the prospect of the sea which would rise twenty feet if the Greenland ice cap melted, as it was in the process of doing. She was a font of information on the settings, and he listened because he liked her company.

After the spot travelogue she was willing to get personal. "How did you get into this business?" he asked.

"I—that is, my original real-life person—wasn't smart enough to make it as a high-powered executive, and not pretty enough to be an actress," she replied. "This offered good money for easy work, and I liked it. It has had its moments, though."

"Moments?"

"Maybe it's easier to show you. Touch my breast."

"What?"

"Reach across. You know where it is, don't you?"

"Yes, but—" Then he remembered; it was an image, not the real woman. It could not be affronted by familiarity. He reached carefully across and poked her left breast through her thick winter shirt. It felt very nice.

"That's what is called a feel," she said.

"Oh, yes! But what's the point?"

"You know this is programed. When you touch any part of me, it feels real, though you know it is merely touch-sensation superimposed on sight-image. There is no person actually here."

He laughed. "Every time I start getting really interested, you remind me it's not real."

"It is real for you. Just not for me. But here's the point: it had to be real for me for the recording. I had to be touched every way I could be touched, with the complicated holo cameras going. So that my figment could be authentic."

That was significant. That would be more intimate than a body cavity search.

"Every way? It must have taken days."

"Weeks, with many retakes. I had no privacy at all. I got poked, stroked, squeezed, goosed, kissed, tongued—everything, everywhere."

"I'm impressed. Those were certainly moments. But there must have been limits."

"No limits."

"You mean—sex?"

"Every variation known to man. So that my figment could be complete."

"And I could—could do this with you, if I follow

the rules of the game?" His erection was already rampant. Fortunately his clothing concealed it. Which made him smile ruefully; he would have been embarrassed for an illusion to see his state?

"Yes," she said. "But I don't come easy. You will have to do a lot of exercising."

"I surely will! Thanks for telling me."

"It's my job."

Of course. Yet he wished it wasn't. "But if we—reach that point, and I feel it all, but you aren't really there—"

"You may have to clean up. Is that a problem?"

Full sex with this lovely, feeling, image! "No." But he cursed himself yet again for a fool. First for seriously considering it, and second for discussing it with her. If the figment had any mind at all, she was surely amused. If there was anything worse than having sex with an illusion, it was having a serious dialogue with an amused one. The young woman was merely a projection of a program, like a video picture.

But he was tiring, and had to end the session, with regret. Crazy as it was, he liked being with Alia, however illusory she might be.

Thereafter the sessions became easier, as his body acclimatized and his arms and legs developed some muscles. The program took him on tours of many lands, and Alia acquainted him with all of them. But it was the more personal discussions following the presentations that really intrigued him. Gradually he got to know her better, and he liked what he learned. She was exactly the kind of girl he would have loved and married, had he met her in life. If she were amenable. As she surely would not be, as there would be scores of better prospects for her. She said she wasn't very pretty or smart, but she was both pretty and smart enough.

Would have loved? He already did. That was perhaps his greatest folly.

He did not push the sexual aspect for a while. It was too nice simply being with her. He was afraid that sex would mess it up, because it would demonstrate that she was after all merely a construct that had no private sensitivities. Her niceness was an illusion he was not yet ready to dissipate.

But in due course he took a step. "You match my pace as I pedal. Will you match my attire?"

She didn't hesitate. "Yes, Spence."

He hunched up his mid-section while pedaling and stage by stage pulled down his exercise trunks, exposing his groin. He no longer was concerned about his erection showing. He was after all in reality alone in his garage.

She pulled down her skirt and panties, baring her legs and belly.

He maneuvered to get his T-shirt off. This was trickier than the trunks because he had to use one hand to pull the sleeve off the opposite arm, without messing up the steering, but in time he accomplished it.

She matched him. Now she was cycling bare breasted. Her breasts jiggled and bounced with the irregularities of the ride, turning him on fiercely.

That was enough. They cycled for some time before he ended the session. "Next time I'll start this way, naked," he said. "Will you?"

"Yes, Spence."

"You're beautiful."

"Thank you."

He stopped pedaling, watching her nude body fade out. Next time—ah, next time!

The following day they cycled nude together. Alia went through the spiel for the locale, which was a quaint English village, complete with people who looked startled at the two bare cyclists. One woman hastily covered her child's eyes as they passed. The program was clearly prepared for this.

Then they reached the dialogue stage. "What do you think of me, Alia?" he asked.

"I think you are committed. You have lost eleven pounds in five weeks, and are healthier for it."

"How do you know that?" he asked, surprised.

"The program tracks your weight on the cycle, and the force you exert when pedaling. You are doing well."

He should have realized that the equipment was following his progress. It was designed to improve his health. Probably it would phone a doctor if he had a serious physical problem while mounted. But that wasn't what he had meant to ask. "I mean personally."

"I like you," she said promptly.

But by this time he was canny. "Is this a programmed response, so that I won't cease exercising?"

She paused a moment. "It is, Spence. But it is also true. That is, if the real me were with you, instead of a copy, I would like you. You're my kind of man."

"How can you know that?"

"By the nature of your responses. You aren't supremely smart or handsome, and you're older than I am, but you are well motivated, open minded, and decent. That would impress me, were I with you personally."

"You know I love you." Oops, he had to stop speaking before he thought.

"Yes. Your physiological readings have indicated that for some time. Fortunately you are realistic about my nature. I can't hurt you by reminding you that I am only a responsively programmed projection."

"Realistic? I'm a fool!"

"A romantic fool," she agreed. "I like that."

He had to laugh. "I'm in love with an understanding illusion."

"Spence," she said, and paused.

"Yes?"

"Do you think it is time to take it to the next level?"

He knew what she meant, but wanted her to say it. "What level is that?"

"You are clearly interested in me sexually. We have come to know each other well, and I return your interest. I think we should indulge."

"How is that possible?"

"I will join you on your cycle. You will have to pedal and steer, having no limbs free, but I can handle that if you wish me to."

"Alia, I'd love it."

"Then hold steady." She guided her cycle close to his, then managed to cross over by a maneuver that surely owed much to facilitation by the program; he doubted it would work in real life. She lay down on him, her back on his chest, her plush bottom on his groin, her legs inside his. She set his hard member up between her legs so it wouldn't get squashed, even in imagination. Her weight felt completely real.

"Now I will steer, if you wish to have your hands free," she said.

"Yes!" It meant the program would steer for him, for this purpose.

She extended her arms to either side of him to reach the handlebars. When he felt her hands there, he released the bars, and put his arms around her torso. His hands found her breasts. They were every bit as wonderful as he had anticipated. "Oh, Alia, you're divine!"

"Thank you. But don't try this at home; the program allows leeway that doesn't properly exist in reality."

"So as to deliver the maximum in exercise rewards?"

"Exactly. A little fantasy can spice things up in a way that reality would not, encouraging further exercise."

"I could exercise like this forever. Figuratively speaking."

She laughed, her breasts jumping evocatively in his hands. "Thank you."

They cycled that way for a while, him pedaling, her steering. He reveled in the sensation of her bare body against his, her buttocks pressing his groin, her hair falling back to tickle his face, and her marvelous breasts in his hands. It was much as he had imagined it in the shower. Surely this was a slice of heaven. He hoped the shifting contact of her thighs against his rigid penis did not make him ejaculate; he was on the verge.

"Spence?"

Had she had enough of this? "Yes?"

"I think you should resume the steering now."

He stifled a sigh. "Of course." It seemed there was only so much non-exercise the program allowed. He let her breasts go and put his arms out by hers. He took over the steering.

"Thank you." Then she put her hands down along his torso, lifted herself up slightly, found his stiff member, and guided it to her crevice. Her legs remained closed, but somehow she made room for him. His member slid between her buttocks, found her vulva, and then her vagina. She let her bottom settle down on it, and the hard rod eased inside the warm slick channel. In a moment it was all the way in.

Suddenly they were intimately connected.

That was it. He ejaculated instantly, pumping jet after jet into her body as his legs pumped the pedals, adding to the effect. "Oh, Alia!" he repeated ecstatically.

"It is nice, isn't it," she said. "You're a virile man, Spence."

The scene spectators applauded. That was a naughty touch, but he was beyond embarrassment.

They rode that way for a time, remaining connected. But the double weight (the program made the pedaling proportionately harder) was tiring, and he had to ease off. In fact, one foot slid off a pedal, and that jolted the other off, and the cycling stopped.

The scene faded, and Alia with it. He was alone, naked, with ejaculate dribbling across his belly. But what an experience it had been!

He mopped up, then showered, thinking about what had happened. The memory gave him another erection. Alia might be no more than a figment, as she put it, but she had certainly delivered. There had been no way she had not seemed completely real, other than her fully obliging manner. Public sex on a bicycle? A real woman would never have done it.

The next day they rode nude again, this time through an abandoned mine with seemingly endless tunnels. He had to avoid a rogue coal cart before finding her standing beside her doffed pile of mining clothes. "Oh, Alia, you were great, last time," he said as she found a matching cycle and rode beside him.

"You were pretty good yourself," she said. "As I knew you would be."

But of course the pleasure had been all his. As a figment she could not have an orgasm of her own, and she had not tried to fake it. This was all his exercise.

They aligned, and she crossed over to join him. This time she faced him, and sat on him upright. Her breasts jogged enchantingly with each bump in the terrain. Then she lifted herself and guided his member into her cleft, allowing her weight to settle comfortably around it. He felt the position completely, inside and outside her body.

He spouted immediately. He couldn't help it. "Alia, you're so great!" he gasped.

She smiled, then stretched out on him without

disconnecting. She lay against him and kissed him, and her lips were warm and sweet. "Thank you."

"But you know, I come so fast, there's no time for you. I'm sorry about that." So was he asking her to fake it? He wasn't sure.

"That's one advantage of being a figment, Spence. I don't know what I'm missing."

"I love you anyway. Alia, I wish I could be with you personally, outside the program."

She shook her head. "Do you know how many men this figment has had sex with?"

"No."

"Forty-three. The program keeps track. That's before your individual case was set up; there may be others elsewhere. They provide a nice royalty stream for the original. If I were with you personally, I'd have to do the same for the others. That would soon get complicated, I think."

He had to laugh, feeling it through to their connection. "How many men has the original you had sex with?"

She looked surprised. "Apart from the modeling for this program, I think none. She's not the type. Being a figment is marvelously liberating. I have indulged in ways she would hardly dream of."

He liked that, obscurely. "I wish I could be with her."

"I suspect she would be far less accommodating than I am. She would not be obliged to keep you exercising."

This time they both laughed.

And of course when the session finished, he had to clean himself up again. But it was well worth it.

He was forty, and had thought that daily sex was beyond his inclination or capacity. Now he knew better.

But the notion was in his mind; what *about* the original woman, from whom the figment Alia derived? He knew her pretty well, from their dialogues. Would it be possible to look her up?

Next session, after another delightful tryst, he asked her. "I'd like to look up your original. Would that be all right with you?"

"Spence, I'm a figment! I have no feelings of my own, so you can't hurt them. You don't have to ask me about anything like that."

"That's the thing, Alia. You're wonderful, but you're not real. I think you're my perfect woman, if only you had feelings. The original surely does."

"Spence," she said seriously, "there may be something you haven't thought of. This recording was made fifteen years ago. I am forever young, but my original isn't."

Fifteen years! That had never occurred to him. She would be pushing forty. That was a sobering realization. "Um," he said, out of sorts.

"Normally, once a man has plumbed his companion sufficiently, fathoming her secrets, he tires of her. You can select another woman and start over with her. You don't need the original. I assure you I won't mind." She reconsidered. "Well, my original would miss the royalties."

"But I love you! And by extension, her."

"You love a twenty-four year old creature who has reason to oblige your passion. I've told you; she would have neither the body nor the incentive. You would be reaching for heartbreak. Take another luscious young image; I understand the teens can be marvelously titillating."

And the system would continue receiving his monthly payments as he pursued the program, having at an imaginary teen girl who giggled endlessly while being plumbed. This was not what turned him on. "No."

"Well, there is more I can offer you. Or if you'd like to indulge with two or more girls together— "

"What is this, a whorehouse?"

Now she looked hurt. He knew it was feeling lessly programmed, but he still felt bad.

"We merely want to encourage you to continue with the program. You have lost three more pounds and are becoming the man you can be. You shouldn't give it up now."

"I'm not giving it up. I just want at least to meet the original. If she's married with five kids, then I'll consider an alternate image."

"She isn't."

He looked at her. "You know this?"

"It's part of the databank. The program keeps track, in case she should be needed to make another recording."

"At age forty?"

"Thirty nine. There is less demand for mature women, but they are available, and she's experienced. You could put in a request."

"No, I want to meet her personally."

Alia sighed. "I fear this will not work out well, but I will give you her address."

"Why are you trying so hard to discourage me?"

"I would prefer not to answer that."

"You are balking? Since when do you do that?"

But she only shook her head, not speaking.

This was different. He put his mind to it. "Is it that you don't want the competition of your older self?"

Now she answered. "No."

"There must be some reason. If you really have no feelings, why don't you just tell me? Maybe you'll persuade me."

She cupped her breasts with her hands. "Let's make love again."

"I'm forty! I can't do it twice, so fast."

"Sure you can, with the right encouragement." She spread herself out on him as he continued to pedal.

It was tempting, but at the moment he was more interested in fathoming the mystery. "You're evading the issue."

She sighed. "I am."

"For a creature without true existence, you're showing remarkable independence. Why won't you tell me?"

Finally she capitulated. "It's complicated."

"It must be."

"She—is me. Everything is programming; I don't really care about you or anyone else, because I have no personal existence. But whatever I am, I owe to her. She is me, unprogrammed. I don't want to hurt her."

"Ah. You're not concerned about me, but about her."

"Yes. She's—innocent."

"Yet this response of yours must have been recorded by her, having been anticipated by the program. She can't be ignorant of the chance that some day some client will want to make it real."

"She's not. She would like that to happen."

"Then what's the problem?"

"I—have more experience than she does. With men. I know how treacherous it is ever to love one."

This was fascinating. "How can that response have been pre-recorded? You're speaking like a real person."

She gazed at him, and tears began to leak from her eyes. "Please don't hurt her. I derive from her; I wouldn't exist without her."

"I'm not going to hurt her!"

"Yes you are."

Was the program glitching? "How?"

"She would like you. I know."

"Well, I hope so. I expect to love her. She's my age."

"And then you would two-time her with a younger edition of herself. That would destroy her."

That made him take stock. He was having an affair with that younger version right now. It hadn't occurred to him to give it up. But what would the real woman think of that? She could indeed be hurt.

"Would it help if I promised never to return to you, after meeting her?"

"No. Either you would break that promise, or you would not get your exercise."

"Suppose I go with one of the alternates, for the exercise, instead of you?"

"You won't."

"Why won't I?"

"Because you love me."

She had him there. "So I can't have both you and your real self?"

"You can have what you choose to have. I can't stop you. But you would be destroying us both."

This remained curious. "What would the exercise system proprietor think of this dialogue?"

"It would terminate me."

"And the royalties would stop."

"Yes. Figments must not evince independence. That's a signal of deterioration."

Maybe it was, but he liked her better this way. It seemed that she did have some small identity of her own, though she had been required to deny it. The boss would consider it a perversion of the program.

Yet the idea of meeting the original Alia-recorder had caught hold of him, and he couldn't relinquish it. "I don't want to hurt you or her. But she just might be the woman I would want to marry. I can't marry you, obviously. So I want to see her."

"Yes, of course," she said sadly. "You will do what you will do."

He hated this, but he had to follow through. "Give me her address."

She did, including her real name, which was of course much less evocative. She lived in another state, but he could get there in a day. "Thank you."

He knew he would be haunted by her sad face as he stopped pedaling and she faded out.

* * * *

It was a small, neat house in a small second-class suburb. Alia-real was not wealthy from her royalties.

He knocked on the door. A woman answered. He recognized her immediately: the older version, heavier set but not unattractive. "Alia," he said.

"Oh, damn! Another stalker."

He was taken aback. "There have been others?"

"You see the copy, and you figure you can just come and mess up the original model. Get out of here."

He had not known what to expect, but not this. "Please. I love your—your younger self. I want to get to know the real you. If you talk with me and still want me to go away, I will. She said you might—might like me."

"She said that?"

"Yes. She didn't want me to come, but I insisted, so she gave me your address."

"You've been exercising with her."

"Yes, with all that implies."

She sighed. "Oh, hell, come in. We'll talk. Then you can go away. I'm not at all the woman I was then."

He entered the house and sat opposite her in her small family room. "I am Spencer Chowder, age forty, a man of comfortable means. I needed exercise, so—you surely understand the rest."

"I'm Janine Stubbs in real life. Call me that, when you mean the real me. So you've had at my figment, as so many have, and you think I'll be amenable to the same."

"No! She told me you wouldn't. She was against this."

Now there was a spark of interest. "Why?"

"She's afraid I will hurt you, Janine. Emotionally.

She said you might—might like me, but then I'd be two-timing you with her. And that would destroy you."

She looked as if she were about to upchuck, alarming him. Then she burst out in laughter. "Oh, that's rich!"

"Did I say something funny?"

"Hilarious."

"I don't understand."

"Come this way."

Bemused, he followed her to her back porch. There was an exercise system similar to the one he had. "You exercise too!"

"With fancy young indefatigable hunks who just can't get enough of me. I am not the woman I was fifteen years ago. My prior self would be appalled. I got the system as a bonus for recording for them, and with no monthly fees. I love exercising!"

This was awkward. "I'm no young hunk," he said lamely. "I'm sorry I bothered you."

"Don't go away just yet. Why did you come here?"

"Well, I did hope that—forget it. I'm a fool."

She did not smile. "Maybe. Tell me anyway."

"I—ultimately fantasy women, however attractive and obliging, aren't quite enough. I want a real relationship. I thought you might be the one."

"That's it exactly. But I don't want to give up the hunks. They really turn me on."

It was a revelation. "So you would understand, if—"

"If you kept on screwing my younger image or some other hot-panted creature. Knowing I'm screwing hunks. Fantasy is fun."

"Yes! But it needs to be supplemented by some reality."

"You got it. Why did Alia think I would like you?"

"We talked a lot. She—she likes me, to the extent she is capable of genuine feeling. You should have some similar tastes, however modified by experience. I think she does have some reality of her own. But she would be terminated if that were known."

"And will you keep the secret?"

"Yes. I love her. I said I'm a fool."

"And you might love me too, as her older version."

"Yes, that was my perhaps ridiculous notion."

"I trust her judgment. I'm not at all the same woman I was then, and I know she would not approve of the hunks, but if she likes you, I will too. Do you want to try it?"

"On your machine? I would be embarrassed."

She laughed again. "Shooting off into the air? I got that. I have to clean up after a session, I'm so wet. But that's not what I mean."

"Then I fear I don't understand."

She met and held his gaze.

Oh. "Where?"

She led him to her bedroom. In moments they were both bare. He was glad that the exercise had removed much of his paunch. She had some excess poundage too, but her exercise had kept her in similar shape. She was appealing enough, considering, especially in the full breasts. It was as though fifteen years had passed in a moment, bringing her to his generation. They were two fortyish people.

He had his erection, and didn't mind showing it, but felt awkward. "If you don't mind, could we embrace first?"

"Why? You're ready." She was gazing at his stiff member without any embarrassment, perhaps comparing it to that of a hunk.

"I am. I do desire you. That's obvious. But I want more. Because sex without familiarity or affection is what I get in the exercise scene. I want someone I know is real. Otherwise what is the point?"

"Damn well spoken! Alia is right; I do like you." She considered briefly. "I have gotten accustomed to the fast urgent kind, knowing that dialogue with a programmed response is intellectual masturbation. A handsome youth does me two or three times in rapid succession, I begin to get my own sensation. It may take me a while to get into a real relationship. How about a compromise: do it fast and furious, get your edge off, don't worry about me; then we'll cuddle until you recover enough to do it again. By that time we should be beginning to know each other."

"That I can do," he agreed.

She lay on the bed and spread her legs. They were good legs, fleshier than those of her younger self, but still evocative. He mounted her and wedged in without preamble, thrusting and climaxing rapidly. Then, belatedly, he kissed her. To his vague surprise, she accepted it.

"That's it," she said. "You could pass for a hunk. But you can't do it again within five minutes."

"I can't," he agreed. "And couldn't when I was

twenty, either."

"The hunks don't have the limitations of reality. They can do it every two minutes if that's what I demand."

"If you demand that of me, I'll fall far short. I didn't even do it every day with Alia."

"You didn't?"

"When I fell for her, I just wanted to be with her. It didn't have to be sexual."

"Well, you've had me now. You can return to her."

He froze. "You're sending me away, Janine?"

"I gave you what you came for. It's like doing a virgin, isn't it? Once you've done it, you move on to the next."

He realized that she had thought he was on a more limited quest. "It's not that way. I want to really get to know you. If you wanted to be rid of me, all you had to do was say so."

"I apologize. If it was that way, I wanted it to happen at the outset. Men will say anything to get a woman in bed the first time."

"I wouldn't know," he said a bit warily.

"Then stay and talk."

They talked, embraced, and it was soon apparent that there was much of Alia in this older woman, and they had common interests.

"You're turning me on," she said. "So I'd better test you before I get too interested."

"Test me?"

"You have had months to get to know me, via my younger self. I have had only this hour to get to know you. I want to be sure you're for real."

"I don't know how I can satisfy you about that. I may be wrong for you."

"Not if you know the answers to three questions."

"I might guess right. That's not a safe shortcut."

She smiled. "Let's try it anyway."

He shrugged. "Ask. But I repeat, if you want to be rid of me, it's not necessary to find a pretext. I want you to want me. For the genuine feeling I can't get from Alia."

She paused. "We'll return to that in due course. First question: what's my favorite flower?"

"Alia loved the gardenia. She said the smell put her into minor ecstasy. I think that's still true for you, because you have a pot of it growing by your bedside."

"You noticed!"

"They reminded me of her."

She nodded. "Second question: what's my favorite pet?"

"None. Alia's allergic to most animals. Except spiders, and she can't stand them."

"You are impressing me, Spence. What's my pet peeve?"

"Men who want girls for sex alone. Alia comes on to her clients because that's the nature of the program, but in real life she wants more. That's one reason she was against my approaching you; you would figure it was only for sex, and be disgusted."

"I did, and was."

"Then why did you—oh, as the easiest way to get rid of me."

"I've had stalkers. I did everything I could to

turn the first one off, but he wouldn't quit. Then I gave it to him, and pffft! he was gone. All he wanted was the conquest. Alia was more to his taste. After that, I just gave it at the outset; it was easier. It's not that I dislike sex; I love it. It's the principle."

"Now I think I understand."

"I think you pass. You do know me well enough, considering. How much money do you have?"

Suddenly he was angry. "The hell! You want me for my money?"

"Isn't it obvious?"

"Then you have changed. Alia hardly cares about money. All she wants is enough to live on. Any beyond that she would give to charities."

"I haven't changed."

He paused, considering. "You don't want to be sought for only sex any more than I want to be sought for only money."

"Now you've got it. Naturally sex and money are involved, as we both need both, but they should be part of a larger emotional package."

"I agree. If you are with me, you can have my money."

"I would just spend it on charities."

"That's the price of you?"

"Part of it."

He considered again. "Okay, Janine."

"You're willing to buy me?"

"I'm willing to take you as you are. You're welcome to take over my finances."

She shook her head. "Oh, Spence, I'll give it all to you without that. I just wanted to be sure."

"If you marry me, you'll have it anyway."

"I'll sign a pre-nup, of course. You can safeguard your money."

"I think there'll be no need."

"Your decision. Now let's just enjoy each other."

But still he hesitated. "We think we have an understanding. That we can accept each other having sex with others in the exercise mode. But we may be fooling ourselves."

"I'm not fooling myself. I know I want both fantasy and reality. But if you have a problem with that, then maybe we do have a larger problem."

"I don't. But I've seen others in denial about their real beliefs, and can't be sure I'm not in denial too."

"Well, there's one way to find out. Watch me make out with a hunk. If that drives you crazy, then at least we'll know."

"I'll watch you if you'll watch me with Alia."

"Fair enough. But I won't be jealous. After, all, she's *me*, younger and prettier."

"I am already coming to appreciate your more mature qualities. She's not prettier, just younger."

She kissed him. "I can live with that assessment. Now watch me with my hunk." She hesitated. "Damn, I hope this doesn't drive you away, Spence. But if it does, better that it happen now than after we have committed to each other."

"It won't happen," he assured her. "You have been completely upfront about it, and I'm doing the same."

"But you want to be sure."

"Yes. Absolutely sure."

"So do I. We've been negotiating as if this is a business transaction. We need to verify the underlying feeling."

They went to the garage, and she got into her rowboat, which appeared as she turned on the unit. It had oars and a sliding seat, with a firm board for her feet to push against. Naked, she took hold. She glanced at him, where he stood to the side, then started rowing. He saw that she had good arm and leg muscles; she had been doing this a lot.

The rest of the holo formed, a complete scene of a boat on a lake. It was a lovely setting, with a forested island ahead and a golf course by the lakeshore. Tranquillity personified. He could see it all, but he knew that she could no longer see him, though she knew he was there.

Janine's thighs flexed with each haul, and her breasts quivered. Spence found this sexy as hell. He had just plumbed her, but this was arousing him again.

Then a powerboat roared toward her. It barely missed her as she shoved to the side, and the wake rocked her boat violently. "Peckerhead!" she yelled back at it.

Spence smiled. This was the same as the car passing too close. The script merely changed the images.

The next one to pass was another boat. A canoe, powered by, sure enough, a young naked hunk with muscular arms and rocklike abs. "Looking for company, you gorgeous creature?" he called.

"Come on over, Bruiser," she called back.

He guided the canoe to the rowboat, then climbed in with her. He gazed into her laboring cleft as she continued rowing. Of course she couldn't stop, lest the scene fade; that was the point of it. "You've got the sexiest cunt on the lake," he said admiringly. "It makes my cock hungry." And his penis was rising.

Spence smiled. The man was right. Those solid bare thighs, that flexing furry juncture—it was about as much of a turn-on as he could imagine.

"I love it when you talk dirty," Janine replied.

"I can't wait any longer. I've got to get into it now."

"You can't, Bruise. I've got to keep rowing. You know that."

"Keep rowing," he agreed, "but spread your legs."

"Like this?" She spread them wide. Now her outer labia parted, giving the inner labia prominence.

"Beautiful!" He got down and put his face to her groin, licking the length of her cleft. The inner labia opened to receive his questing tongue. His member was at full erection, dew forming at its tip. It was a large, thick one, really too big for her to accommodate.

"You've certainly got the touch," she said as he lapped her. "I could do this forever."

"But I can't," he said. "I'm about to burst." He lifted his head, moving his body up so he could take a mouthful of her left breast. He sucked, and she sighed. His huge rod was dripping goo.

Spence's own member was dripping. He had never before watched a live performance like this, for all that Bruiser was only an animated figment. Was he supposed to be jealous? He was fiercely turned on.

"Can't wait," Bruiser gasped. He got himself up

against her, set his penis, and rammed it in full depth. Some remained outside; it was indeed too big. He thrust, and thrust again, urgently kissing her mouth at the same time. Her vagina seemed to be sucking on his embedded member, eager to take it all in. And with each thrust, less remained outside; it was hammering the hole deeper. In real life that would have been painful for them both. But this was fantasy.

Janine groaned and squeezed his torso with her thighs, though she never stopped rowing.

The man continued thrusting: five, six, ten, twelve times. How long did it take him? Spence would have spurted by the third one. Then he realized that realism was not the point; the woman needed more action to get there, and the image was providing it.

At last, after what in life would have been an interminable effort by the man, she got there. "Oh! Oh! Aaaah!" she cried, pressing as closely as she could considering that her arms still drew on the oars.

Only then did Bruiser go into his own climax, bucking savagely into her and groaning appreciatively, his full member finally inside. Then he collapsed on her, lying between her legs as they kept flexing with the effort of rowing. "What a fuck!" he gasped.

"What a fucker," she replied, laughing. "You really plumbed me that time, Bruise. But I did manage to take in all of you, just as I promised last time."

"You sure did! No other woman can manage it.

They're either too shallow or too narrow. I just can't get enough of you, you ravishing creature."

"I bet you say that to all your women."

"Yes. But you're the best. I close my eyes and picture you when I'm clasping them."

"Thanks. It was great. See you again tomorrow?"

"I am eager for the hour."

"Bye now." She stopped rowing, and the scene faded. Bruiser had never had the chance to dismount.

"Wow," Spence said.

Janine got out of the boat, putting a sponge to her cleft. There would be no ejaculate, just her own juices. "Now you've seen it. Are you jealous?"

"Yes, of the experience. I can't plumb you like that."

"No one could. I'd need surgery if a rod that size jammed into me that hard. But what fun to pretend! There's just something about a really big, hard fuck."

"It certainly turned me on." He glanced down at his erect penis, which was drooling.

She laughed. "So you can handle it."

"I'd like to do you right now, but it would be a let-down for you after that performance."

"Don't worry. I know the difference between fantasy and reality. That's the point of having both, isn't it? But hold off on having me now; I want you to save it for Alia."

He had forgotten that. "Yes, of course."

She turned to the machine. "What are your settings?"

"Recumbent bike, and Alia."

She made them on the console. "What's your unit number?"

"Oh, at home? Why?"

"Because the units are separate. The Alia of this one won't know you from that one, unless they are tuned in to each other. Then it will be just like home."

That did make sense. He gave her the unit number, and she entered it on a special pad.

"Done. Go to it, lover."

There was the bicycle. He got on it and started pedaling. The forest scene formed.

Soon Alia was there. She joined him, but held back from the embrace though she saw his stiff member. "Did you do it, Spence?"

"Yes," he replied. "I went to see her."

"And?"

"And we hit it off. I like her and want to be with her. She can handle it. In fact, she exercises too."

"She does!" She looked shocked.

"With handsome, virile young hunks with huge anatomy. We agreed not to interfere with each other's exercises."

"She must have liberalized considerably."

"Yes, she has. In fact, she's watching us now."

"Now?" She drew back. "How could you!"

"Well, it seemed natural to observe each other, so we know there's no jealousy. There isn't, as far as I know."

"What does jealousy have to do with it? This is an invasion of privacy."

"You are her younger self," he explained patiently, wanting to get through this so he could clasp her and explode within her. "She might resent my doing it with you. So we're testing that, to be sure she doesn't. Once we're sure, we can marry."

"Marry!" She looked outraged.

"Well, it is natural for people who love each other."

"You're dumping me for her!"

This set him back. Since when did a figment care about outside relationships? Or about anything else that wasn't scripted? But he carried on. "No, I want both of you."

"Me for sex, her for meals, housework, and laundry," she said scathingly.

"Her for sex too. We can hire a housekeeper, and eat out; there need be no drudgery."

"Her for sex too? She turns you on?"

"Oh, yes! Especially when she exercises nude. When she does a hunk. She's *you*—only my age. Please, Alia, try to understand. I love you both."

"The hell I will, you lecherous voyeur! Go screw some other figment. Stop pedaling this instant."

How could this be happening? "Alia—"

"Go away!" She was in tears of rage or pain.

What could he do? He stopped pedaling.

Reality returned. He turned to Janine. "You heard?"

"Every word. The girl's got spunk."

"What happened? I thought she'd be glad I didn't hurt you. Instead she seemed angry."

"Come to bed, Spence."

"That won't solve this. I can't go to a different girl. Alia's the one I love."

"So I see," she agreed, leading him away. "You had a real, live, lover's quarrel."

"But *why*? I don't understand at all."

"She's young, Spence. She has sexual experience

galore, but not enough general relationship experience. After you're hurt a few times, you develop a broader perspective. She doesn't understand that love can be shared. She thinks that if you love me, you can't love her. That was probably why she didn't want you to come here."

"But she said—"

"That it was me she was protecting. She may even believe that. Actually she was afraid that I would alienate you from her. She saw my presence at your tryst as confirmation. She thought I was savoring my victory, knowing she couldn't satisfy you as I could."

"I never thought of it that way."

She put her hand on his arm tolerantly, as if calming a child. "You are after all a man. This is not a male nuance."

"If I have to choose between you, I don't know what I'll do. You are two aspects of the same woman."

She kissed him. "You don't have to choose. You can have both."

"But—"

"She'll come around, in time. I'm in a position to know."

For Janine was Alia, older, wiser, battered by hard experience. She was surely correct. "That's a great relief."

"Now we have some time to pass. My guess is that three sessions with Alia should do it, especially if you take pains to reassure her of your love. She needs that. She does love you, in her fashion."

"I will!" He gazed at her. "I thought I could love

you. I think I already do. You understand what I need."

"I do, Spence. At the moment you need sex."

She was right. He had been highly turned on throughout, as she was so well aware. "*You* are what I need. Alia is the girl. You are the woman."

She smiled appreciatively. "This one is for you. You don't have to make me come. You are not competing with the hunk, you are complementing him."

"I want to take you with me, if I can."

"Oh, you can, but that will take more time." She glanced at his turgid member. "I don't want to torture you. It will give me pleasure to give *you* pleasure. My turn can wait."

"With her, I would take that offer. Not with you."

She did not argue further. He had the impression he had pleased her.

He stroked and kissed her breasts, and licked her vulva, and slowly she responded. She had, after all, had an orgasm more recently than he had. "But put it in me when I come," she said. "I don't like getting there dry."

That was interesting. "Tell me when." The oral sex was turning him on in a way the straight fast sex had not; there was a greater depth to his passion, filling out the urgency of his penis. He tickled her clitoris with his tongue, the way Alia said she liked.

Her breath quickened. A pulse showed in her neck as he glanced up. Her thighs spread wide, then closed, and spread again, reminding him of her session with the hunk. That was not a turn-off.

"Now!"

He got up on her and plunged in. Then it was like riding a bucking bronco as she suffered her long slow orgasm, bringing him off in the process. It wasn't like sex with Alia; Janine was too preoccupied with her own feeling of the moment to pay attention to his the way Alia did. But that was part of the realism of it. He was not her whole object, but merely a partner in pleasure. Alia had never climaxed with him, even in pretense—and this was no pretense.

At last she subsided. "Oh, that was great, Spence! You didn't know quite how to make it perfect, and that's what's perfect about it, you know?"

"I know, Janine," he agreed. "For perfection, we go to the exercise."

She laughed in agreement. "Side by side, in parallel machines. We understand each other. Do we have a future together?"

"I think we do. I believe I could love you, as I said. In fact, I'm getting there already. *Am* there. I'm repeating myself. You're so like Alia, only more mature."

"She and I have this in common: we want to be wanted," she said. "By a real person. *As* a real person."

"I want you, Janine. Not just sexually. In fact sex isn't really the point. I want a compatible companion, and I think you are that. Just as I had hoped."

She kissed him. "Just as I had hoped too."

"You?"

"That some day one of Alia's clients would want the more mature version. Not a stalker seeking sex. A sincere man. I knew it was foolish, but still I hoped, even as I approached the dread blank wall of age forty."

They talked further. It was the beginning of a permanent relationship. And by no coincidence, thereafter, they both continued to exercise regularly and thoroughly, often watching each other do it. They did not share this news generally; others would not necessarily understand.

* * * *

I wrote this story in March, 2006, expecting it to be a brief one. But I wasn't satisfied with the simple version: boy meets phantom girl, makes it with her older self. So I kept returning to it, amending it, and it kept growing until it became a novelette. Okay; stories sometimes seem to have wills of their own, like figments, and need to be obliged.

I exercise seriously myself, not because I enjoy it – I don't – but because writing is a sedentary occupation and I know I'll go rapidly to pot if I don't act to prevent it. It seems to be working; I maintain my college weight though some settling around the middle seems impossible to eliminate as I enter my 70s, and a crushed disk gives me a chronic backache. So exercise doesn't prevent all ills.

For several years I tried the exercycles and rowing machines, but inevitably they broke; it seems those things aren't made to be forcefully used. So I moved on to straight running, cycling (including an adult scooter), archery, and dumbbells. But the idea of a cycle-powered virtual reality scene stayed with me. I first thought of it when I first used the rower on January 25, 1993. I had thought the rower could be chased by wolves or dragons and barely escape, and maybe that would have made a good story, but in the end I decided on human interaction.

Would I like to have an exercise system like this? You bet, though I'm not sure my wife would understand.

Heaven

Elmer could see it was Heaven, because of the huge pearly gates rising out of the surface of the cloud bank. He was not entirely dismayed; he had been getting old, and that last illness had been a bad one. He had lived a good life, to the best of his ability, so wasn't surprised to wind up here.

In fact, he expected soon to be reunited with his dear wife of forty-some years, Ellen. The last few years alone would have been intolerable, if not for the company of the parakeets.

Ah, the parakeets. He hoped to be united with them too. They had all been good birds, well worthy of eternal reward in the Afterlife. All of them with P names: Peter Parakeet, Paul, Patrick, Perry, and of course the females Penny, Pearl, Polly, Pam. His favorite had been Paige; it almost seemed that he had been able to talk with her. Her death had left him and Ellen desolate for days.

But he had immediate business; no sense in drifting off into reveries. There should be time enough for that, in Eternity. He approached and lifted the ornate door knocker. It made a melodious clang, announcing his arrival.

The Angel Gabriel appeared. It was clearly him, because he was shiningly noble, with a halo, splendid wings, and a nacreous name plaque. "Yes?"

"I am Elmer Allen. I trust you have me on your list."

Gabriel checked the scroll that appeared in his hands. "Oh, yes. We have been expecting you."

"That's nice."

The Angel frowned. "That's odd."

"Odd?"

"I thought you were a good man. This shows how deceptive memory can be."

"Well, I thought I was a good man. I certainly tried to be."

"Ha, ha, ha," Gabriel said, unsmiling.

"I beg your pardon?"

"Don't try to play innocent with me, you impostor. You have a rap sheet a league long. What made you think you could come here?"

This was really odd. "I don't think I understand."

The Angel read from the scroll. "Car theft. Child abuse. Murder." He paused as Elmer stood stunned, then read the ultimate: "And you cheated on your taxes."

"I never cheated on my taxes!" Elmer protested indignantly. "Or any of the rest of it."

"We have the testimony of the car owners, and of the children." He frowned, reading the ugly details. "Your daughters trusted you, and you did that, you pervert. Shame on you; you certainly belong in Hell."

"We never had children," Elmer said. "It was one of our deepest regrets. The parakeets became our family."

The noble brow furrowed. "No children? Then

how could you have molested them?"

"I couldn't have. You've got the wrong information."

Gabriel focused more closely on the scroll. "Now I see it! Identity theft! We must have let a criminal into Heaven, while his crimes were put on your record. This has to be straightened out."

"I should think so," Elmer agreed dryly. "Meanwhile, you might seek the testimony of my wife Ellen, or even the parakeets."

"No animals in Heaven," Gabriel said absently as he studied the rap sheet.

"No pets?" Elmer asked, shocked. "What happens to them?"

"The dogs go to Hound Heaven, and the cats have their cat house. I'm sure they're well taken care of."

"And the parakeets?"

The Angel shrugged. "No birds here. They leave droppings. There must be a cage for them somewhere. Look, I'm trying to untangle this glitch. Return tomorrow."

"There will be no need," Elmer said stiffly. "I am withdrawing my application."

"But you may qualify for eternal bliss."

"Not without my friends. I doubt Ellen would have cared to reside here either; she loved those birds as much as I did."

Gabriel checked his scroll. "No Ellen Allen listed here."

"Precisely." Elmer walked away, leaving a surprised Angel.

Now where was he to go? He did not fancy Hell,

in significant part because he was sure that neither Ellen nor the parakeets would be there. Was he doomed to wander unsettled forever?

A bird appeared before him. It was a blue parakeet. In fact it was—

"Paige!" he exclaimed, putting out his hand.

The bird landed on his forefinger. He brought her to his face and kissed the top of her head. "I'm so glad to see you, Paige!"

"Peep," she said.

"Oh, you were looking for me? I really appreciate that. But if you're not in Heaven, where are you?"

"Peep," she queried.

"Of course I'll go with you, wherever that may be," he said. "I don't care if it's a perpetually foggy bog. I'm just so glad to see you. Are the others there?"

"Peep," she agreed, taking off.

"All of them!" he exclaimed, delighted as he followed her. "This is so wonderful."

"Peep."

"And Ella too? My heart overflows. I have to admit I was somewhat disappointed with Heaven. Imagine a place with no birds. It must be dull as—-well, Hell."

Then they came to Paige's home. It was a giant beautiful aviary filled with parakeets of every description.

"Why this must be Parakeet Heaven!" Elmer said, amazed. "It's absolutely lovely. But I can't enter here; there must be a rule."

"Peep."

"You say it's missing something to make it

complete? Whatever could that be? It seems to have everything."

"Peep."

"It is missing me? That's very flattering, Paige, but surely the parakeets wouldn't want a human messing up their Heaven, any more than the Human Heaven wants birds."

Now other parakeets approached, and behind them a human woman. "Ella!" he cried, running to embrace her.

"The parakeets have invited us to reside in their Heaven, dear," she said after kissing him. "They say that we, especially you, have been so good to them in life, they want our company in the Afterlife. Please agree."

"Of course I agree," he said as the sheer wonder of it took him. "There's no place I'd rather spend eternity."

Then he was almost buried in parakeets, as all his friends clustered about him.

* * * *

So what's your notion of Heaven? I think I'd prefer Parakeet Heaven, though I fear I wouldn't qualify.

My original idea note was recorded September 23,2005, but it's not my first story relating to parakeets. I wrote "Beak By Beak" in the 1960s partly in memory of the parakeets we had had. I have liked birds since 1952, when my high school roommate Peter Wickham was a serious bird watcher, and my aunt gave me Peterson's Field Guide to the Birds. That summer I learned all the birds of our farm in the forest of the Green Mountains in

Vermont, from wren to pileated woodpecker, and over 50 years later I still know those birds – and very few others. I got distracted by incidentals like college, marriage, and my writing career. These things happen.

There had better *be birds in Heaven; don't you agree?*

Seconds

Byron wandered through the "seconds" section of the store uncertainly. Did he really think that buying a new jacket would solve his problem? Yet how else was he to start?

A striking young woman approached him. "Excuse me, sir. I need a favor."

He gazed at her a moment before answering. She was as lovely a creature as he had seen in real life, with an hourglass figure and classic features. Whatever could she want with him? "What is it?"

"I want to buy my boyfriend a jacket as a surprise, but I don't know his size. He's about the same as you, though. Would you mind trying this on?"

So it wasn't a pickup line. Too bad. But actually this might fit the profile of what he needed. "Of course."

"Thank you so much."

She held it up, and he put his arms through the sleeves and shrugged it on. "It's a little tight in the shoulders."

"Oh. If it's tight on you, it would certainly be tight on him. He's pretty well developed."

So was she. "Maybe you should get his measurements."

"But then he might catch on and ruin the surprise."

"Your chances of getting a perfect fit by checking it on another man are remote. It would probably not fit well, and he would be put in the awkward position of having to tell you that or conceal the problem. Also, a second is not the ideal gift."

"It's what I can afford. But you're right; I'd better reconsider." She put the jacket back on its hanger and hung it on the rack. "Thank you."

"You're welcome."

But she dallied. "Actually, it's a different favor I want. You seem like a nice man."

This was becoming interesting. "I hope so."

"Are you single?"

Most interesting. "Yes."

"It's a different favor I need to do for my boyfriend. I need to find a man."

Oh, yes, the boyfriend. So this wasn't a romantic come-on. "I don't think I understand."

"It's—unusual. You may not be interested."

"If you are thinking of a threesome, I am not interested. I'm rather conventional in that respect."

"Oh, no! Nothing like that. It's that he and I can't be seen together. So I need a man to—to seem to date, on a double date, so we can be together without others knowing."

Extremely interesting. "You want to keep company with me in public, so you can be with him in private?"

"Yes. Would you be able to handle that?"

Byron pondered briefly. Suppressing his own interest to promote that of another man. Could this be what the doctor ordered? It was worth finding out. "Yes."

"Oh, wonderful!" she exclaimed, taking his hand and squeezing it. "Can we go somewhere and talk, to set it up? A snack bar? I'll pay."

Yet she was shopping for seconds. She didn't have extra money. "I'll pay."

"No, that's part of the deal. You get paid. I can use Shawn's card for this."

Byron shrugged. "As you wish."

They adjourned to a connected snack bar, and she bought them organic sandwiches and mugs of the shop's specialty ale. Evidently she ate right, to protect her appearance.

"It's like this," she said earnestly. "Shawn is black." She paused as if expecting a reaction.

So he gave it. "I don't have a problem with that. It's your romance."

She relaxed visibly. "I am Karoline, with a K."

"I am Byron, with a B."

They smiled and shook hands over the table.

"Shawn was a pro athlete, and now is organizing investing in black enterprises. His people would think he was betraying them if he associated with a white woman. He needs the right reputation, or they'll consider him an Oreo."

"Oreo?"

"It's a cookie. Black on the outside, white on the inside."

"Oh." He repressed a smile.

"So we have to date in secret, for now. I love him, and I'll do what I have to. Which means being with a white man, while he is with a black woman.

Interracial friends, to show he's not prejudiced. He isn't, obviously, but it will be dismissed as a show so as not to alienate white investors." She smiled briefly. "The show is not exactly what it appears. Maybe someday we'll be able to date openly."

"I appreciate the problem. I gather we'll be seen in public. To what extent should I seem to be your date?"

"No kisses. No feels. But you must be clearly with me. If more is required, I will take the lead. But do not get ideas."

"I will be a gentleman," he agreed.

"We'll attend a play or an opera, and sit so that I am on your right, and he is on my left. The white couple and the black couple. If anyone else is likely to see anything, nudge me. You understand?"

"This will be a hot non-date in the center."

"Exactly. He's a passionate man, and I want all of him I can get, anywhere, anytime. But we can't afford to be seen. Then we'll eat at a fancy restaurant with a similar pattern. Then maybe an evening dance." She looked at him. "You can dance?"

"Depends on the type. But why bother, since you can't dance with him?"

"Good point. Scratch the dance. We'll finish at his place. White friends visiting, pure social courtesy. You'll be on your own until midnight, when you and I depart. There will be free liquor at the house, but don't get stinking drunk. Shawn covers all expenses, and you and the girl will each get two hundred dollars for your help. Do you have any problem with any of this?"

"It should be a good date."

"It should be," she agreed with a smile. "Dull for you in the evening, but there's a good stock of videos you can watch, any rating you want. Any questions?"

She really had this organized! "I gather I'll be with the leftover black girl. What's her name?"

"Celie. She works for Shawn in some lowly capacity. She's a nice person; don't abuse her. She needs the money."

"I promise," he agreed, unsmiling.

"I'll need your number and address."

"I don't get yours?"

"I'll call you about the timing, and pick you up. You are free Saturday?"

"Free."

"Wear a conservative suit. And don't talk about this to your co-workers or friends. We want you anonymous."

"Got it. No one will know." He gave her his number and address. "I'll be waiting by the street at the right time, so you won't have to look for me."

"Excellent." She smiled. "It's a pleasure doing business with you, Byron."

"I hope it's a good play."

"It will be. Shawn wants nothing but the best. I'm helping him with the culture aspect."

They finished the snack and parted. Byron returned home, bemused. He was doing a considerable favor for someone, one he would never have thought of himself. He hoped that qualified.

But not at the expense of natural caution. He picked up his phone. The number answered immediately. "Yes, Byron."

"Susan, do a fast background due diligence on

three given names and call me back. Shawn, who is a former black athlete now organizing investments for black enterprises, Karoline with a K, who is white and beautiful, and Celie, who is a lowly black employee of Shawn. Off the record."

"One hour, Byron." She clicked off.

An hour later Susan called back. "Shawn Johnson, rising track star, sidelined by injury, but the insurance settlement left him worth a million dollars. Legitimate entrepreneur on his way to a second million. Karoline Singleton, sometime model/actress, occasional feature in tabloids, presently not associated with any man by her preference. Celie Green, exactly as you described, deep in credit card debt through no fault of her own. She's a clean girl, honest to a fault. I have further detail if you require it."

"No, that's fine, Susan. Thanks."

"May I ask what your association with these diverse people might be?"

"I'm double dating with them. Keep that private."

There was a brief pause, which was significant for her. "You are dating now, Byron?"

"It's a special situation. I'm anonymous."

"Not for long, if you are seen with Karoline. She's a magnet. So is Shawn."

He laughed. "It will do my image good."

"You surprise me, Byron."

"Good. Bye." He hung up.

So the information Karoline had given was accurate. It was a legitimate double date.

He called his psychiatrist, and left a message

with the service. "Dr. Yondar, Byron here. I am about to indulge in a double date as a personal favor to three strangers. I'll get a free show, meal, and two hundred dollars. Does this qualify?"

Fifteen minutes later Dr. Yondar called back. "Depends on your motive, Byron."

"White woman wants to be with black boyfriend, but his image prevents it. So I will go out with her, but she'll be holding hands under the table with him. I'm doing it because she asked me."

The psychiatrist laughed. "It qualifies. See how you feel after it's done."

"Seems like odd therapy."

"You may be surprised. Play it through and find out."

"Thanks, Doctor." He hung up, relieved that he had guessed right on this. Dr. Yondar was known for unusual therapies, but he had a sterling reputation for success.

Karoline called him Friday, setting up the schedule for Saturday. He was ready at the proper hour, suited and standing by the street.

A limo pulled up precisely on time. The door opened. "Come in, Byron," Karoline called.

He climbed in and the limo got in motion. There were two others with her: a solid black man, and a petite black woman. "Byron, meet Shawn," Karoline said, and he shook hands with the black man. "And Celie." He shook with the woman.

"You got the picture?" Shawn asked.

"I'm with Karoline in public," Byron said. "You're with her in private."

"Right." Shawn pulled out his wallet and

counted off four fifty dollar bills for him, and the same for Celie. Then he wrapped his arms about Karoline and kissed her. "The limo is private."

Byron was left sitting with Celie, who glanced at him and shrugged. They knew their roles. She was in a rather attractive dress that showed off a good figure. Byron realized that she must have been picked in significant part for that, so as to be credible as a date with the boss.

"You look tight," Celie said.

"I beg your pardon?"

"Your muscles are tense. I can help that. Turn around and take off your jacket."

He turned to face away from her. He pulled off his jacket. She put her small hands onto his shoulders and massaged them. The effect was immediate; it felt good, and he felt his tension easing.

"How did you know?" he asked as she continued.

"I have a feel for it. People are often unconscious of stress, but it can be eased."

"You have the touch," he said. "I can't remember when I have felt so good, so quickly."

"It's a gift."

"It certainly is."

In seemed only a moment before the limo drew up to its destination. Celie helped him back into his jacket. His shoulders and back felt enormously refreshed. "Thank you, Celie."

"You are welcome."

There was a line, and the limo had to wait. Shawn and Karoline hardly noticed, wrapped up in each other. "I had no idea who you were, Celie,"

Byron said. "Now I am glad I met you."

She shrugged. "All in the day."

"There is something about the way you talk. I can't quite place it."

"I talk white."

"That's it. If you were on the phone, I would have no idea of your color."

"I was adopted by white parents and raised white. Now it can be a problem with blacks. They think I'm putting on airs."

An Oreo. "I have no problem with it. But then, I am white."

"I noticed."

"I meant no offense. I— " He spread his hands. "I apologize."

"Don't bother. I know you didn't."

He still felt awkward. "I haven't been out socially in a long time. I may be clumsy."

"You're what—two years out of college? Tied up with the new job? It probably feels longer than it is."

"I'm thirty."

"You're fooling!"

"No."

"Now I'm embarrassed. You certainly don't look it. I'm only twenty-two."

"I try to stay in shape, physically."

"So do I."

Then the limo made it to the gate, and it was time to disembark. "Nice meeting you, Celie," he said.

"Mutual."

Shawn got out first, then turned to assist Celie, his nominal date. Byron followed, doing the same for

Karoline. "Bit of blouse untucked behind," he murmured.

"Thanks." She fixed it as she straightened out.

The show turned out to be *The Phantom of the Opera,* so well known that even Byron had heard of it. They had four seats in the center of the main section. As they made their way down the crowded aisle, a sharp-featured woman spied Karoline. "Ms. Singleton! You're dating!"

"My private life is none of your business," Karoline said curtly and pushed on.

Then the woman spied Shawn. "Shawn Johnson! Whatever are you doing at the opera?"

"My date's got better taste than I do."

The woman glanced at Celie, who smiled deprecatingly. "He needs a bit of culture, don't you think?"

"Understatement of the week." She moved on.

"Newsbitch," Karoline murmured. "Works for a tabloid called SNOOP. With luck she won't catch on that we're a foursome."

Byron was coming to appreciate why Shawn was so cautious. The tabloids would have a field day with a Karoline-Shawn affair, and it would not be ideal for either of their reputations.

They reached their row, and Byron led the way to their seats. Karoline followed, then Shawn and Celie.

"I am beginning to appreciate the virtue of anonymity," he told Karoline.

"You said it. If any of them pester you for gossip about me, buzz them off."

"Gladly."

Then the opera began. Byron expected to be bored, but found it fascinating. It was one great, dramatic story, with some very nice music. "I love this!" he said in wonder.

Karoline patted his hand. Then she tuned him out as Shawn's hand slid under her skirt. Her interest was not in the opera.

Byron wished he had a woman as eager for his attention. But his social skills in that respect weren't much, and the women he knew were mainly business professionals. In any event, he had never had the time to spare. Which was much of his problem. The psychiatrist had ordered him to make time.

After the opera the limo took them to a top-flight restaurant where they were served courses Byron couldn't even pronounce. He had to get Karoline's help selecting his meal. He had eaten often at restaurants, but generally avoided the fancy ones.

While they waited to be served, Shawn and Karoline's hands disappeared beneath the table while they both maintained straight faces. Byron and Celie, seated cornerwise from each other, discussed the opera, maintaining the dialogue and keeping eyes out for any nosy intruders.

"That was one phenomenal experience for me," Byron said. "I've never been to an opera before. I was surprised."

"I haven't either," she agreed. "I absolutely loved it. Even the gory parts. And the music!"

"The music was enchanting," he agreed. "When they hauled up that chandelier—"

"I was afraid it would fall on our heads. But then

I got involved in the story and forgot it."

"Same here." They continued reviewing it, discovering a new common interest.

The food arrived, and Shawn and Karoline had to free their hands for it.

It was one sumptuous repast.

In due course the limo took them to Shawn's mansion. "The place is yours until midnight," Karoline informed them. "Stay inside and downstairs." Then she and Shawn went upstairs.

"It seems we have three hours to ourselves," Byron said. "I'll look around; I'm not much for videos."

"Neither am I. I believe there's an exercise center."

"Now that appeals. After a big meal it's not ideal, but if there's a running track I could jog."

"So could I. It can be hard to squeeze it in on a working day."

They found it: a complete gym and circular track. Then Byron thought of something. "I discover a problem: we're in our good clothing. That won't do for jogging."

"He probably has jogging clothes we could borrow."

They checked, but discovered that those supplies were locked up. "Damn," Byron muttered.

Celie glanced sidelong at him. "I have an idea you may not like."

"Do it naked?"

"I can handle it if you can."

He considered. "You are not an unattractive woman. The sight of you jogging nude could give a man ideas."

"Do you have those ideas?"

"I fear I do. But I can go watch a video until you are done. Then you can watch it while I run. Can you trust me that far?"

"I trust you already. We can run together; that's less boring."

"You're sure?"

"You're a chained tiger, but you wouldn't force a woman."

"How can you know this?"

"I have a feel for such things."

"This suddenly becomes much more interesting. Suppose I promise not to touch you?"

"That is good enough for me." She started removing her dress.

He started to do the same, but stopped. "This dialogue, and the prospect of nudity, is giving me a reaction," he said, embarrassed.

"I've seen it before, elsewhere. I promise not to look. Running will abate it."

"Good enough." He stripped, revealing his erection. It seemed the natural thing to do.

Without further comment, she began circling the track. He joined her, pacing her. She was, as she had indicated, jogging, not running; it was an easy pace.

"You're fit," she remarked. "You're not straining at all."

"It's a matter of discipline. I can't say I enjoy exercise, but I know how strongly it benefits the human body."

"Same here. But you know, I'm enjoying this. There's a freedom, naked and in company."

"I feel it, too," he agreed, surprised.

They circled the gym several times, maintaining the easy pace. Byron had never imagined doing something like this, but it was fun.

"I need to walk," Celie said. "I'm not as fit as you are."

"You're fine," he said, slowing to a walk.

"Thanks."

She was breathing hard, and it did things for her breasts. He was in danger of getting the reaction again.

"You called me a chained tiger. Do I give off vibes?"

"You do," she agreed. "My guess is that you're a workaholic with a lot of drive. I can't figure what you're doing here, being a second."

"A second?"

"Shawn and Karoline are the primaries, the ones this is really all about. We're the seconds. The leftovers, the imperfects, the ones who don't matter. We're thrown together randomly, having no other connection to each other."

There was a tone creeping in. "Are you bitter?"

She was silent a moment. "If I talk to you, will you talk to me?"

"I don't want to seem dull, but I don't think I properly understand."

"If I answer honestly, you could use it against me and get me in trouble. I don't want that."

"You are asking whether I will keep your secrets?"

"More than that."

"Whether I will keep yours, and share mine?"

"Yes. There's something about this situation that makes me want to bare my mind as well as my body. Maybe I'm being foolish."

This interested him intensely. "I think I am not free to tell you all my secrets, but I will give you an edited version that will not be inaccurate. And I will not seek to embarrass you by betraying your confidence. Will that be sufficient?"

She paused. "I think it would be simpler just to have sex and leave out the dialogue."

"Damn! I was hoping you wouldn't notice my erection. All I can do is remind you that I promised not to touch you, and I keep my promises."

"I meant me. You're a man; you'd be turned on by any bare woman, wouldn't you? It's nothing personal."

"Any attractive bare woman, yes. But it *is* personal. I am coming to know you."

"And you're about to know me better. Yes, I am bitter, to an extent. I work for Shawn, and I do what he tells me, or I'll lose my job. If he wants me to fetch a file, I fetch it. If he wants a spot poke, I hoist my skirt. If he wants me to go on a fake date with him so he can make out with his real girlfriend, I do it. I'm used, any way he wants. I need the money. But I wish I had my own life."

"I don't know what to say."

"Well, you asked. Now tell me why you are here. I'm pretty sure you don't need the money."

"I am what you might call a high-power executive. I make monetary deals that bring my company a good return on its investments. I can afford anything I want. But I'm depressed. You may not understand the kind of hold depression can have on a person. It is independent of status or money."

"I do understand. Go on."

"My psychiatrist told me I'm headed for burnout if I don't take steps to abate it. He told me to relax and take life easier, but I'm not made that way. I am, as you surmised, a workaholic; I can't change my nature. So he told me to come at it obliquely, to submerge myself and get involved in helping someone else, or to undertake some worthy cause that would in no way benefit me. He said that might solve my problem. I am dubious, but I'm giving it an honest try. When Karoline approached me, I realized that this might be an opportunity to do that. So I'm here, trying to help someone else without doing anything for myself. The free opera, meal, and the money are nothing to me. Well, actually I did like the opera; it's the first time I've watched something just for the fun of it. I didn't count on your healing hands on my shoulders, or on running nude with a lovely woman. Those are totally new and novel experiences, and I like them better than I could ever have guessed."

"Your psychiatrist knows what he's doing. He thinks you're too self-involved, so he's making you try to tune out yourself and help others. It's bound to make you happier."

"It already has."

She smiled. "We've cooled now. Let's get dressed and talk some more."

"Gladly."

They did, and did. She had him lie on his stomach while she gave him a fuller massage while they talked. Her hands were like magic, relaxing him wherever they touched.

"What were you doing when Karoline approached you?"

"I was shopping in the seconds section of a clothing department, looking for a jacket."

"You're joking!"

"I'm not. It's sheer coincidence that you see us as seconds, after an encounter in a seconds section helped put us together."

"So you were looking for bargains."

"Not really. I—my company provides a tailor and seamstress, and we get fitted suits. I wanted to get something on my own, privately, just for the experience of doing for myself, so I went where I thought it unlikely I would be recognized."

"Did you find anything?"

"No. I'm not very good a shopping for myself."

"I could help you there. I know how to shop."

"You surely could."

"I'd have to pretend to be your girl Friday. I could do that."

"Why would you have to pretend such a thing?"

"I'm black."

"Am I missing the point?"

"You're serious?"

"Yes."

"To an upper class white man, a black woman is good for only about three things: to fix his meals, wash his laundry, and to bare her bottom when he gets a notion. No way is she his social equal."

He was surprised. "You are serious?"

"I've been there. Shawn's the same, except for

color."

"That makes it better?"

"Not really. But he pays better."

"I realize that I never had much personal contact with blacks, so I'm neutral. You're a person to me."

"Thank you. I think I knew that when I first saw you in the limo. It's why I reached out to you."

"With your magic touch."

"Add it to the list: we also massage."

That made him react. "I didn't mean to put you in that category."

"I know you didn't. You're not a racist. But racism is all around us regardless, and we can't avoid it. You and I can talk alone as one person to another, but in public that social climate would make it impossible. It reminds me of a line from a poem, that hidden current: 'I would I could know what swimmeth below when the tide comes in.' That's all I know of it, but it speaks to me. There are dangerous things that don't show on the surface, and you'd better be careful of them."

"So in public I shouldn't treat you like a person?"

"That's about it."

Midnight approached. "If Karoline asks me, I'll do it again," Byron said. "Will you?"

"Oh, yes! I have to."

That reminded him. "Take my share of the money. I don't need it and you do."

Now she became guarded. "I don't want to take your money. It has implications."

"I promised. I'm not trying to buy you. I just want you to have it. Please accept it in the spirit offered."

She paused, then acquiesced. "Thank you."

Shawn and Karoline came down. Wordlessly they showed the way to the waiting limo. It took Byron home, and went on to deliver the others.

Byron returned to his solitary suite, thinking about Celie. He had never before interacted seriously with a black woman. He liked her, and hoped to meet her again.

With that in mind, he made a call. "Susan, I need to identify a line from a poem. It goes 'I would I could know what swimmeth below when the tide comes in.'"

"Got it."

She called back within the hour. "It's from *The Marshes of Glynn* by Sidney Lanier, an American poet of Civil War days. I'm emailing the full text to you, together with background on the poet. He's an interesting fellow."

"Thanks, Susan."

The following week went well. Byron made the deals as always, and was as hard-nosed as always, but now he had a larger vision. He was aware of the way the other parties saw it, and that was an additional advantage.

But more privately important, he was buoyed by the seconds date. He had succeeded in submersing himself, in doing favors for others, and felt better for it. The therapy was working.

And he wanted to see Celie again. There was something about her.

The call came Friday: "Date for tomorrow, same terms?" Karoline's voice asked.

"Same deal," Byron agreed. When he hung up

the phone he raised both arms in a Victory gesture. He truly wanted this.

The limo picked him up. The other three were there. Shawn detached himself from Karoline just long enough to hand out the $200 payments, then disappeared into his rapture.

Celie touched his shoulder. He removed his jacket and turned away. She kneaded his shoulders. "You're not as tight," she remarked.

"I had a good experience last week."

"So did I."

This time they attended an excellent play, and Byron sat beside Karoline. "I forgot to ask," she murmured. "Did you and Celie get along okay?"

"Just fine. We jogged around the track."

She shrugged. "Each to his own taste."

After the play they went to another posh restaurant. This made Byron nervous, as it was one he patronized when required to entertain prime prospects. Sure enough, the maitre d' recognized him. "Why hello, sir," he said, surprised.

Byron quickly pressed a fifty dollar bill into the man's hand. "Mistaken identity," he murmured.

The man was naturally quick on the uptake. "Of course. I took you for someone else."

While they waited for the entrees, Shawn and Karoline sat with their hands under the table, largely oblivious to anything but each other. On impulse, Byron took Celie's hand under the table. Her eyes widened, then narrowed. She had misunderstood. He quickly let go.

Then they were at the mansion, alone together for three hours again. "Why did you take my hand?"

Celie demanded.

"I apologize," Byron said. "I meant no offense."

"Why did you take my hand?" she repeated.

He sighed. "I have never been a foolish or impulsive man. I plead guilty to both this time. I'm sorry."

"Why did you take my hand?"

She meant to have the truth. "I've been thinking about you all week. I just wanted the contact. I shouldn't have presumed."

She changed the subject. "Let's exercise."

They went to the gym. "Oops," he said. "I forgot to bring clothing."

"So did I."

There was a pause.

She smiled. "Same terms?"

"Same terms," he agreed, relieved.

They stripped, and he embarrassed himself again with his stiffening member. She pretended not to notice.

They jogged. "I didn't really forget," he confessed.

"Neither did I."

"You wanted to do this again?" he asked, surprised.

"I've been thinking about you too."

"You also? I thought it was just my own foolishness, reading something more into the situation than exists."

"I'm foolish too."

"I'm trying to follow my psychiatrist's advice. What can I do for you that won't benefit me?"

"I told you how I have to do what Shawn wants."

"Yes. That's how I met you."

"So you know I've given him sex on demand."

"Yes."

"Do you still want me?"

"Yes, as I think my member has already signaled. It isn't as though I'm virginal myself."

"Then take me."

"Now?"

"Now."

"There's an exercise mat in the corner."

"Got it."

They jogged to the mat. She lay on it and spread her legs. He hesitated. "I have an awful urgency. Do you mind if it's fast?"

"Any speed will do."

He got down on her and kissed her. Then he entered her slick channel and exploded.

"Now what can I do for you?" he panted as his member softened.

"You've done it."

"No. That pleasure was all mine. You didn't come."

"I didn't need to. You kissed me."

"Well, yes. That's part of it." He slid down and kissed her breasts. "So is that. Thank you for obliging me. But I'm supposed to be doing for you."

"You kissed me."

"I don't understand."

"No white man ever kissed me before. Even Shawn didn't bother. You did."

Byron took stock. "They would have sexual intercourse with you, but would not kiss you?"

"That's right."

"But that made you like a—" he stalled out.

"Like a whore."

He did not like that word. "Like something unclean."

"Why did you kiss me?"

Now he caught on. "All they wanted was the sex. They did not respect you. I care for you, though I have not known you long. I want to kiss you. I did it without thinking."

"You showed respect."

"Oh, yes, Celie! I—think I could fall in love with you. If that repulses you, tell me now."

"You're a high-powered exec. What would you want with a black girl?"

That set him back. She was no part of his societal framework. "I don't know."

"Yes you do."

He had to put a name on it. What was sex with love, without marriage? "A mistress. I don't think I can offer more than that. I'm sorry."

"I will settle for that. It isn't as though I am unfamiliar with the problems of interracial liaisons."

"That puts such an ugly face on it."

"It's an ugly world."

"Damn it, Celie, I'm attracted to you. I just hadn't thought it through far enough. I should not have touched you."

"Byron, I felt the pull toward you the moment I saw you. I knew I was going to wind up in bed with you, if you wanted me. I'm not ashamed of that. I know my place. I'll take what you can give me, and I won't make any trouble for you. I'm just glad you care enough to value me."

"Oh, I do! But this—this is simply using you. That's no good."

"It will do. I've never been had before by a man who actually cares for me. I know it won't last forever, but I will revel in it while it does."

"You have far too generous an attitude."

"I'm a giving person. It's my nature."

"You are," he agreed. Then a revelation struck him. "I can learn from you!"

"Not much, I think. All I have is a high school education. I'm not high-power anything."

"Let me explain. My psychiatrist told me to learn to give, to tune out my own gain in an effort to do something to benefit others. To submerge myself. I tried, and it helps. But this—you're giving to me. I need to learn how you do it, and do it myself."

"You won't make many sharp money deals that way."

"That's business. I mean personally. How can I emulate you?"

She laughed. "You mean like giving me a massage?"

"Yes!" he said, seeing it. "You must get wound up too."

"I was joking."

"I wasn't. Roll over."

Bemused, she rolled onto her stomach. He put his hands on her shoulders. "You will have to help me to this extent; tell me how to do it."

"Just sort of knead the muscles. Feel which ones are tight, and work them loose. You have to get a feel for it."

He kneaded. "There?"

"Yes, but not so hard. You're stronger than I am."

"Sorry." He kneaded gently. Her muscles *were* tight, but soon they relaxed. He moved to her arms, and to her back, getting the hang of it.

"Ooh," she said. "That feels so good."

"I know. You did me, remember?"

"I remember," she agreed. "But you surprised me."

"Oh—there's something else. That line you know—it's from *The Marshes of Glynn,* by Sidney Lanier."

"You found it!"

"Not by myself. I asked the company researcher."

"Do you know any more of it?"

"Yes. He lived in Georgia, and wrote about the marshes by the sea there. He drew a parallel between the tide and sleep, as if hidden thoughts were swimming there. It's not actually a racial commentary, though surely it can be taken that way too. It concludes: 'And I would I could know what swimmeth below when the tide comes in/ On the length and the breadth of the marvelous marshes of Glynn.' I brought a printout of the whole poem for you."

"Oh, Byron! How thoughtful!"

"I'm learning from you."

He did her whole back and legs, skipping over her pert bottom. "Muscles there, too," she said.

"But your buttocks turn me on."

"You know what you can do about that."

"But that's not giving, it's taking."

"Something about giving," she said seriously. "It

gives back almost as fast. Do it, turn me over, take me. It's a fair deal."

"That's my language." He massaged her buttocks, and his penis stiffened. "But I want you to get your climax too."

"Okay." She turned over part way, and lay on her side, her knees forward. "Put it in from behind, easy, so you don't come yet. I won't make it if you leave me behind." She chuckled. "Is that a pun? Don't leave my behind behind?"

"Maybe. It's really nice anatomy, regardless."

"Enough with the flattery. Ease it in."

He obeyed, lying on his side behind her, sliding his member into her vagina. His recent orgasm slowed his response, so he could do it without immediate culmination. The feel of her bottom against his groin as he achieved full entry was amazingly pleasant.

She lifted her upper leg and set her foot on the mat beside her other knee, so that her thighs were parted. "Now reach around me and tickle my clitoris with your finger. Gently."

He did, finding her cleft with his fingers, and the little knob within it. It was slick with moisture.

"Stroke down farther, then up to it. Lightly."

He did, running his fingertips along the channel of her vulva. He had never done this with a woman before, and it was exciting, apart from the sexual aspect.

She began to react as his finger reached her clitoris. Her vagina tightened around his member, clasping it rhythmically. With each pass of his finger, she reacted more, until suddenly she went into the clenching pulsing of her orgasm. She put her hand on top of his, pressing it tightly down against her groin, stopping his motions. "I love you!" she gasped.

"And I love you!"

Her climax set off his. He thrust repeatedly, and jetted into her, the squeezing of her vagina wringing extra pleasure from him. He had never before had an orgasm like this!

"You're right," he gasped. "It gave back!"

"I never came with a man before. It's great."

"So I'm your first in this respect?"

"My first," she agreed.

"Then you were a virgin, for me."

She laughed. "For you."

They lay there, remaining connected. "What you said," he asked. "Did you mean it?"

"I shouldn't have said it. I just got carried away by the feeling and lost control. I'm sorry."

"I'm not. I want your love."

"I guess you have it. But what we feel in the middle of an orgasm isn't necessarily what we'll feel when we're sober."

"True. So we'll make allowances for exaggeration. But Celie, I'm happier right now that I've been in years. You make me feel whole."

"You feel my what?"

"Complete," he said quickly.

"I was teasing."

"I know." He pulled out of her, put his hand on her shoulder to turn her onto her back, came down and kissed her mouth. "Stop me when you get bored."

"When hell freezes over?"

He moved down to her breasts, kissing them all over. "I never wanted to do this with a woman before. Not after sex. I just want more of you."

"Same here. I love having you do it."

"I live an austere home life," he said between caresses. "My whole world has been my business. Now I feel I have a personal life too. Because of you."

"It certainly feels like love."

"It does. Celie, do we have to wait for the primary dates to see each other again?"

"Byron, I've got a job, and shopping, laundry, and everything else to do. The weekends are all I have free."

"Then when you're shopping. Let me come with you."

"I can't. If you were seen with me, no one would say a thing. But word would reach your office at lightspeed, and they'd marginalize you out. They'd find other reasons, anything but the truth. Your career would be quietly gone. I can't do that to you."

"No it wouldn't."

"You haven't been there, Byron. I have."

And of course she had. He might be able to persuade her if he told her everything, but that had its own danger. He had to find another way.

"Come spend nights with me. I'll send out for anything you need."

"That would be expensive. I can't afford it myself, and I wouldn't foist it off on you."

"Forget the expense! The thought of spending the night in your embrace overwhelms me. Please."

She wavered. "I shouldn't."

"Tomorrow! I'll pick you up. Just give me the

address."

"I hope I don't regret this."

"I hope you don't too." He returned to her face and kissed it avidly. "I've spent my life without knowing love. Now I'm afraid I'll wear you out."

"I'd love to have you try."

He tried, and she seemed indefatigable, as eager as he. It was new love, burning brightly.

In due course they came to sex again. This time she sat on him and took his member in vertically while he fondled her breasts. "But I can't get at your clitoris very well in this position," he said after a while.

"You want me to come again?" She seemed surprised.

"Oh, yes!"

"I can do it myself, if you don't mind."

"Yourself?"

"Stop me if this bothers you." She put her own hand down to her groin, just above his embedded penis.

Interested, he watched. She stroked herself, and soon he felt her vagina reacting. Masturbation—it had not occurred to him that it could be done in conjunction with coupled sex. Yet it made sense. It was also a considerable turn-on in its own right.

Her clenching intensified. She lifted on him, and pressed down, causing the base of his member to emerge, then disappear back into her, doing his thrusting for him. His eyes were fixed on her bouncing breasts. He ejaculated into the storm of her orgasm, another wrenching, intense, divine fulfillment.

Breathing hard, she straightened out her legs and came down on him without losing the connection. He wrapped his arms about her, holding her close. "But you may not get much sleep, at my suite," he warned her. "I won't be able to keep my hands off you."

"I'll risk it."

The time was getting late. They disengaged, took a shower together, dried and dressed. When Shawn and Karoline came down, they were pristine.

Two days later he brought Celie to his suite. She walked through it, assessing its virtues and liabilities. "You've got more space than I'd know what to do with, but no carpets, pictures, decorations, nothing. It's like a vacant showcase."

"Like my life, before I met you."

She checked his refrigerator. "There's no food in here, just water."

"I eat at a restaurant."

"All meals?"

He nodded.

"I can't do that. They'd see us together."

He had forgotten. "I'll have it delivered."

"Meals for two? They'll know someone's here."

"I guess I didn't think it through very well."

"I'll stay out of sight. They'll assume Karoline's with you."

The white woman. "I don't like sneaking around. Maybe we should do it openly after all."

"No. That's more mischief than we can handle at the moment. I'll be anonymous, and they can guess what they want. But next time, order the makings—I'll give you a list—and I'll make you a decent meal."

"But I don't want to make a cook of you."

She smiled. "I'll do your laundry too. So as to complete my usefulness."

"Celie—" He broke off. "You're teasing."

"Yes. But I really do want to do these things for you. As a woman, not as a black. So as not to be good for only one thing."

"Celie—" He smiled ruefully. "Got me again."

It worked out. Soon enough they were together naked in his bed, making desperate delicious love. Despite his warning, they did sleep most of it. He realized that every time he woke and reacted to her body, she fitted herself to him and brought him efficiently to climax, and then he drifted off to sleep again. "You're managing me," he said as it happened in the wee hours.

"Do you mind? I don't want you to lose sleep, so I put you down quickly."

"And what about yourself?"

"I'll get by."

"You're giving again."

"It's my nature," she repeated. "I love being here and doing for you."

"I love having you here. But *I* should be doing for *you*."

"You are, Byron. You said you're happy with me. Well, I'm happy with you. I like being your mistress. The tide is in his ecstasy."

"What?"

"That poem you found for me, *The Marshes of Glynn*. I read it all. It speaks to me in new ways. Such as love: 'How still the plains of the waters be!/ The tide is in his ecstasy./ The tide is at his highest height:/ And it is night.'"

"And it is night," he echoed, clasping her again. Time would confirm it, but he knew already that he was utterly in love. Maybe that wasn't what the psychiatrist had ordered, but it had abolished his depression, and he knew he was no longer heading for the meltdown of burnout. Not while Celie was in his life.

In the morning he tackled another matter. "You need money. I want to help you. Will you take money from me?"

"I'm not doing this for money," she protested.

"Please. A mistress takes money."

"I can't be your mistress free?"

"Give me your wallet."

She dug it out of her purse. He opened it, saw she had only six dollars. He turned away from her so she couldn't see, and put ten hundred dollar bills in. He closed it and returned it to her. "Don't look."

She threw up her hands. "Maybe that's best. As long as you know I came because I wanted to be in your arms all night. That's all the payment I need."

"Sometimes you just have to take, as well as to give."

"As long as you know," she repeated.

"I do."

"I'm not looking. You have to tell me. What did you put in there?"

"I want you to have it."

"What did you put?"

He sighed. "One gee."

She froze for a moment. "*Now* I'm looking." She brought out her wallet and looked. "Byron, you know I can't take this!"

"Celie, I love you and want to help you. I'm not good at giving. I know you need it. How can I do it?"

"How do you know I need it?"

"You've been open about that. You do what you have to, to survive, without necessarily liking it. You bare your bottom for Shawn, to keep your job. How is this worse?"

"It's money. It's bad enough I took your two hundreds. This is that much worse." She took the bills out and laid them on the table.

"Celie, I want so much to help you, but I don't know how. You say we can't be seen together. At least let me give you the money."

"You can buy me, Byron, but I wish you wouldn't. I'd rather be your friend."

He thought of an angle. "If your services for a night were up for auction, I'd bid that much for them."

"You wouldn't!"

"I'd bid more. Much more. Please. I don't know how else to help you."

"But you'll go broke!"

"I won't. But I would gladly go broke, for you. Look, Celie, I'm not good at giving; I'm trying to learn that from you. You're not good at receiving. Accept your value on the market, as it were."

She gazed at him half in bafflement. "You're serious."

"Oh, yes."

She decided. "I'll compromise. Half." She took back five of the bills.

"Half a night," he said, smiling.

"Take me home." But she was not angry.

He took her home. She kissed him lingeringly in the car before getting out. "But I value your love more."

"Welcome. I had no private life. You have become it. I would proclaim it openly if you let me."

"I love your naiveté."

The Saturday routine continued, but now Celie spent one or two interim weeknights with him. They did not mention this to the others. She also accepted money in five hundred dollar increments, though expressing concern about the drain on his resources. "Once I get my credit cards paid off, I won't take any more."

"When," he agreed. "Meanwhile I'm in heaven."

"So am I."

Then the bomb dropped on them.

When Byron joined the three in the limo, Karoline produced a copy of the tabloid *Snoop*. "You folk probably don't read this junk," she remarked.

Three heads nodded agreement.

"Well, listen to this. It's this week's cover story." She unfolded the tabloid and read. "Remember how Shawn Johnson has been dating his employee, Celie Green? In the company of a white couple, Karoline Singleton and an anonymous white man? So we all can see that Shawn is not the black racist some have called him? Well, that's old news, and only the tip of the iceberg. We were looking at the wrong couple. That white man turns out to be Byron Brevard, scion of the Brevard clan, who inherited three hundred million dollars six years ago and is said to be well on the way to doubling it by shrewd business dealings.

'He'll be a billionaire before he's forty,' a dismayed rival says. He lives a Spartan, celibate private life, spending nothing on himself. His whole life is business, and he's a genius at it. Now we know what Karoline sees in him; she has an unerring nose for money." She paused for effect.

Shawn and Celie were staring at Byron. "You been sponging off me, when you had that?" Shawn demanded.

He was in for it, and it wasn't Shawn he was worried about. "I delivered a service for a price," he said evenly. "I honored our deal. I'll refund your money if you are unsatisfied."

"I thought you were—not that rich," Celie said.

"It has no bearing on my feeling for you."

Shawn pounced. "So you're knocking off a little black ass on the cheap?"

"As you did?" Byron snapped back.

Karoline picked up on that instantly. "You're banging *her*?" she demanded.

"Not since I met you, babe," Shawn said defensively.

Karoline faced Celie. "True?"

"True," Celie agreed tightly.

"Then you're his ex. That's too much temptation. I want you out of this party. And I don't want you working for him anymore. I want you all the way out of his life."

"Please," Celie begged, tears streaming. "I need this job."

"Hon, she don't deserve this," Shawn said. "She only did what she was told. She's a good girl."

"I'll bet. Get rid of her."

"She was just a passing piece."

"An incidental black fuck?"

"Yeah."

"And what am I?" she demanded furiously. "A fancy white fuck?"

Shawn smiled uneasily. "I love it when you're jealous."

She slapped him. "Turd!"

"It's not like that, Kar. I don't want her hurt for what's not her fault."

"Which means you still have feeling for her. That's why she has to go."

Shawn turned to Byron. "Okay, Mister Big Deal Man. How you going to make a deal to fix this mess?"

"It's possible," Byron said. "But first I'm waiting for the other shoe to drop."

"What other shoe? This ain't bad enough?"

"That snooping reporter didn't research enough to learn my identity without learning more. See what it says."

Karoline lifted the tabloid. "I didn't finish it; it just arrived. You think there's more?"

"I fear there is."

She resumed reading to herself. "Oh my God!"

"What's going on?" Shawn asked.

"Listen to this: your girlfriend's sneaking out to see my boyfriend."

"What are you talking about?"

"Celie's been visiting me between times," Byron said.

"So? What do I care if you hit it off with her?"

"They think she's your girlfriend," Byron

reminded him. "So she must be cheating on you. That's a scandal."

"For shit's sake!"

Karoline read further. "This supposedly chaste, loyal young woman comes to Byron's apartment and spends the night once or twice a week. Maybe they're working late?"

"The snide bitch!"

"I'm lost," Celie said, the tears still flowing.

"Why do you think that?" Byron asked her, hating to see her grief.

"Because now you'll have to dump me."

"Why?"

"You're in the stratosphere. I'm nothing. You can't be seen with me."

"It was bound to come sooner or later," Karoline told her. "You didn't think he was serious about you, did you? A fabulously rich white man? You were just something to pass the time while he waited on us."

"That's not true," Byron said.

"He said he loved me," Celie said brokenly.

"They all do. So the girls will spread their legs without making a fuss. Standard male operating procedure."

"Hey, I never did that," Shawn protested.

"The hell," she snapped at him. "It worked on me."

"I do love you, Kar!"

"But not enough to be seen with me openly."

"It's a special situation. You know that."

"It's only a moment before the bitch'll catch on that you and I are dating," Karoline said. "Then the fat's really in the fire."

"All because you screwed up," Shawn said savagely to Byron. "Why'd you have to fuck around here?"

"He was slumming," Karoline said snidely.

They were not equipped to understand. "Celie," Byron said, reaching for her hand.

She jerked it away. "Get away from me! I was such a fool!"

What else would she believe? He cast about for a way to reassure her.

The limo slowed, reaching its destination. "Keep driving!" Shawn yelled at the driver beyond the partition. Then, to Byron, "So fix it."

Then it came to him. "I believe I can fix it, my way. But there will be a price."

"I'll pay it! Not that you need the money."

Byron turned again to Celie. She faced away from him, mopping her eyes. "Listen to me," he said.

She did not respond.

"Everything I told you is true. I said I had enough money. I didn't say how much because I feared you would react exactly like this."

"It would have been kinder to tell her at the outset," Karoline said. "Before she fell for you. But then you'd have missed out on some fine free fucking, right?"

"God, you're bitchy when you're mad," Shawn said with rueful admiration.

Byron ignored them. "Celie, all of it was true. And so is this: I love you. You are the most giving person I have encountered, and I am still learning from you. I am fulfilled in your presence, and empty in your absence. You—complete me. I want you to be with me always. Openly and proudly."

She turned her head to face him, but made no sound.

"Celie, before these witnesses, I am asking you to marry me. To be my wife."

Her mouth fell open. "You can't do that."

Now he could afford some fire. "The hell I can't!"

"The hell he can't," Shawn echoed. "Who's going to say boo to him, with his clout? He can do what he damn well wants. He could marry *me*, and no one would peep."

That broke Karoline up. "They'd poop, not peep! Poop their pants."

"It was a damn figure of speech. But true."

Celie looked beseechingly at Karoline. "Can he really?"

"You know, I think he does mean it," Karoline said, surprised. "Sure, he can do it. Only he needs your agreement. Probably on an armor-plated pre-nup contract."

"Pre-nup?" Celie asked blankly.

"So that you can't just marry him and divorce him next week and take half his fortune," Shawn explained.

"I wouldn't do that!"

"It is a necessary thing, in my position," Byron said. "But you will have a lawyer to represent your interest, so you will be fairly treated. You will never again be poor, regardless." He paused. "But first you do have to marry me."

Celie struggled. "I—I—oh, God, I will. I will."

"Kiss her," Karoline said. "It's traditional."

Byron took Celie in his arms and kissed her wet

face. She melted, but he could feel the lingering tension in her. She was afraid she was having a dream that could still turn out badly.

"That's nice," Shawn said. "But what about *our* problem?"

"That is the corollary," Byron said, disengaging minimally. "You are about to suffer the enormous public humiliation of losing your black girlfriend to a rich white man you thought was your token white friend. Never trust a white man! You may even have to settle for taking his white girlfriend, who is being similarly dumped after being similarly deceived. She is no more pleased about being so used than you are, and might take up with you as much for spite as interest. At first. Then, possibly, it might become real."

"I'll be damned," Shawn said. "I've been screwed."

"Royally," Karoline agreed. "It does make sense."

"But then we'll be seen in public," he protested.

"So why don't you marry me, and make it okay?"

"Damn! If he can do it, so can I. Okay, let's do it."

She glanced sharply at him. "That was an acceptance, before witnesses?"

"Yeah, sure. No more pussyfooting around secretly." He grabbed her and kissed her. "And you know something? I'm glad."

"So am I. But we had better rearrange the seating for the play. I still don't want her next to you."

Celie smiled wanly at Byron. "I suppose I won't need that job anymore."

"You won't," he agreed. "You will have a more difficult one: learning to be a socialite. Handling money."

"I can handle money. I'm paying off my cards."

"Real money."

"Like a slush fund of a million dollars for petty cash," Shawn said.

"Oh!"

"Choosing a house for us," Byron continued. "Trying to get some sleep at night."

She laughed, faintly. "I'll manage."

He held her close. "You know something? We're not seconds any more."

"Not any more," she agreed. Then she kissed him.

She might never believe that she was still giving him more than he was giving her. She was giving him the missing half of his life.

* * * *

Here's a curiosity: I'm sure the basic notion for this story was in my Idea File for years or decades; I remembered it and sought to look it up for the details. I couldn't find it. So I wrote it from memory, and it amplified nicely. The essence is of course the "seconds" couple, the leftovers, there to provide cover for the primaries, two unimportant people thrown together by coincidence, and then discovering their own romance. As I tackled it, it developed its own ways. For example, it wasn't intended as an interracial story; there were already others in this collection. But when I pondered why a couple should go to such lengths to conceal their love, the choices were limited. Different religions no longer have such force, at least in America, and neither do differing classes. Color was the easiest. We try to deny it, but there is a deep continuing current of racism in our society. So the problems of race are recognized here, and of class/money, but the point is the seconds. Who are, as they realize, no longer seconds.

While writing this story, I looked up a comment on novelist Mark Twain for another purpose, and on the way there saw one on Sidney Lanier, another American figure. It reminded me what a great poet he was. I had serious reference to him in my 1969 novel Macroscope; that seemed long enough ago so that I didn't have to worry about repetition. So I let my admiration show again.

Empathy

She called on his home Sunday morning, knowing he wouldn't be in church. He answered the door in his pajamas, unshaven. He paused when he saw her, as she was a stunning beauty, by no coincidence.

"Jim Bessimer?" she inquired dulcetly, knowing he was. "I am Hellene."

"Oh, shit! Not another Hell recruiter!"

She smiled fetchingly. She could be extremely persuasive when she tried, without even saying a word. She was trying now. "The same. May I come in?"

He was already fighting a rear-guard action. "Look, I told the other girl I'm not looking for that kind of action. I'm a respectable man."

"Gainfully employed as a postal clerk," she agreed, opening her blouse to show some breast. "I merely want to talk with you."

Still he resisted. "No! I'm not going to Hell!"

She opened her blouse the rest of the way, exposing both breasts. They were the best that Hell could craft, guaranteed to compel the ardent gaze of any normal mortal man. "Here is my offer: I will accommodate your interest in any manner you choose, as long as you hold a fair dialogue with me. I will depart once we come to a determination, one way or the other."

He gazed at her excellent rondure. "What if it takes a week?"

Hellene smiled again. "I was thinking of today, but I will stay longer if the dialogue remains productive. Normally it can be concluded within two hours."

Jim was obviously of two minds, but her appearance nudged him forcefully toward acceptance. "You'll do sex?"

"If you choose."

"Why wouldn't I choose?"

"Because you may not want to be unduly influenced, in a decision that could affect your eternal afterlife. I understand that men's emotions tend to follow their sexual indulgence, sometimes clouding their perspective."

"Damn!"

"Precisely." She knew she had him. She had never been a man, but her extraordinary empathy enabled her to appreciate his burgeoning desire for her perfect body. His judgment was already being distorted in exactly the way she described. Women desired many sensible things, generally in moderation; seventy per cent of a man's desire related to the body of a woman, and not in moderation. Seeing his readiness, she almost wanted to have sex with herself. Certainly she would soon be obliging his body as she carefully roped and bound his soul.

He had to laugh. "Okay, come on in. But I'm not committing to anything, regardless." He opened the door for her.

Hellene glided in. She took a seat on his living room couch opposite his recliner, crossing her legs. Her short skirt tightened, showing her thighs. "If I may inquire, where did the prior recruiter go wrong?"

"I told you, I'm not into Hell."

She lifted an eyebrow.

"You're pretty damn savvy," he said. "But I guess you mean, why did I kick her out instead of stringing her along for some free sex."

"We do like to identify our errors," she said. "We do not like losing prospects. Lucifa, the Mistress of Hell, does not look kindly on that sort of thing." What she did not clarify was that Hellene herself was an approximation of the physical image of Lucifa. It was one of the perks of her position, once she had earned the name.

"She was a blonde. I'm not into blondes."

"No even for free sex?"

"My mother's blonde. My three sisters are blondes. We don't get along."

"Ah. It feels incestuous."

"Not even that. I just don't like blondes."

So it seemed the failure had been sheer chance. The other recruiter had not done her homework, confident that her bombshell appearance sufficed. Hellene, of course, had done hers, and knew about his preference. But she had felt it better to evoke it from him directly. It was nevertheless a pretext, a reason he gave himself for something he could not explain. The right blonde could have overridden his reticence. The recruiter had surely misplayed it in some manner, turning him off. Hellene would not misplay. "So you prefer blackheads."

He paused, then laughed. Her hair was midnight black. "Yeah."

Hellene adjusted her pose, setting her right ankle across her left knee so as to provide him a view of her nether thigh all the way to her unclad groin. She did not need X-ray vision to see his developing erection; it pushed out his pajamas. Empathy: It was as if she were looking through his eyes, peering under her skirt, feeling her groin heating. "We have all kinds in Hell, of course, and they can be fiendishly obliging."

"But once you've got a man in Hell, you burn him to death. Or whatever."

"Not necessarily. It depends on the contract."

"You can cross off the hellfire?" he asked, amazed. "And torture, sleeplessness, thirst—all that bad stuff?"

"If so specified," she agreed. "That is part of what we shall be discussing: terms of engagement." That word had more than one application, being technically correct while putting in his mind the wild notion of being maritally engaged to her. Peripheral persuasion.

"But isn't Hell for eternal punishment?"

"No. Hell is for those souls that do not go to Heaven. There are assorted reasons. Some are hopelessly corrupt, of course; those are confined to the nethermost regions to stoke the fires. This is selection rather than punishment; they need to be isolated from those they might degrade. Some are, if you will pardon the expression, relatively angelic;

they could go to Heaven, but prefer Hell. Some of those are missionaries; some simply see themselves as undeserving. Most are in between, to varying degrees." She shifted her angle to give him a more direct line of sight under her lifted thigh.

Jim seemed to be having trouble focusing, mentally. So did she, to a lesser extent; her evocation of his passion was making her eager to consummate it. That was a consequence of empathy. "Some are angelic? Why the hell should they choose Hell?"

He had not picked up on her explanation. That was another signal of his distraction. So she tried again. "Well, it is more varied and interesting, for one thing. More bad girls are there, and they are, to adapt your phrasing, bored as hell. That appeals to some men."

"And they put out?"

"Eternally. Some of them like to emulate the Muslim Heaven and team up seventy-two to a man, each perpetually virginal despite frequent indulgence."

"That sure does sound like Heaven to me!"

"Something we need to clarify," she said, using her hands to lift her ankle further above her knee so that he did not have to hunch down to get the best view. He thought he was having an objective discussion, but his desire made it rhetorical. He would be getting into her pantingly soon. "Too much of anything becomes unpleasant, including sex. Those seventy-two expect to be serviced every twenty-four hours."

"All of them?" he asked, amazed.

"All. Inaction is dull."

"But that's, that's six per hour. Ten minutes each. When does he sleep?"

"There is no sleep in Hell. The action is continuous."

"But no man could possibly do that! After the first couple, maybe three, he'd have to rest for a while."

"There is no rest in Hell."

"But then how—?"

"After the first two or three, as you say, his potency wanes. But they have ways to force ejaculation regardless. After a few repetitions it turns blood red, but he does perform. Failure to do so summons demons with hot pokers they are eager to apply to his nether sphincter."

Jim whistled. "I think I begin to see. It *is* Hell."

"And if he did not specify that the virgins be young and shapely, they may be gross and hideous. Some have hymens that can be breached only by heroic effort and pain. It doesn't matter; he will perform if he values the integrity of his own anatomy."

"Muslim Hell!"

She smiled a trifle grimly. "The advertising literature does not go into such details. But if such is your desire, you may specify in your contract their age and shape, and extend the time for each. Perhaps a leisurely one per hour. They will not be pleased, but contract terms are rigorously honored."

He hauled his eyes from her groin to her face for a moment. "If you don't leave loopholes. And I'll bet they are legion. It would take a legal genius to eliminate them all. So he'll be screwed regardless."

"So to speak," she agreed equably. She forced herself to be patient; premature sex would be a waste. "But there are standard boilerplates that cover the exigencies. Hell does not need to cheat or deceive or renege."

"But isn't Hell the place of lies?"

"A canard propagated by Heaven. Hell has never violated any promise made. In contrast, Heaven often does."

"Now hang on a minute there! That's got to be the biggest lie of all!"

"Heaven is the liar," she insisted, jogging a bit on her bottom, feeling the echoing pulses in his rigid penis. Then her patience snapped; she couldn't wait longer. "But if I may pause for a moment, I believe you are in danger of soiling your pajamas. Are you sure you wouldn't like to proceed to sexual activity now? It may clear your mind."

"But you're using it to trap me! To get me so hot I'll sign anything."

"By no means. I am offering to take off your edge so that you can think clearly before signing anything, if you choose to sign."

His mouth worked. "I can have it without signing?"

"As I said at the outset, my purpose is to keep you in dialogue until you are clear about the full nature of our offer. The best way to demonstrate my good faith at this point is to abate the sexual interest I have evoked in you." And in herself. Her vagina was burning.

"Okay," he said.

She went to him immediately, squatting on his

chair with her knees spread wide to either side of him, her skirt up around her waist. She expertly worked his pajamas with a tug at the cloth to loose his straining member, then lowered her open split to take it in to a partial depth. It slid along like a greased piston, opening the snug channel as it proceeded. Then she paused.

"What?" he asked, confused.

"I have frozen physical time in the key region," she said. "I want you to see that this penetration is entirely at my discretion. Look down."

He looked. "I'm halfway into you—and I can't move it."

"Were I inclined, I could tease you, preventing you from completing the act until I obtained what I wanted from you. But I am not doing so. I have no need of coercion. Do you understand?"

"I—I guess so." He strained to achieve greater depth, but could not. None of the rest of his body was touching her; she was acrobatically poised over him.

"Now I will give it to you." Animation resumed, her bottom descended to his groin, and his penis disappeared all the way into her. O, joyful distention! She milked it internally, and it jetted powerfully within her core. Each hot spurt was like balm, easing the agony of her thirsty channel without giving her an equivalent orgasm. Empathy: the satisfaction of his lust was the fulfillment of hers.

When it was done, she lifted herself off and stepped quickly back to land on the floor, her skirt dropping back into place, her breasts remaining exposed in the open blouse. Her vagina was the only part of her that had touched him. She had a goodly deposit of ejaculate she was busy absorbing, cleaning out her love channel and digesting the protein. She would be ready for another shipment well before he was ready to deliver it. A busy recruiter could go a long time without eating, sustained by the protein donated by her clients.

"God," he gasped.

"This particular contact was not an act of God," she said. "Note that only the essentials touched. Imagine how it could be if you had access to more of me."

"Yeah." He was plainly awed.

It was going well. This client should be good for several milkings.

"And you will have that access, in the course of our dialogue, unless you prefer to break it off now and send me away." As if he had any choice.

Jim stared at her, not speaking.

"In that case, we shall resume our discussion. We were addressing loopholes and lies. Hell delivers exactly what it agrees to, much as I am doing now. But because it is not a temporary liaison, more care must be taken. Would you like to review some sample contracts?"

"No! I'm not going to Hell!"

"Naturally not," she agreed. "But you are reviewing what we offer, so as to decide whether this is a deal worth making. If you conclude it is not worthwhile, I will depart without further ado. Have you come to such a conclusion?"

His mouth worked. "No. Not yet. I want to see your offer. But losing my soul to Hell—I don't like that."

"Here is the thing about that," she said, sitting and re-crossing her legs. His sexual interest was already returning, albeit muted; young men were marvelously resilient. Men might have aspirations of continuous sex, but they were after all subject to natural limits. Continuous stimulation, however, was another matter. "The contract does not actually commit you to Hell."

"It doesn't? Then what's the point?"

"The contract merely sets the terms of the deal: what we provide, what the limits are once your soul reports to Hell. Your actual residence there is determined by a more basic thing: whether you deserve it."

"And who decides whether I deserve it?"

"You do."

For an instant his gaze left her groin and touched her face. "You're joking."

"By no means. There is a color gradient from white, which is positive, to black, which is negative. This has nothing to do with skin pigment; it is all in the soul. Pure white is bound for Heaven; pure black is doomed to Hell. Most folk are in between, neither perfect nor perfectly imperfect. As they progress through life, the balance shifts, according to their good and bad deeds. If there is more white than black at the time of death, it is Heaven; if more black than white, Hell. You can look at your color chart at any time by visiting the www.purgatory.org web site and clicking on your name. So it is in your interest to do more good deeds than bad, to check your tally at reasonable intervals, and to be sure it is positive as you near the end of your life. The worst contract in the world has no power if your final statement is positive. Since living folk have certain powers over their destinies, they really make their choices themselves, as will you. You will go to Hell only if life corrupts you sufficiently." She adjusted her legs again, to be sure she had him properly hooked. He was hers for the taking; she knew he would sign. She just had to be sure not to let him slip the hook.

"Then why bother with a contract at all? You know anyone you sign will skip out after taking the enlistment bonus."

"Not necessarily. Oh, I agree that virtually all men intend to void the contract by shifting their balances to the positive, after reveling in sin early in life. But few actually do."

"I don't see that."

She spread her legs while leaning forward earnestly, so that both bare breasts and open thighs came into play. She could almost see them reflected in his pupils. "Few do see it. They all convince themselves that they will be the exceptions, avoiding terminal corruption. Generally speaking, they don't. You see, corruption is insidious, and they are not on a river in Africa."

He blinked. "Not where?"

"Denial. It is not a river in Africa," she said, smiling.

"De Nile," he said, getting it. "But you're not denying me anything."

Oops, he had missed the larger point. Hellene got up and climbed onto his lap, taking in his thickening penis again. It wasn't ready to spout yet, but this would encourage it. "I am not denying you anything," she agreed. "In fact I am proffering you a marvelous bargain, can you just firmly grasp it." She took his hands and set them on her breasts, as something to grasp. She felt his penis surge within her. Neither science nor philosophy had ever quite decided whether breasts or buttocks had the greater evocative appeal for men. It seemed to depend on the quality of each, and on the individual man. Feeling his hands on her and his member in her, she was still unable to tell. But the combination had special force.

"So what's being denied?" he asked, perplexed alongside of his quickening sexual interest.

"Your propensity for corruption. It is not a sudden process; it is gradual. You are hardly aware of it, unless you keep a constant check on your balance of good and evil. You will tell yourself that what you are doing is all right, perhaps even necessary. You will refuse to believe that you are being corrupted. And in the end you will go to Hell."

"Never!"

"Precisely. You're the exception." She shrugged, causing her breasts to move within his grasp, which in turn made his penis expand another notch within her groin. Like a magma chamber filling beneath a volcano, it was getting ready to erupt, and great would be the force thereof. She reveled in that force. "So you can safely sign our contract, certain it will never be implemented."

"But why should I sign your contract at all? You're giving me this great sex free."

"I am only for an hour or a day," Hellene explained patiently. "Hell is forever. So is Heaven, if we lose you. We are playing the long game, seeking to channel you our way. You will sign because of what we offer."

"But you just said this great sex is only for today."

"Jim," she said persuasively, "I am not the only evocative woman in the world. We are prepared to offer you a woman a day for life, if that's what it takes. So for you sex can be perpetual. This is merely a sample."

That fazed him. "But what women could match your appeal?"

Technically, none. But there was an angle. "Any woman could. We can, if you wish, duplicate this body and have it animated by a woman of Hell who will be your absolute love slave, doing anything you crave, whenever you want it."

"Anything?" he asked, intrigued.

"Anything sexual. Any digit, any orifice, any process. She will be expert. You will have no complaint."

"But why should any woman put up with that? I've got some pretty weird ideas."

She knew; it was part of the research. Penis thrust down throat, penis thrust into anus as far as it would go. What he thought was weird was standard male fantasy. She would gladly indulge it if the occasion warranted. Any orifice sufficed to take in the jets of healing liquid balm of passionate commitment. "Jim, she's in *Hell*. This would provide her the chance to interact with a live man, and to live in a manner on Earth again. It's far better than what she otherwise faces."

"So you do torture souls in Hell."

"Some," she agreed. "It depends on how much they need it. Only considerable emotional and physical pain can clarify some souls."

"Suppose I want more?"

"Sex, power, recognition—all can be yours, to the degree you desire."

"Why would you offer all this to an ordinary postal clerk? It doesn't make sense."

She paused, drawing on his penis with her trained vagina. The effort was effective; she evoked the eruption, and it spewed violently into her. This time she did not withdraw as it ebbed; she closed her organ around his member, clasping it securely, massaging it, savoring it, commencing the next evocation. She did not have to pretend to like amorous interaction; she truly enjoyed it, because it equated with success. Jim did not, of course, protest. He had never before had sex like this.

Now she spoke again. "Perhaps I can clarify it best with a historical example. In the early 1900s in war-torn Europe there was an aspiring architect. He wasn't getting anywhere, but Lucifa recognized his potential for mischief, and signed him up. Like you, he had high aspirations and was sure he would not be corrupted. We gave him the gift of oratory. The first time he addressed one of the socialist groups he frequented it turned out that he had phenomenal evocative power to persuade others to join his cause. He became a political leader. He tried to stage a coup, and got arrested and punished, but he persisted, and in time he was able to take over the government of Germany. Then his power corrupted him, and he led his nation into a war that engulfed much of the world and generated conditions that sent millions of people to Hell, and finally himself, when he suicided. His name was Adolf Hitler."

"Never heard of him."

Hellene suppressed her irritation. What passed for education these days? "The point is, Hell seeded him, and reaped an enormous payoff. Now we are seeding you."

He laughed, his limp but not entirely diminished member jerking inside her. He was thinking of seed in another sense. "I'm going to bring on a world war that kills millions?"

"We don't know exactly how it will play out, just that you are a key potential player. We want you on our side. These things don't always work out, but at least it is possible with you. We will see that you have the resources to accomplish it if you are going to. So now let's negotiate; what do you want?"

He sighed. "I'd rather complete the third fuck before telling you. You're so good at it."

"You fear I will abruptly depart?"

"Yes."

"Then let's accomplish it."

"It will take some time. You're brought me off twice already."

"We shall see." She opened his shirt and leaned into him, setting her bare breasts against his chest. She sought his mouth with hers, kissing him first lightly, then solidly, then with tongue. She augmented this by measured breathing that caused her breasts to stroke across his flesh, and peristaltic massaging of his embedded member. "You underestimate your masculinity," she murmured between kisses.

Actually he had underestimated her proficiency. Stoked by the fourfold stimulation of lips, breasts, vagina, and flattery, buttressed by her own evident desire, he rebounded rapidly, and before long was geysering into her again. The orgasm was not as intense as before, but lasted longer and was deeply satisfying. She could tell by the way his body reacted. Fulfillment, again, also for her.

The challenge completed, she drew off him and reassembled herself. "Now tell me."

He had no choice but to oblige. "I want to do good in the world. I see news about how many are hungry, even starving, especially in third world countries, and I want to feed them. I know how to do it, too: cultivate new kinds of fungus that can grow on any garbage, literally, so it's cheap and available, and produce nutritious substance that can be shaped and flavored into anything. So there wouldn't be any more hunger in the world."

Hellene nodded. "This is a worthy ambition. We can facilitate it. But there may be complications."

"I'd still lose my soul?"

"Not directly, if you follow through honestly. But consider this: you would rapidly become a formidable political force, because those who support you would be fed, while those who do not will continue starving. Are you ready to wield political power?"

That set him back. "No. I don't know anything about politics. I guess I'd have to hire someone to handle that."

"The man you hire will be corruptible."

"Well, I'd hire an honest one."

"I could corrupt him, for the benefit of Hell."

He considered that. He had developed a healthy appreciation of her potential. "Maybe some other way."

"Such as enlisting the aid of the World Bank, which is in business to assist third world countries in need?"

"Yeah, I guess."

"It is already thoroughly corrupt."

"Oh."

"Still, you could hire a financial and political adviser to steer you past such potential shoals. I am merely showing you that it is not as simple as developing and growing your fungus, though we can provide you with the essential strain."

"You can?"

"There is fungus all over Hell, and it mutates like crazy. The barest touch of magic could produce the strain you want."

"I'd sign the contract for that!"

"Surely you would, and that may be what happens. But there are other challenges. Suppose the fungus mutates, as it may when produced in the quantities you will require? It might graduate from eating garbage to eating live flesh, and take over the world after consuming the last human being."

Jim froze. "If Hell can make the right strain, it can turn it into the wrong strain. And so I would destroy the world."

"Not necessarily. An amendment to the contract would cover it, requiring Hell to keep the strain pure, on pain of nullifying the deal."

"Which side are you on, anyway?"

"The side of Hell. I am merely showing you that you will want to consider the contract carefully. Saving the world from itself is no careless matter."

"I don't think I can afford to make the deal. Too many ways I can be mousetrapped."

Hellene adjusted her posture to reinstate the lure of partially-viewed flesh. Jim did not notice consciously, but it kept him in the dialogue. "You merely need to make sure it is a fair contract. We will help you there."

"But why bother, when you can torpedo the world by playing on my ignorance?"

"Because it is your soul we are after. We would not get it if you made an honest mistake. Neither would we obtain the souls of all those killed by that mistake. They would be perishing as innocents. So it behooves us to ensure that the contract is fair. That way you will corrupt yourself in your own time and fashion, and we will reap the harvest."

"This is weird! You're trying to make it easy for me to do it right, so I can escape Hell after getting the benefit from it."

"Exactly." Hellene measured out another peek of thigh.

"Why?"

"So that there will be no question of malfeasance on our part when you become corrupted and your soul comes to Hell. The minions of Heaven are adept at saving souls on technicalities. Frankly, we have had a bellyful of that, and want no more of it. You must corrupt yourself. Then there is nothing Heaven can do."

Jim shook his head. "You're some woman."

She showed more thigh. "Thank you. I try to be."

"I mean intellectually." But his eyes were on that thigh. Now that he knew exactly what pleasure it could deliver.

"Of course."

"So why are you so sure you'll get my soul?"

"If you make the deal, and Hell gives you the power you seek, it is highly unlikely you will not corrupt yourself. So it's a relatively safe bet."

"I don't see it. I'm not going to corrupt myself."

"Let me take you on another verbal experiment. Let's assume that you are successful in building an organization that not only feeds the world, but suffers no erosion of integrity. That you accomplish your mission."

"Yes!"

"With no hunger or starvation, the population of the world mushrooms, no pun intended. All the resources of the planet are used up, but there are still more people. All the other creatures are exterminated, squeezed out by the burgeoning mass of humanity. Now at last even the garbage runs out, and people begin to hunt, kill, and eat people. All because of your initially successful effort to abolish hunger. It is ironic, isn't it?"

That set him back. "I guess I didn't think that far ahead. There would have to be population control. Maybe a contraceptive can be built into the fungus, so nobody reproduces without getting the antibody."

"And here I am, a woman desperate to conceive and bear my own child," she said. "I know you have the antidote. Give it to me."

"No," he said uneasily.

She approached him. "I did not hear you. I will do anything to get that medicine." She lifted her skirt.

He had done it three times in fairly rapid succession, but now his member hungered for a fourth. She knew it, being well familiar with the imperatives of members. "Someone else will have to dispense it, not me. I could set that up."

"I will seduce him for it. He's a man, isn't he?"

"Then a woman!"

Hellene smiled. "Hell has skilled men, too. They can wrap women around their fingers, or whatever other digits they choose. Few mortals are truly incorruptible."

"I'll find those few."

"That quest will divert you from your primary mission of feeding the hungry."

"But what else is there?"

"There are ways. For example, the contraception might be partial, with no antidote. There would be a reduced number of conceptions, causing the population to decline and eventually stabilize at a sustainable level."

"Yes!"

"But there will be a formidable shortage of babies. Those who bear them may have them stolen, or may even be killed for them. The babies themselves may be killed by those who, being denied, refuse to let anyone else have them. There will be no safety for children. All your fault."

"God, I don't know what to do!"

"God won't help you in this. You will be

inevitably corrupted by the power you will have to wield, and we will garner your soul."

"So I shouldn't even try?"

"You should try. You just need to consider the matter more carefully."

"I think maybe I should back off the whole idea."

"Don't do that. That would cause me to forfeit your contract." She smiled. "Hell has no fury like that of a woman scorned." She approached him, opening her blouse.

He was defeated. He had to have her again. "What do you advise?"

"There are safeguards. It is not as if this question has not been asked before. We'll come up with a contract everyone is satisfied with, never fear." She kissed him, savoring the victory she had won.

For a strain of fungus that grew so plentifully in Hell that one of the torments for damned souls was the assignment of periodically cleaning it out, she had garnered a client.

Jim Bessimer might or might not save the world, but his soul would surely be coming to Hell. Because he would have remarkable power, and his chances of escaping its corrupting influence were remote.

* * * *

When Hellene returned to Hell's Annex for her next assignment, there was a surprise. The familiar Recruiter station remained unchanged, with its plaque: THE WAY TO A MAN'S SOUL IS THROUGH HIS PENIS. Yes indeed: she had just demonstrated that yet again. On the side for the male recruiters was a similar plaque: THE WAY TO A WOMAN'S SOUL IS THROUGH HER MOUTH.

That meant more than one thing: women liked to eat, especially sweets. They also liked romance, so a fervid, feeling kiss by a handsome man could work wonders. Naturally the male recruiters were highly romantic. They faked it, of course, just as the women faked sexual interest, but were just about as effective.

Actually Hellene herself didn't have to fake the interest; she had it, because of her empathy. Her desire was akin to that of the average man, and she indulged it freely when recruiting. It was one of the things that made her the best operative Hell had. She suspected that the top male recruiters didn't have to fake romantic inclination either.

The surprise was her next client: Heaver. "I know of him!" she exclaimed. "He's the enemy!"

She went to the assignment office to protest. The demon supervisor received her gruffly. "Got a case you can't handle, strumpet?" His little horns steamed.

"This is an agent of Heaven," she said. "I recognize the name. In fact, he's their top operative, to carry the name, just as I'm Hell's top. He's absconded with some of our best prospects. How the Hell did he get on my date list?"

He gazed at her soberly. His eyes were fire-red. "So you know. Deal with it."

"What is the matter with you?" she demanded. "We don't date the enemy!"

"We do on this occasion. He asked for you."

"*Asked* for me!"

A parchment appeared in his hands. "According to the Cosmic Protocol, such contacts must be accepted at least once a year. We could seek one of theirs if we chose."

"Why would we ever choose? They're intolerably self-righteous holier-than-thou bigots who think sex is a dirty word."

He smiled grimly. "Maybe you can make him see the dark." His gaze flicked to her skirt.

"This is a blessed waste of my time and expertise."

"Twenty-four hours," he said. "Then you're free for at least a year. We're done here." The parchment burst into flames as he faded out.

She realized that she was stuck with it. But she was curious; what in Hell could Heaven want with her? She had deprived Heaven of more prospects than any other recruiter. She should be anathema.

Then a small thought insinuated itself. Heaver surely knew of her, just as she knew of him, mainly by reputation but possibly also by sight. After all, she emulated Hell's most beautiful woman, Lucifa. Could he have developed a personal interest in her? By most accounts sex was discouraged, if not actually forbidden, in Heaven. Could he have developed a hankering for what he was missing?

Hellene licked her lush lips. What a challenge, to use her alluring sexuality to draw in and convert the leading agent of Heaven! Success would make her forever infamous.

She smiled. Suddenly this outrageous assignment had become a phenomenal challenge.

She reported to the specified address exactly on time. It was an undistinguished home in mortal suburbia, designed to be that way so that the locals would not catch on. A nexus where the agents of

Heaven and Hell could meet privately when they chose. As was the case now.

She dismissed the taxi and walked to the front door. She didn't need local transport, of course, but was being especially cautious. So far it was like any other recruiting appointment. But this one was likely to be the challenge of her life. Heaver was no gullible pushover. He was an experienced agent like herself. And just as talented. Also, he had actually sought this encounter. That spoke obscure volumes. He knew what he was up against.

She knocked on the door. It opened immediately; naturally he had been expecting her. "Heaver, I presume?" she inquired with a crafted smile.

His smile seemed sincere. He was a handsome man, as light of hair and feature as she was dark. "The same. Heaver of Heaven. And you are Hellene of Hell. You look charming, and I am charmed."

Damn, he was good! She really did feel charmed. She would have to study his technique. Meanwhile she drew on her own, fashioning a sincere smile. Her appreciation was for his technique rather than his mission, but that would do. "Thank you."

"I have prepared a snack," he said. "Please come this way."

"As you wish." She took the seat he indicated, and crossed her legs for good effect. If it was temptation he wanted, she would provide it. But she was well aware that he could have obtained that almost anywhere else, yet he had asked for her. That suggested a larger ambition on his part. "I am yours for a day and a night." For of course she would give him sex; it was her mode of persuasion.

"Perhaps." He poured a glass of champagne, her favorite brand, and proffered it. He had evidently done his homework.

"You did me the honor of requesting my company," she reminded him as he poured his own champagne. "You are surely aware of my parameters of expertise."

"I am. That is why I requested you."

Hellene made a moue. "There are ways and ways we can do this. We can take our time, verbally fencing. Or we can get promptly to the point. The choice is yours."

"We shall do both, of course," he replied easily. "The point is simple: I mean to recruit you to the side of Heaven."

"The side of Heaven!" she exclaimed, feigning more amazement than she felt. So he had a big ambition too. "I am a creature of Hell. You are wasting your effort."

"Perhaps," he repeated. "You are Hell's most effective recruiter. You have brought in so many men who would otherwise have been ours that it threatens the balance of the spheres. We have to nullify you. And I personally would like to win you, as you are matchless."

"Oh, pshaw! There are hundreds of women with classier figures than mine, and thousands with greater intelligence. You could win a harem of them with far less effort." For Lucifa had not seen fit to allow her minion to be quite as lovely as the original. Hellene well appreciated the expediency of that.

"Dozens, and hundreds," he said, smiling. "But

only five who exceed you in both aspects. None of them work for Hell. They are therefore irrelevant to my purpose."

"You *have* done your homework," she said, for his figures were on the mark. She knew exactly where she stood among mortal women; it was part of her own homework. She intended never to be surprised by superior talent.

"Now that we have established the mission," he said with a winning grin, "shall we proceed to the combat?"

"You aren't much for euphemism," she said.

"It is a matter of integrity. I would not care to recruit you on any false premise."

"You aren't going to recruit me at all! But if you persist, I may recruit *you*."

"You must be the fabled snowball in Hell."

She smiled, turning on the allure. "I'm not that cold. Just realistic. If we must truly tangle, we need to understand the rules of the game."

"As you wish. I will attempt to romance you into love with me, while you attempt to seduce me into cooperation with you."

"You are at a disadvantage. Men are more readily subject to sex appeal than women are to romance. A man can be turned on by any display of shapely flesh, while women are more discriminating." She displayed her legs up to an interesting region. "Are you sure I can't tempt you? I understand that Heaven is a bit uptight about sex for its own sake. A healthy man like you must be starved for it."

"Heaven prefers to save it for a committed

relationship, rather than wasting it on superficial contacts."

But she knew she had quickened his interest. "Well, we have committed for a day and a night. We are not going to convert each other, so why not at least enjoy it? I can give you an experience you are unlikely to find in Heaven."

"And you will try to use it to corrupt me. In fairness, I have to say that will be ineffective."

"You don't desire me?"

As Heaven's representative, he couldn't lie. "I do desire you, for your ability as much as your form. But your wiles will not convert me, so it would be wrong to give you false hope."

"My hope is as realistic as yours."

"Perhaps. But I think I have superior motive."

"Come on, Heave! You get the same perks and benefits I do. We both want to retire with our nice bodies and enough wealth to give us freedom for the rest of our mortal lives. I doubt you want that more than I do."

"Heaven will grant you those things, Hel, if you join."

"And Hell will grant you the same. Neither of us will benefit or lose significantly by changing sides, and both of us have the discipline not to do anything foolish. So this whole business strikes me as an exercise in futility."

He nodded. "True. I see I must reveal another level."

She gazed at him with mock shock. "You mean you have not told me the whole truth? For shame!"

He did not laugh or smile. "I did not feel it was

sufficiently relevant to our dialogue. But now I see that it is. I apologize for holding back."

He was genuinely apologetic; she could tell. That foolishly touched her. "Heave, I was only teasing. You don't need to tell me anything that makes you uncomfortable."

"But I do," he said grimly. "It is this: the reason you must be stopped is that your efforts threaten to put Hell far enough ahead in acquired souls to give it a clear majority. That must not be."

"Why must it not be? Do you begrudge the victory to the side that plays the best game? It isn't as though it will make any immediate difference to the mortal realm, and the balance may shift the other way in time. It's an ongoing game."

"No. It is not."

She looked at him, for the moment forgetting her spot exposures. "And your reasoning is?"

"If either side achieves a clear majority, guaranteeing it the victory, it will terminate the game at that point. The competing sides do have that power. The mortal realm will cease to exist."

That froze her. "You are serious?"

"Quite. That is why you must be stopped."

"But by that reasoning, Heaven must not be allowed to get ahead either. That would also doom the mortals."

"Yes."

"Then this exercise is really pointless! Neither of us can afford to convert the other."

"Not so. Hell is threatening now, while Heaven threatens at some nebulous point in the future. The game could proceed for millennia more."

"And with both of us working on the same side, the balance could shift rapidly, putting Heaven ahead much sooner. What would you do then?"

He hesitated. "I don't think I can answer, lest I compromise my position."

"Face it, Heave: if either side wins, and abolishes the mortal realm, neither one of us will have a job any more. Do you want that?"

"No."

"What, you can achieve your reward of everlasting bliss in Heaven, and you don't want it?"

"You are making this difficult, Hel."

"I mean to. The reasoning of Hell is insidiously persuasive. I think you should answer."

He made an effort. "It is not the kind of bliss I crave."

She flashed a bit more flesh. "Because there is no decent sex in Heaven?"

He smiled. "That, too, you winsome creature."

"There is something else?"

"It is that the mortals do not deserve such a fate. They are struggling to eke out their lives for good or ill, and to abruptly throw them away in mid-cycle seems unfair. I do not care to achieve my bliss at the expense of theirs."

"Yet this is the nature of the game, isn't it?"

He shrugged. "It is not a thing I would expect a creature of Hell to appreciate as I do."

"I am in this game to win. Naturally there are losers."

"Naturally," he agreed sadly.

She felt a tug of sympathy. She fought it. Was he expertly playing her? "So we are in a personal contest, which you have to win. I can win in effect by refusing to play. I may be locked in for twenty-four hours, but I don't have to play."

"True."

"I remain ready to give you some fun in that time."

"I believe it, and I am tempted by it. But I fear that this, too, is not the kind of fun I crave."

This was interesting. "Then let's find an alternate means of engagement."

He eyed her warily. "What do you have in mind?"

"Challenges. We challenge each other to do difficult things, and see who best succeeds. It won't decide the issue of Heaven or Hell, but it will pass the time and might lead to some insights."

He considered. "I am not sure where this will lead, but if it keeps us in dialogue, I am amenable."

Keeping them in dialogue. Of course that was part of his aim, as a recruiter. Well, she could make it a truly challenging dialogue.

"Okay. I suggested the game, so you can have the first turn. Challenge me to do something against my nature."

"Why? I mean, why not something that is merely rigorous, like climbing a branchless tree?"

"Because that's not an emotional challenge. It is in the difficult emotional decisions that character is best revealed."

"Such as whether to pursue a course that means the end of mortality?"

She laughed. "Save that for later. Something more personal."

Heaver spread his hands. "I think I don't properly understand. Perhaps you should take the first turn."

Hellene shrugged. "As you wish. Rape me."

"I beg your pardon?"

"You heard me, son of Heaven. Unlimber that stiff cock and jam it in my cunt until it pukes golden gobs."

He paused momentarily. "Must we employ such terminology?"

"Correction: impose your knowledge of my privacy without my consent."

"This is not a thing I would ever do."

"That's the point, Heave. The challenge is to do what is against your nature."

"That's not a challenge. That's an impossibility."

She oriented on him purposefully. "I will talk you through it. We are playing a game, not indulging in reality. It can't be actual rape when I tell you to do it. No man can rape me without my consent."

"Isn't that an oxymoron? If you consent, it's not rape."

"It is a simulation," she agreed. "You try to hold me down and have sex with me while I try to prevent you. We both know that we have both had sex many times before with others and are willing to do it with each other; there's nothing virginal here. It's a challenge to see whose will will prevail. That will reveal character."

"This is not the sort of game I care to play."

"Which is the point. It's the easy game that is pointless."

"You may call it a game, but it seems too much

like actual abuse."

"When you play checkers you kill them by jumping over them. When you play chess you kill chessmen by taking their places. These are war games with their own special rules of combat. You do what it takes to win or lose. That does not make you a killer or a warrior, merely a player."

"Still, those are merely pieces," he said. "Symbolism is not reality."

"Physical sex is reality."

"That is my problem. Forced sex."

"Game sex is not rape."

He paused again. "Point taken."

"But it is a challenge, for you. Can you rise to it, pun intended?"

"I doubt it. I could not indulge in something separated from an ugly reality by mere words."

"You're an athlete, right? You play manly games. Climb mountains, race races by foot, bike, car? Box, wrestle, martial arts, weapons? Swordplay, shooting? Violence?"

"It's not the same."

"When you wrestle you try to hold a man down until he surrenders. Imposing your will on him. That's physical."

Heaver shook his head. "It's not the same."

"You are rationalizing. A game is a game."

"As extraordinary one."

"Precisely. An easy game— "

"Does not reveal character, as you pointed out," he concluded. Then he made a decision; she felt it. "You realize that if you require this of me, I may then require something similarly difficult of you?"

"Oh, yes."

"That may similarly expose your underlying character."

He was getting it. "Yes."

"Then let's establish the rules of engagement, as you put it. I presume that what you mean when you say rape by consent is that you will not use vicious measures to defend yourself. No knife or gun."

"Or brass knuckles. No nails, bites, butts, gouges, knees. You in turn do not use drugs, pain holds, violence, threats, fraud."

"Threats, fraud?"

"The threat to kill my family and friends if I do not submit. Or pretending you are a doctor doing an examination."

"Oh, of course."

"And I will not gouge out your eyeballs or bite your tongue off if you try to kiss me. Just wrestling, with a different kind of pin. It ends when you ejaculate into me, or admit you are unable to. Your victory or mine."

"I begin to see the appeal. One further proviso: if at any point you wish to end the contest, you may say so and it will end without conclusion."

"Ditto for you."

"Perhaps we should leave our clothing behind, as it is bound to be damaged in such a struggle."

"Naked, both of us," she agreed. "On a suitable surface, so as not to damage the furniture."

"Mattress on floor?"

"Bed will do. Shall we say that if I succeed in getting off the bed, the hold is broken? So you can't flatten me against a wall."

"Of course. Maintain contact with the bed."

"Shall I do a strip tease, or merely doff my outfit?"

"We have time. Let's attend to any sanitary facilities we require, then you may do the tease."

"Do I get to strip you, too?"

"If you wish."

"But the contest does not start until I get on the bed."

"Agreed."

They attended to the sanitary matters, then she did a dance, languorously removing items of clothing one by one. She alternated hers with his, finally pulling down his drawers to expose his erect member. He was a beautiful specimen of manhood in every way, as of course he would be; he was her opposite number. His body would resemble that of God.

Naked, she stepped into him, drew him close, stood on tiptoes, and kissed him. His hot member was squeezed between their two bellies, by no accident. Then she stepped back, turned, and made a little leap onto the bed. "Come and get me, brute!" she cried, spreading her legs toward him. "Or do I mean get me and come?"

He followed immediately, coming at her headfirst. But she closed her legs just before he got there, and used her feet to push his chest away. He landed on the bed beside her.

He reached for her shoulders, to hold her down. She turned into him and kissed him as she skated her torso away from him, leaving them connected only at the mouth and shoulders.

He moved his torso to cover hers. She slid down and lifted her legs to circle his thighs, locking him into place over her. But his member was up against her belly, unable to reach her groin. He tried to slide down, but her leg-lock held him fast.

She kissed his chest, tantalizing him. This was fun!

He did a pushup, lifting himself off her. Then kneeling, he put his hands on her shoulders and hauled her up and toward him. He had a lot of arm power; in a moment he could have her groin up where his member could reach it.

She unlocked her legs. Her torso jumped up under the force of his lifting. Then she locked her legs around his waist. His member was safely below her, again unable to reach her groin. She kissed him.

Heaver laughed. "You are good at this."

"I have done some wrestling too, though that is not what it is normally called."

Still kneeling, with her attached, he put his hands on her thighs and pried them apart. In a moment she would have to slide down into position.

She released him and twisted her body, landing on her back on the bed with her legs now straight and locked together. He dropped on her, pinning her, but again his member was not in position. When he tried to lift and guide it with his hand, she twisted back out of position, kissing him on the way. He was unable to complete the act.

He continued to struggle, but she continued to counter him. Finally he paused. "I fear I must yield the point. I am unable to possess you."

"Don't give up yet," she urged him

mischievously. "There are several ploys you haven't yet tried."

He shook his head. "There may be, but I am ignorant of them. I must say, however, that it has been a pleasure making the effort. You are a remarkably fit woman. Thank you." This time he kissed her.

That got to her disturbingly. "You are being too damned decent, Heave. At least have the courtesy to be annoyed."

"I am most annoyed, and frustrated. But I honor the rules of the game. You have won the point."

"I have not won! You've been too blessed gentle."

"I would never seek to hurt you or any woman. It's not my nature."

"That's the damned challenge!" She was swearing too much, but couldn't stop it; he had succeeded in putting her off her pace. "To go against your nature, at least a little, for the sake of the issue."

"I am sorry."

"Damn it, pick me up like you mean it. Flip me over, flatten me prone, break me over the edge of the bed, and have at me from behind. You can do it, you know."

He was taken aback. "Oh, I would not indulge in sodomy."

She still could get surprised by details. He had never used the rear position? Heaven *was* uptight! "I didn't say sodomy, Heave. My cunt is accessible from the rear, especially when my legs bend forward."

He gazed at her, embarrassed and perplexed. "Why are you telling me this?"

"Because I don't think you're man enough to do

it anyway. I don't want to leave you any pantywaist excuses like not knowing the right technique."

"But then I might win the contest."

"Not if I'm right. You'll get to the point, then freeze. That's my victory."

He shook his head, bemused. Then he got up, lifted her into the air, turned her over, and laid her firmly on her stomach. He came down on her, preventing her from moving. His groin was now at her bottom.

She felt his hard penis nudging her wet cleft. The struggle had worked her up; she was more than ready for sex. But of course he hesitated, exactly as she had predicted. Even game-rape violated his decency.

"I dare you," she said.

He remained in his agony of indecision.

"Chicken!" she said. "Buc-buc-buc-BAWK!"

That did it. He set his member and rammed into her. He thrust and thrust again, his hot large rod distending her avenue, setting her off. She felt his urgency and reveled in it. She clenched her flesh around his, swallowing it, seeking the most sensation.

He climaxed, and that set off hers. She felt as if she were riding a joy pole, floating through deep space, drinking in his pulsing essence. Thrust after thrust, spurt after spurt, as though the universe were focused around that nova bursting in that black hole, infinite energy encompassed.

At last they both subsided. He lay against her legs, bottom, and back, his head nudging hers, breathing hard.

"Also," she murmured, "you got me so worked up I had to finish it. Well done!"

"Thank you," he said faintly. "I never did that before."

So she had gathered. He had had sex, of course, but not simulated violence. "It is just a taste of what awaits you in Hell."

He stiffened, and not sexually. "This was an inducement for conversion?"

"Well, I *am* a creature of Hell. I don't do anything without being aware of the manner it affects my mission."

He withdrew, and not just sexually. She had hurt him. That hurt her.

She turned, catching his retreating hand. "Heave, I'm sorry. I did enjoy it. I wanted you to do it. That was more personal than calculated."

"You are a creature of Hell," he repeated, sitting in a chair. "I should not have forgotten, even for a moment."

"Never forget," she agreed. "You are not dealing with an innocent girl. I am what I am. But I'm proud of you for coming through."

"Now it disgusts me. The more so because I find myself starting to like you."

Exactly. A man's emotion followed his sex. "Well, you are as *you* are. But there is nothing disgusting about honest sexual desire or expression."

"You made me simulate a rape, believing that it would incite in me a taste for more of the same."

This was not going well, so she changed her approach. "And did it?"

And he could not lie. "Yes." He would not meet

her gaze, ashamed.

Suddenly her empathy overwhelmed her. "Oh, Heave, trust me this far. I accomplished what I wanted, but I am sorry. I wanted to free you, not humiliate you."

"I am nevertheless humiliated."

She stepped into him, standing, and drew his face into her bare bosom. "I feel your humiliation. I should not have done it. I apologize."

He might have argued, but her breasts were in his face, working their special magic, seducing him in a way that went beyond sexual. He allowed her to comfort him.

"It's my empathy," she continued, stroking his hair. "I feel what you feel, to a considerable extent. It is my prime talent. It hurts me to hurt you."

"Empathy," he agreed. "It is my prime quality too. The ability to put one's own consciousness into another being, by imagination. But it failed me this time. I thought you truly desired me."

"I do, Heave, I do. But nothing is a hundred percent."

"What percent was calculation?"

Hellene considered. "For the simulation? Perhaps ten percent. The rest was unmitigated passion. You did not misread me there." She pressed his face into her warm cleavage. She was actually rather touched by his reaction; it was not typical of a man who had just achieved violent sex.

Not typical at all.

She jerked away from him. "Son of Heaven, are you playing me?"

Heaver smiled ruefully. "A little, perhaps. I, too,

am what I am."

"Trying to draw out my motherly instinct? To make me desire the generosity of Heaven?"

"Perhaps. To a degree."

"What percentage?"

"Ten."

She had to laugh. "The mirror of mine. We are indeed two of a kind." She paused to wipe herself clean, then returned to him, proffering her breasts again. "Take anything you want."

"Thank you." He stroked them with his hands and licked the nipples. His touches were evocative; he was good at this. "You are, if you will excuse the expression, divine."

"I will excuse it." She nudged her breasts more firmly into his face. She was evoking his romantic desire, but also getting herself interested in sex again, with more than a touch of her own romance. The two did tend to interact.

"Now it seems I must require a challenge of you. Something against your nature."

"Can it wait?" she asked. "Your caresses are, if you will excuse the expression, fiendishly effective."

"It can wait," he agreed. "May I proceed?"

"You may." She was breathing harder, and not entirely to stimulate him.

"There are things I wouldn't do with a woman destined for Heaven."

That was a question. "Do them with me."

He stood and guided her back to the bed. He laid her on it, on her back, and separated her legs with his hands. He licked her cleft. Her clitoris responded with a tingle of incipient pleasure. She closed her knees gently about his head. This was fantastic.

He paused. "This pleasure is guilty."

"Only in Heaven," she replied. "I am completely incorruptible—by definition. And I understand male passion. You are becoming natural."

He nodded. "Perhaps I am." But he was also becoming emotional about her. She was offering him the kind of sex Heavenly women would not.

He continued, and soon enough evoked her second climax. She groaned in urgent ecstasy as his tongue continued stroking. Her orgasm was long and intense, transporting her.

When it was done, she sat up and wordlessly pushed him onto the bed, on his back. She took his erect penis in her mouth and gently sucked on it, licking the underside. He became uneasy. "Is this natural?"

"Oh, yes, in Hell."

She slid her mouth down onto it, taking it all the way into her throat. He did not protest further as it swelled larger. She milked it, and in due course caused it to spurt ardently into her mouth and throat. She had tamed him to that extent.

"A woman of Heaven would not have done that," he said.

Duh. "There are advantages to being another kind of woman," she said. "A man of Hell would be far less intriguingly reticent."

"There are ways in which we complement each other."

"As every man and every woman complements the other," she agreed. "Only more so, with us."

"Oh, Hel, I could get to like you too well."

"And I you. But I ask you to believe me, this is not artifice on my part. I am enjoying this experience with you." And she was. Perhaps too much.

"I believe you. Empathy governs."

With each feeling so much of the other's pleasure or pain. She had not before interacted with a man who matched her in that respect. She had expected to be challenged, as by a rival weapon that matched her own. Instead she was merging with him, emotionally more than physically.

But they were not finished. "Now you need to make your challenge to me. Something against my nature."

"Do a good deed with no prospect of advantage for Hell."

Hellene spread her hands. "I have no idea how to proceed."

"As I did not with the rape simulation."

"Fair enough. So guide me. Name a deed."

"Let's see what offers." He went to turn on the TV.

He thought commercial broadcasts would inspire him? But she made no objection. She went to join him on the couch before the TV, taking his hand.

"You are friendly," he remarked.

"It's my nature." She lifted his hand to her mouth and kissed it.

"You have already seduced me," he reminded her with a smile. "Twice, if I have not lost count."

"There can never be too much seduction." She set his hand on her breast.

"As you wish." He took her hand and set it on

his limber penis. That was considerable progress, for him. He was loosening up, appreciating sex for its own sake.

Then they leaned into each other and kissed.

Hellene was sure she was making an impression on him; for one thing her fingers felt his penis reacting. But he was also affecting her. They were made for each other.

"...bearing down on the village of Avoca," the TV news was saying. "The power is out, water can't be pumped, and the wind is rising. There is little hope for the inhabitants." The picture showed a line of fire sweeping toward outlying houses, the black smoke roiling. The image was shaky, evidently being taken from a helicopter.

"People will die there," Heaver said.

"You know we can't stop the fire," she reminded him. "We are limited to one-on-one solicitation. We can promise mortals their desires, but can't do history-changing acts as such. We are not supposed to interfere with the normal course of mortal events."

"Not directly," he said. "But we do enable particular mortals to affect human history."

"A loophole," she agreed. "We exploit it freely."

"Perhaps that is why Hell has gained recently. Heaven has been less apt in this respect."

"Perhaps," she agreed. "We both know that the great majority of souls go to Heaven or Hell according to their records in mortal life. Our competition is for those few that can go either way, with the potential for significant effect in the mortal realm."

"Exactly. So we try to influence those few. Hell

corrupts them with power or material things; Heaven with visions of the larger good they can do. It is not merely their souls in question, it is the souls of so many others they may influence."

"So the news is the news," she said. "No inspiration there."

"Oh, but there is. Go there and save a child without proselytizing for Hell."

"Oof!" she said, emulating a reaction to a punch in the stomach. "Can't I interest you in some really wicked sex instead?"

"You can, but not instead. Are you forfeiting the challenge?"

"By no means. I will go there now."

"I will go with you."

"You don't trust me?"

"I trust you to follow your nature. But I like your company."

"Then let's go together. But perhaps we should dress first."

He laughed. "Perhaps we should."

They stood and made one more nude embrace and kiss. She guided his hands to her bottom, and pressed them into a squeeze. There was something fetchingly quaint about his slight diffidence in the face of robust desire. Then they dressed and focused on the televised fire. It was a thousand miles away, but they were able to sense it via astral projection.

"Soul travel," he said. Heaven had its own terminology.

"We send our souls out as astral projections," she agreed. "To locate a suitable spot to land. So that we don't land in the middle of a wall or tree."

"Then we exchange places with our souls," he said. "And when we are certain, we recall our souls to our bodies."

It was the way Hellene had traveled to this region, before catching a cab for the last few blocks to the house, and surely he had too. Mortal transportation was not always feasible. For one thing it required money, and they preferred not to use it themselves. For another, it was time-consuming and unreliable. So they quietly teleported, hiding it from mortals.

They embraced again, clothed, and oriented on the fire. Their images landed on a cleared slope a few hundred feet ahead of the fire line. "This seems apt," Heaver said, disengaging. "The grass is too short here to sustain the fire; it will bypass this spot."

"Apt," she agreed. It seemed to be a play area, worn down to dirt. Indeed, the fire would skip it in favor of richer harvests in forest and housing. She summoned her body. Now she was physically here. She looked around.

The fire was bearing down on a row of houses to the side. She extended her image toward them, and sensed people. They were scrambling to carry their most treasured possessions from the houses, but the wind was carrying the fire there too rapidly. It must be a fluke gust taking the fire in an unexpected direction, so that folk who had thought they were safe were suddenly in danger.

In one house there were struggling parents and two children. They were trapped inside by fire that had already invaded the interior.

"There are two," she said tersely. "I can save only

one."

"I will save the other," he agreed immediately. Of course he would; it was his nature.

She projected inside the house. There was a little boy, about six years old, standing terrified. "Come with me," she said, bringing her body there.

She stepped forward to pick him up, holding him close to her bosom. Then she transported back to the slope outside. She set him down, unharmed.

Heaver appeared, holding a little girl, surely the boy's sister, about five years old. She was crying, but safe.

"Mommy!" the boy cried.

The house collapsed in flames. It was too late for the parents.

They were left holding the children. They exchanged a glance. The parents were horribly dead. The children were orphans.

Had there been more time, they might have warned the parents, so that they could get out of the house before it collapsed. Their focus on the children had limited them. She felt guilt for that, and knew Heaver shared it. Yet had they not come, the children too would have died.

"They will be in shock," she murmured. "We must divert them, giving them time to adjust. The first hours are critical."

"They need new parents," he said. "We have not truly saved them yet."

She agreed. Her challenge was not yet done. "Guide me."

"They will need a new family. If they are turned over to the state, they will be put in an orphanage, then in foster care. This does not seem ideal."

Hellene shuddered, now feeling for the children. "I agree. That is worth avoiding. But what else is there?"

"I need time to consider prospects."

"You have some?"

"I may have, if I can sift out the right ones. Meanwhile yes, we must divert them."

"How?"

"Music."

"Soothes the savage breast," she agreed. "But I am not a musician. I can sing and dance, though."

"What kind of song and dance?"

"Bawdy songs, dirty dancing."

"That won't do."

She considered. "I agree, for this purpose. What kind of songs and dances do you know?"

"Hymns. Ballet. The minuet."

She formed a subdued laugh. "We have a problem."

"Mommy!" the little boy sobbed again.

Hellene got down on her knees and hugged him close to her. That seemed to help. He needed the comfort that only a grown woman could provide. "We'll keep you safe," she told him. She had had little experience with children, but things were coming naturally, as her empathy came into play.

"There must be some songs we both know," Heaver said as he did the same for the little girl.

They discussed it while comforting the children. Soon they discovered a compromise: one of his hymns had the same tune as one of her unhappy love songs: "Greensleeves."

They set the two children on the ground, facing away from the burning house, and prepared for the song. Heaver produced a harmonica and played the melody. He was good; the music was enchanting. She had not before realized how lovely such a simple instrument could be, when played well.

Hellene sang. She was good, too, at this particular thing, and his apt support made her better.

Alas my love you do me wrong
To cast me off discourteously
When I have loved you so long
Delighting in your company.

The children were paying attention, listening, though this surely was not their type of song. What counted was not the words but the sheer delight of the melody. They went into the refrain.

Greensleeves was my delight;
Greensleeves was all my joy
Greensleeves was my heart of gold
And who but my Lady Greensleeves?

They went through the whole sad song, and the children were rapt. Hellene suspected that it was partly because it was a beautiful song, expertly played and sung, but mostly because its expressed grief echoed theirs. There really was magic in song, quite apart from the kind that she and Heaver practiced when questing for souls. The human species had evolved—Heaver would say had been made—to appreciate the social power of it.

When they completed it, they both were surprised to discover several other people, fire-refugee families, standing by. "We heard the music," a man explained. "It was the one positive thing amidst this desolation."

"The fire surrounds us," a woman said, holding a sobbing child. "Only this field is clear. It will be hours before the road is cleared for rescue."

"The kids are freaking out," the man said. "Please, do another song. They'll listen. Just as Dick and Jane are."

The woman glanced at the collapsed burning house where the children had been, and winced. She knew what had happened. "Please," she agreed.

Hellene looked at Heaver. "Do we know another song?"

"I will consider."

"I don't recognize you two," the man said. "Visitors?"

"Friends of the family," Hellene said, and Heaver kept silent. She was able to lie, as he could not, but it was only partial, as they had just become friends in their fashion. "We'll take the children to relatives." And that was of course what they would have to do. It was turning out that saving a child was not as simple a matter as she had supposed.

More families were approaching. There did not seem to be any other deaths, but all were destitute in this moment, having lost their houses and all they contained. Some had pulled their cars up to the edge of the field, but with the roads closed by the fire, they could not escape.

"Red River Valley?" Heaver asked.

He had successfully zeroed in on their scant common base: unhappy love. "I know it," Hellene agreed.

He played his harmonica, and in a moment she sang.

From this valley they say you are going
We shall miss your bright eyes and sweet smile
For they say you are taking the sunshine
That brightens our pathway awhile.

The parents sat down around them, forming a kind of circular theater stage in the center, holding their children, listening. Many were nodding, remembering the song. The simple beauty of folk songs had been largely lost in the age of electronic entertainment, but their evocative power remained.

Heaver paused in his playing. "Why don't you join in for the refrain? Hellene can sing it the first time, then you do it for the repetitions."

Several parents nodded appreciatively. He was getting the group involved, helping them be distracted too. His empathy encompassed the whole group. Hellene felt a sudden warm surge of emotion; he was a nice man. She wasn't sure how to cope with the unfamiliar feeling, so focused instead on the song.

Come and sit by my side if you love me
Do not hasten to bid me adieu
But remember the Red River Valley
And the girl who has loved you so true.

Then they had the parents sing it, as Hellene led them and Heaver played the melody. Their rendition was uneven, but also authentic; it was truly a group effort, bringing the people together when they most needed mutual support.

Thereafter she continued with the other verses, and the families sang the refrain with increasing competence and feeling. Hellene felt it too; it was easy to imagine herself as a girl being left behind by the man who was going out into the world. He was taking part of her heart with her.

She tried to fight it, for it was dangerous ever to get emotional about a prospect, which was really what Heaver was. But she could see that this good man was getting to this bad girl, and she couldn't stop it.

They discovered other common songs, and went through them. But now the children were getting restless. Their attention spans were brief, and what interested them for a while could not do so indefinitely. They needed to do something else—something that might involve the children.

"Dancing," Hellene suggested. "Do we have any in common?"

"The waltz?" he inquired, taking her in his arms.

She liked being held by him, but this wouldn't work. "The children wouldn't be interested."

He considered. "I fear they would also not care for ballet, or the minuet."

"And the tango or dirty dancing would not be appropriate," she said with half a smile. "What do we both know that they could do?"

"If folk songs work, perhaps so would folk

dancing."

"Square dancing!" she said, remembering her childhood. "From before we—assumed our positions."

"My memory is vague. But as I recall, there was a caller who instructed the couples as the dance proceeded, so that anyone could pick it up. The promenade, swinging your partner."

"The bow, the balance, the do-si-do," she agreed, also remembering. "Standard elements. We can make up the rest."

They presented the notion to the parents. "We can establish a dance, then have the children do it," Hellene said. "It may take some time to get it right."

Several nodded. Time was what they needed, until the rescue caravan cleared the road and came for them.

The made up a square dance: "Greensleeves." Heaver perked up the melody to make it sprightly, with a beat. They reviewed the motions, so they could be done when called. Heaver and Hellene demonstrated them, starting with the slight formal bow: honor to your partner. Then the swing: a straightforward holding and turning, the man supporting the woman, who leaned into it, causing her hair and skirt to flare. Again, she discovered herself liking this too much. They had had sex together, and were rival recruiters, yet this simple closeness and unity of motion and purpose girlishly thrilled her.

Then the do-si-do, wherein they crossed their arms and circled each other without changing orientation, so that they were back to back before returning to their places. And the balance, wherein they faced each other and swung their legs in a mannered shifting of weight, seeming pointless when done alone, but elegant when mirrored by a partner. And the promenade, a linking of hands before the bodies and doing the sashay, a kind of skip-step around the larger circle of the formed square.

Each individual motion was simple, and she as the caller called them out so there was no confusion at any time. But as the square shaped up, and the motions were performed together, the larger art of the dance became apparent. Dancing was for viewing as much as performing; everyone enjoyed it.

Once the adults had remembered the basics, they formed the square: four couples, standing at the sides of an imagined square, the men on the left, women on the right. Heaver played the melody, and Hellene called. "Sets in order." There were now enough people for two squares, eight couples, sixteen people, with a number of women left over. In fact, some women had to assume the male roles, as it was mostly women who were at home in the daytime with the children. It didn't matter; the role was everything. They made the squares square.

"Honor to your partner." Each person faced his or her partner and made the little bow.

"And your corner." Each turned to face the closest partner of the adjacent side of the square, bowing. Several children tittered; they thought it was funny to see their parents paying attention to the spouses of others. That was good; an amused child was not a terrified child.

"Swing your partner." They did, and did it well. Married couples knew how to do this sort of thing together.

"And your corner." That really set off the watching children, who regarded it as downright naughty. Square dancing, more than most, was a social exercise; people constantly interacted.

"Balance to your partner ... and your corner." They did. "Do-si-do with your corner ... and your opposite." For the first time people addressed members of the couples across the square, eliciting another series of childish giggles.

"And promenade the hall." They linked arms and sashayed around the square.

The watching adults applauded. They had successfully completed a dance.

Then they got the children involved. Each adult took a child of the opposite gender as partner and guided them through the basics. Each adult kept a perfectly straight face. The children found this hilarious. The bow, balance, and do-si-do were easy, but the swinging was problematic because of the size differentials in some cases.

"Like so," Heaver said. "You and I will demonstrate," he said to little Jane. He picked her up with his right hand around her back and his left hand holding her right hand up at his chest level, and solemnly turned in place. She giggled throughout. It wasn't really embarrassment or humor, so much as the fact that he was an extremely nice man to be close to. He affected women of any age much as Hellene affected men.

Then Hellene demonstrated it similarly with

Dick, setting her left arm firmly around him and taking his left hand in her right. She turned gracefully. "You swing well," she told him. There was a friendly chuckle around them. The little boy actually blushed.

Heaver resumed his harmonica playing, and Hellene resumed her calling. It was ragged, but they got through the dance. After that they changed partners and did it again, and again. The children were rapidly becoming proficient. Everyone seemed to be having fun.

There was a honk in the distance. A red fire truck appeared, red lights flashing.

"They cleared the road!" someone cried, immensely gratified.

"What, in half an hour?" a woman asked, surprised. Then she looked at her watch. "Two hours!" she said, amazed.

The truck pulled up and halted. Firemen piled out. "Here we thought you'd be dying, and you're dancing!"

"We had a good distraction," a man said, laughing. "For the children." But perhaps for the adults, too.

The evacuation began. People returned to their cars, to form a caravan led by the fire truck, as the fire was not yet done. Portions of the highway were single-lane, and there were staging areas for trucks to pass. Special housing was being arranged in town. The worst was over, but much remained to accomplish, including the reorganization of shattered lives.

"I ache with their pain," Heaver murmured.

"So do I," she said, and felt tears on her face. Empathy, yet again; it could be painful.

They held each other for a moment, with perfect understanding. The two orphaned children helped comfort them.

Several parents came to thank Heaver and Hellene. "You gave us what we needed in our hour of crisis," one woman said. "You saved our children from freaking out. Surely God sent you both."

Hellene kept her mouth shut. "To a degree," Heaver agreed. "We are glad to have been able to help."

Privately, he told her, "You did well. I am satisfied that you accomplished your challenge. You are not evil."

"I never claimed to be. I merely work for a different employer."

"Yet you rose to the occasion and did a deed contrary to your nature."

"Not really. I could never hurt a child."

He gazed at her. There was something intangible in his expression. "At such time as we are alone again, I would like to kiss you."

That was far more significant than it might have seemed to an outsider. He was expressing sincere emotion, not sexual desire.

"I will welcome it." So was she.

There was activity all around them, but in effect Heaver and Hellene were left alone with the two children. They questioned them, carefully, about relatives—and learned what dismayed them. It was a limited family; there were no suitable relatives. One uncle was alcoholic; a cousin was in prison. Other relatives were in no position to assume the burden.

"I remember a worthy couple," he said. "Devoutly religious, but unable to have children of their own. It's a shame, because they both love children, and have much to offer them."

"Religious," she said. "They would be indoctrinating the children into their worship of God."

"They would. It is their nature. Do you wish me to look elsewhere?"

She wrestled with her perspective, disliking this. Then she realized: her challenge was to do a good deed without consideration of any benefit to herself or Hell. Her deed was not yet complete, despite his acknowledgment.

"We'll take them there," she said. Having made the decision, she felt relief and gratitude. Heaver was coming through for the children, and she loved that. And, perhaps, him.

He did not reply. Instead he took Jane's little hand and led her around behind a fire truck. Hellene followed with Dick. Unobserved, they embraced the children and touched hands, projecting their souls.

Their images appeared in the other scene. It was a nice suburban residence in a nice neighborhood. They walked to the back of the garage, then changed places with their bodies. Because they were embracing the children, they came too.

That simply, they were physically there, with the children, who were surprised. "You know you can't go home," Heaver said to the children.

Grimly, they nodded.

"These people will take good care of you," he

continued. "They are very nice."

"But we want to stay with you!" Jane cried. She was becoming more expressive than the boy, as some girls did.

Oops.

Hellene intervened. "We are special people, without homes of our own. We love you in our fashion, but we can't take care of you. These folk can. But if you don't like them, we will not make you stay." She caught Heaver's eye to get his agreement.

"Okay," the child said reluctantly.

"I will inquire," Heaver said. He left the children with Hellene, and walked to the front door.

She kneeled and put her arms around both children. They hugged her and cried. She found herself crying with them. It had never been possible for her or Heaver to keep the children, but now she was sorry for that.

A kind-faced woman of middle age returned with Heaver. "Oh, my, yes!" she said. "Dick, Jane, we have ice cream inside."

Both children looked at her with sudden interest. She took each by the hand and led them toward the door. Heaver and Hellene remained where they were.

Jane hung back a moment, conscious of the significance of the shift. "But will you visit?" she asked plaintively.

Heaver took Hellene's hand, asking a silent question. "Yes," she said through her tears.

Jane pulled away from the woman and dashed back to hug Hellene. It was an amazingly sweet moment. Then she returned to the woman. The three went into the house.

"She hugged *me*," Hellene said, belatedly astonished.

"She had already hugged me," Heaver said. "You agreed to visit."

"I think she took part of my soul with her."

"Children do."

"Will there be any problem about adoption? This isn't any normal mode of placement."

"There will not be a problem, God willing."

"And God is willing," she said, catching on. "You are using your power."

"I am free to do so," he reminded her. "This is not my challenge."

"It is mine," she agreed. "I am not soliciting for Hell. I just want what is best for the children. Both of them."

"Your attitude becomes you."

"We must go home before I change my mind about leaving the children here."

He took her hand, and they projected to the residence where they had met, and in a moment exchanged their bodies there. It was of course unchanged.

"The children," he said. "The way you related to them with genuine caring— "

"I confess it," she said. "Though it destroy my image. I love those children."

"My view of you has altered," Heaver said. "I am not certain how to express it."

"Please," she said urgently. "I want to make love."

"May I kiss you first?"

"Kiss me," she agreed, entering his embrace.

He kissed her, and it was as though a tender fire radiated from his lips to hers and spread throughout her body.

After a fleeting eternity he drew back a bit. "Now I believe I know how to express it," he said with a rueful smile. "I love you, daughter of Hell."

There it was. Her remaining emotional restraint vanished in a figurative puff of smoke. "And I love you, son of Heaven."

"There is something else. We both have strong empathy. It enables us to better relate to our clients. When we encountered each other, we related with twice the power."

"And fell in love," she agreed. "Because we relate to each other better than any other two people can."

"And with that love comes yet more, it seems," he said.

"Telepathy," she said, reading his mind.

"We have truly become almost one."

"Fortunately with two bodies."

Then they got out of their clothes and on the bed, and made love, sharing bodies and minds. Sex was only a small part of it.

"We have a problem," he said as they lay beside each other, hands clasped.

"Perhaps not. I will change sides for you."

"As I would for you. That is not the problem."

"The balance of souls," she said, understanding.

"The end of mortality. Did we place those two dear children with a loving couple only to facilitate the early termination of their entire realm?"

"The Hell we did! We can't let it end."

"Yet if either of us changes sides, it will lead to the more rapid conclusion of the issue between Heaven and Hell."

"Have you considered resigning?"

"Have you?"

"As of this moment, yes. Without us, it may take millennia for the balance of souls to shift sufficiently."

"Much could happen in that time," he agreed. "But there would be a personal cost."

She nodded. "We would lose our looks and special abilities. I was a completely ordinary girl, when mortal."

"Never that! They would not have enlisted you."

"I had empathy," she agreed. "And discipline."

"As did I. But my appearance, my manly abilities—all would be forfeit."

She turned on her side, propping herself on an elbow. "We have spoken of love—but we have never seen each other truly naked. I mean, as we were."

"As we would be again, if we quit."

"So maybe we'd better show each other that."

"I looked like—" he shimmered, and was replaced by a somewhat pudgy, homely young man with acne. No Adonis, by miles.

She did the same, revealing her similarly pudgy, homely young woman form. Her breasts sagged somewhat, and her thighs had cellulite. "This," she concluded.

"But we are unchanged in what counts," he said.

"Are we?"

He caught hold of her and drew her in to him. He kissed her mouth repeatedly, then her breasts, and put his hand down to guide his hardening penis into her un-evocative cleft. She cooperated, bemused. Could this be real?

His member found the place, and pushed, but there was pain. She winced.

He paused immediately. "You prefer not?"

"It's my hymen. I am still a virgin in this body."

"I did not realize. I will desist."

"No, do it, Heave. I want it."

"But I want never to cause you pain."

"The hell with that! Do it."

He penetrated her, thrust, and thrust again repeatedly, not climaxing. Obviously her present body did not turn him on in the manner her enhanced one did. Yet she appreciated his effort, though she was somewhat dry internally and uncomfortable, apart from the sting of her ruptured hymen.

"We just made love," he reminded her. "My original form lacks fast rebound power. Have patience; I'll get there."

Oh. Of course. She participated with a will, ignoring the rawness, and slowly they both built up to a pitch. At last his orgasm came, like toothpaste oozing through a clogged tube, heaving its way through the conduit to spread at last in her channel. His body lacked the ability to gush with force. She didn't react sharply; it was more of a curtailed, frustrated pleasure. As sex went, it was third rate.

"Magnificent," he said.

She laughed. "The effort, maybe. Not the achievement."

"But we did it in our own un-enhanced bodies,

right after doing it in the great ones. As a test of mutual passion, it was perfect."

"I suppose it was," she agreed, seeing it. "If we can do it handicapped, it must be real."

"So we have nothing to fear from reversion. We can relate to each other as we are."

"So we can. I have been spoiled by the good body. But if you can address me without it, I don't need it."

"It is your real self I love."

"But thank you for making that effort." She reverted to her sightly body.

"Welcome." He reverted too. "Something I wonder, belatedly: why did God assign me to this mission, knowing the risk of my succumbing to your charms?"

"He thought you would conquer me—as you did. Now I wonder why Lucifa allowed me to meet you. She could have caused endless bureaucratic delay, stalling."

"She thought you would conquer me—as you did."

"Each was perhaps overconfident."

"Is that typical of omniscient beings?"

"Hardly."

"So the question returns: why? It seems at best a waste of effort on both sides, and at worst a loss to both sides."

"It does," she agreed.

"Let's review history, in case there is a hint. In the beginning, for this purpose, God trusted Lucifa above all others, until she betrayed him by trying to seize power and had to be expelled. Now she still tries to rival him for power from her base in Hell."

"Hell's version differs. God was always lusty, taking advantage of his position to seduce any appealing soul-woman he fancied. Only Lucifa resisted his advances, so he booted her out as an object lesson and vilified her. Thereafter no other female in Heaven had the temerity to resist his harassment."

Heaver laughed ruefully. "That version does differ! I wonder which one is true?"

"We can get a notion by examining the present. Does God still seduce pretty women?"

"Oh, yes! He has infinite appetite and potency. We theorize that the main reason for sexual diffidence in Heaven is to keep the women clear for his approach. But what of Lucifa: does she remain virginally pristine?"

"Hardly. Her line of lovers extends back to the beginning of her descent to Hell."

"So why would she have resisted God's advances?"

"I don't know. She revels in sexuality. Maybe it is to spite God, to show him what he is missing. I am crafted in her image in both appearance and passion, to a fair degree. I would have sex with God if he came to me without demands for conversion to Heaven."

"And I am crafted in the likeness of God in physical and emotional aspect, though of course falling considerably short of his effulgence. I think Lucifa is the epitome of illicit temptation, and I would surely revel in an affair with her, however guiltily. My potency is not at all as great as his, however."

"Nor is mine as great as Lucifa's. But I don't need it to be; I can seduce and oblige almost any mortal man without the need to have my own orgasms. Actually I can enjoy it, as his pleasure becomes my pleasure."

"Because of your empathy," he agreed. "I also gain pleasure from giving women pleasure, though this is not necessarily sexual."

"Empathy," she agreed. "It defines us both."

"Accounting for our success as recruiters. And now for our identification with the mortal realm." He turned to her again. "Yet even were it not for that, I believe I would want to retire with you. You understand me."

"And love you," she agreed. "Is there any reason to delay?"

"I know of none. I do not care to return to Heaven without you, or to transfer to Hell."

"It will not be easy to make a living together, especially considering the likely wrath of God and Lucifa."

"Whose purposes are it seems not ours," he said grimly.

"Then let's do it."

He nodded. Holding her hand, he faced the ceiling. "I, Heaver, recruiter of souls, hereby resign from my compact with Heaven, eschewing promised rewards, to exist hereafter in the mortal realm."

Her turn. She faced downward. "Go to Hell, Lucifa. I quit."

Heaver laughed. "Your expression is more direct, but the essence is the same."

"Yes. Now kiss me before we lose our bodies and powers."

He drew her to him and kissed her. She kissed him back. They both paused expectantly.

Nothing happened. They retained their good bodies. They extended their souls and found they retained their astral or soul-traveling abilities.

"Good is omniscient," Heaver said after a time. "He surely heard."

"So is Lucifa." Then she had a nasty thought. "Do you suppose they require formal, in-person resignations?"

"That may be," he agreed. "But if we go there, even in soul travel, they may not let us return to the mortal realm."

"Imprisoning our souls until we change our minds," she said. "We are valuable recruiters."

"I do not want to be kept apart from you, now that I have discovered in you my life fulfillment."

"That goes double for me." She pondered a moment. "I have an evil idea."

"Perhaps. Let's hear it."

"Let's take each other's places. That is, I go to Heaven, astrally, and you go to Hell. They can't hold us there, because we are not *of* those opposite realms. I'll tell God of your resignation, and you can tell Lucifa. Then we can revert to the mortal realm."

"You're right, beloved! That is a devilish idea. Perfect for the occasion."

"But we'll need to help each other. I don't know my way around Heaven, and you surely are unfamiliar with the layout of Hell."

"True. But we can maintain soul contact

throughout, guiding each other. It should be an interesting experience."

"It should be," she agreed. "Especially if they don't want us to succeed."

"And surely they don't. Yet what else is there?"

"Nothing much I can think of at the moment."

"We must do it now, before we realize the impossibility of success."

"Agreed. But can we make love again before we go to what may be our doom?"

He considered his limp penis. "Sex, I think not, but love, yes."

"Let's embrace and travel. Our connected bodies will connect our souls reliably."

"I must face Hell," he said. "You must face Heaven."

"No problem. Get on me."

He assumed the position, resting his body on hers while supporting part of his weight on his hands and legs. He kissed her. "I love you, Hellene."

"I love you, Heaver."

Then they traveled. Her soul passed though his body and ascended into the sky, while his descended into the ground.

"What's the route?" she inquired, her mental linkage feeling like normal dialogue.

"There is a small pink cloud. Pass though it."

She spied the cloud. "I see it. Meanwhile, you look for a small blue magma dome. Pass through that."

She flew to the cloud, which looked completely ordinary apart from its faint color. But of course the portal to Heaven had to be concealed, lest mortals discover it.

She circled it, then dropped in from above. And found herself on a broad golden avenue girt by flowering trees. At the end of the avenue was a set of huge nacreous gates.

This was truly the entry to Heaven.

She paused, daunted. "Do I just walk on in?" she asked Heaver.

"And announce that you're from Hell, looking to interview God? I would hesitate."

But she was intrigued. "Maybe the truth wouldn't hurt. It's a legitimate mission. Meanwhile, how are you doing?"

"See through my eyes."

She did so. He was standing in a motley group beside a flaming river on which a ferryman was slowly poling his boat toward them.

"That's the River Styx," she said. "Take the boat across. You don't want to swim, even in soul form; it hurts."

"Take the boat," he agreed.

She dropped to the avenue and walked toward the pearly gates. She seemed to be alone, which surprised her; surely there were throngs constantly coming to Heaven.

"There are," Heaver said. "But each soul is alone until admittance. Even then contacts are few; obvious crowds are frowned upon."

"In contrast to Hell," she murmured, proceeding.

Soon she reached the gates. She looked for the gatekeeper, who she understood was called St. Peter. There was no one. "Anybody home?" she called.

When there was no answer, she tried to rattle the

gate for attention. But her hand passed through it without resistance. She considered a moment, then walked on through. Now she was in Heaven Proper, it seemed.

"That's odd," Heaver said, when she told him. "Maybe it's because you are not on the registry of angelic souls. So you aren't being tracked."

"That being the case, I will just fly up to the highest level and brace God," she said.

"Perhaps you had better delay until I reach the lowest level of Hell," he said. "I may not be on the registry of damned souls, but neither am I able to walk through the furniture."

"Apt point. Souls often try to avoid or escape Hell, so it is more firmly constructed. No one tries to escape Heaven."

"I can't think why," he said, laughing. "No, I wasn't talking to you, sir."

She looked through his eyes again. He was facing a grizzled drunkard with an aggressive aspect.

"No talking on the boat!" the ferryman snapped.

"Ah, go fuck yourself," the grizzled man snapped back.

The ferryman touched him with the tip of his pole. The man collapsed. So much for talking back.

"You don't have to speak aloud to me," she reminded him. "Just vocalize in your mind and I will hear."

"I know," he mentally vocalized. "The distraction of Hell made me forget."

"That's better."

The craft approached the other shore. Demons were lined up with pitchforks, grinning. The other damned souls flinched. Obviously the souls could not be killed, but they surely could be made to hurt.

"Is there a way to avoid this unpleasantness?" he asked.

"Not for the damned souls. But the forks should pass through you with no effect, if your presence in Hell mirrors mine in Heaven."

"That would give away my nature. Would it help to approach the supervisor and state my mission? I am not after all a damned soul."

"I fear the brute would not listen," she said. "Hell is full of souls trying to pretend they are exceptions and don't really belong there. I think you'll have to lie."

"I can't do that!"

She sighed. "I love that incapacity, but it is ill-suited for Hell. Let me rephrase: you will need to employ subterfuge."

"Even so, it is difficult."

"Think of it as a game whose rules require some concealment of purpose. The challenge is to get through to Lucifa without getting Hell into an uproar."

"Perhaps so," he agreed reluctantly. "What do you recommend?"

"That you use a shortcut I know. The human souls are relegated to many set layers of discomfort, tortured by demons and hunted by monsters. You can assume the form of a monster and bypass the layers."

"So much for avoiding torture in Hell," he said ruefully.

"Those we recruit sign contracts that forbid

torture. They are all right. But these present souls you are among don't have contracts. They spent their lives doing evil and were always destined for Hell. They richly deserve their fate."

Now the raft was landing. Demons were jumping onto it to prod souls forward, who were exclaiming with pain.

"That is hard to believe."

"That lout you spoke to accidentally, who told someone to fuck himself? I just checked his file. He abducted little girls, raped them, and throttled them. They went to Heaven, of course, where they became eternal children. Their families lived on in muted grief. You want to forgive him?"

"No."

"The others have similar crimes on their scant consciences."

"I withdraw my objection."

"Step onto the land. Once you are free of the raft you will be able to change form. Become a vulture and fly to the nearby dark forest."

"Not a flamingo?" he asked with an attempt at humor.

"No lovely flamingos in Hell."

He stepped across just ahead of a pitchfork and became a vulture. "Hey!" the demon behind him cried.

"Go fornicate with your own anatomy," the vulture said.

Furious, the demon stabbed at the ugly bird. But Heaver had already launched into clumsy flight. The demon couldn't chase him; there were other souls in need of immediate punishment. But he did not look pleased.

Hellene stifled a chortle. Heaver was learning.

He reached the forest. A dinosaur with many teeth spied him and snapped at him. He tried to avoid it, landing and running into the forest, but it followed.

"Become another saurus," Hellene said. "Blend in."

He became a similar monster. The other assessed him, then approached, snarling. "What do I do now?" he asked, alarmed. "If it touches me and finds nothing, my disguise is spoiled."

"Make yourself solid," she advised. "You can do that by drawing on a bit of your mortal substance."

"But then I'll have to fight it."

Hellene laughed. "Not so. You are a handsome male saurus, your nature manifesting even in that form. She's being friendly."

"Friendly! How can I make her go away?"

"Fuck her."

"I wish you would dispense with the ugly language."

"I'll rephrase: have sex with her. That's what she wants."

He was appalled. "But she's a beast!"

"So are you, at the moment. Act like one."

"I—I can't—"

"Think of her as being me. I would gladly have sex with you in that form."

The saurus nudged him. Heaver hesitated again, then made his decision. He got behind her and angled his swelling member. She cooperated, lifting her tail. He found the place and nudged in.

Now commenced a dance like none other. The saurus put her head down to brace herself against the ground, keeping her rear elevated. She shoved violently back against him. Heaver rammed in forcefully, lest he be shoved back into a tree, his body crashing against hers as his member penetrated to full depth. Pound! Pound! Pound!

"Oh, I wish I was there!" Hellene exclaimed ecstatically.

"So do I," he muttered.

Soon he spurted what seemed like a few pints into the nether maw, and the monster was satisfied at last. She pulled off and took off, saving her tankful of juice.

"Well done," Hellene said. "That was better than fighting her, wasn't it?"

"It seemed so real."

"It *is* real, just not mortal. Don't the souls in Heaven seem real too?"

"Yes, of course. In the eternal realms, souls seem as solid as the bodies of mortals. We'd both seem solid too, if we were in our proper realms. Which of course is the point; we can't be trapped."

"We hope."

"A well-founded hope."

"Follow the nether trail to its end. That will be Lucifa's throne room. Then coordinate with me."

"On my way." He found the nether trail, which started on the forest floor and spiraled down into the ground.

Hellene assumed bird form and flew upward toward the Divine throne room. She passed through all levels as though they had no substance, which was convenient. She saw many shining angels in passing, but ignored them, staying clear. Her business was with God alone.

In due course she reached the apex: the Holy of Holies. She assumed enough solidity to perch on a glowing chandelier, and contacted Heaver. "Where are you now?"

"At the nethernmost access," he replied. "I think Lucifa is near."

"Oh, she is," the voice of Hell's mistress said. "Assume your normal form, Son of Heaven, so that I can address you."

Then Hellene's attention was taken by her own setting. "You too, Daughter of Hell," God said.

She dropped to the floor, becoming her beautiful human form. "You know me," she gasped. She had expected to introduce herself, surprising him.

"I am omniscient," he reminded her. Now she saw his form.

"Heaver!" Except that he was larger, more handsome, and shining.

"I am the original whose likeness he assumed. Just as you assumed the likeness of your infernal mistress Lucifa."

She marshaled her composure. "I am here to tell you—"

"Of course. Now let me address your mistress directly."

Hellene tried to protest, but suddenly a dark presence assumed control of her body. Lucifa had taken over.

"So we meet again, after six millennia," Lucifa said. Her body—Hellene's soul-body—now was shrouded with form-fitting darkness. Nothing else. It was an extremely sexy outfit.

"It has seemed like six eternities," God replied. "You are surpassingly beautiful, as ever."

"Don't try to tease me with your lies," she snapped. "I know better."

"What lies? You are the deceiver. You deserted me in my hour of need."

"Come off it, rogue! You had at every woman in Heaven in descending order of appeal, reaming them all in turn before dumping them, and left me for last. I refused to be humiliated that way, either by being last or being dumped, so I departed. Then you lied about me, vilifying me before everyone."

God had the grace to wince. "Gabriel put out a public relations story to account for your departure. What was I going to do—fire him?"

"You could have told the truth."

"The truth was that I tackled the maidens in ascending order, leaving the best to last, so that the others would not be slighted."

"Hold forth your hand, wretch! I can tell a lie by touch." She put out her own hand.

"No need," God said ruefully. "I forgot that you, too, are omniscient. I will try again. The truth is that when you departed, and I saw what you wrought in your own domain, I realized that I had misjudged you, and sorely regretted it. There is no woman to match you in either realm; you should have been first on my list." And now he held out his hand for verification.

Lucifa considered, then withheld her own hand without touching his. "No need. I like that version better."

"As you wish," God agreed, seeming relieved.

"So are we at peace at last, after six thousand years of war?"

"I believe we are. There is no further need to vie for supremacy, recruiting for mortal souls."

"So shall we fold the mortal realm now?"

Hellene felt shock. Had her mission here merely facilitated the thing she feared?

"No need," God said. "There are an unGodly number of mortals there now."

"They breed like flies," Lucifa agreed.

"The rush of souls would overwhelm our facilities. I prefer a measured assimilation, as is the case at present."

"Fine by me." Lucifa eyed him. "Do we have any other business before we separate?"

God eyed her similarly. "Are you going to make me say it?"

"Yes."

"I still desire you. I want to possess you."

"That's nice." But she made no move toward him.

"Are you going to make me beg?"

"Yes."

He laughed. "Hell *does* have a fury like that of a woman once scorned!"

"By definition," she agreed.

"You have beauty and fire like none other. I have longed for you for six millennia. My passion is higher than Heaven, deeper than Hell. I beg you, indulge me."

She melted slightly. "And what of those other

women in Heaven?"

"What of those other men in Hell?" he asked sharply.

"Mere substitutes for you. They were inadequate."

"That's it exactly. With each woman I tried to imagine it was you in my embrace, but none sufficed. Only you can truly be you."

She nodded. "I think that will do. Come to me, OmniPotent."

He came to her and clasped her. A bed formed, and they fell on it, their clothing vaporizing. They kissed, and Heaven flickered with lightning while Hell sizzled with rising magma. He stroked her marvelous breasts, and every volcano on Earth swelled dangerously.

"Oh, my love, my love!" he breathed. "With you I am complete at last!"

"Darling," she whispered. "Only you can truly fulfill me."

His giant member addressed her opening cleft. Mountains shook and earthquakes shuddered open across the mortal planet. He slowly penetrated her. Hurricanes formed over enormous whirlpools. He thrust. Continents jolted against each other, enormous ledges of rock jamming down into tight subduction zones. He ejaculated—and the realms went wild.

In Heaven every male angel clasped every female angel. In Hell every demon clasped every demoness. The male and female souls united ardently. And on Earth every male creature clasped every female creature. It did not matter whether they were old or young, married or single, human or animal. All that mattered was that they were of opposite genders and close enough to come together within seconds. In private rooms, public places, or in between, male and female, they mated with desperate passion. There were some interesting scenes aboard airplanes in flight, and in movie theaters. Some of the most dramatic, fittingly, were in halls where dances and operas were being shown. On-stage and off-stage, people desperately clasped each other. There were also complications where the genders were not approximately even. Monasteries joined with nunneries. Prisons exploded in riots.

Meanwhile every volcano erupted violently, jetting hot stone and gases to unprecedented heights. Every river surged its waters out across the surrounding landscape. Every piston-driven motor turned on and operated at high velocity, the pistons constantly driving into the cylinders.

Then it was done, and impromptu couples stared at each other, appalled. What had come over them? What had happened to the world?

"That was almost worth six millennia of frustration," God gasped, relaxing. "What an experience!"

"Almost worth the wait," Lucifa agreed. She was overflowing with God's copious emission.

"And our minions performed well," he said.

Lucifa laughed. "They thought they were acting on their own initiatives."

"It was the only way we could tryst without scandal. By encouraging Doppelgangers to connect us via their soul bodies, so that we did not have to leave our domains."

"While their physical bodies remained in the mortal realm," she agreed. "We had better release them now."

"To a degree," he agreed. "First one more kiss."

She met him, and they kissed ardently.

Hellene was suddenly back in her own body on Earth, kissing Heaver. She jerked back. "The nerve!" she snapped.

"I feel so used," he said, understanding perfectly.

"We *were* used—to provide the physical bodies for their phenomenal copulation," she said, disgusted. "Because they have no mortal bodies of their own." Now it was her body overflowing with his emission. Used, indeed.

"I thought we were going there to resign our commissions."

"So did I. But now I realize that we were too quick to decide on that course. When Lucifa possessed me I picked up some of her mind."

"I too, with God. They put that thought in us, to make us go to them. So they could use us."

She shared his anger. "And they facilitated our entries to Heaven and Hell. We should have realized that it was too easy."

"We were fools."

"Or at least dupes."

"Yet our decision was good: to resign our positions."

"Let's resign them now."

They did so—but again nothing happened. They remained beautiful people, with special powers.

"I fear they are not yet through with us," Heaver

said. "I am remembering another aspect of God's mind. They want to make similar trysts, now that they have established the conduit, borrowing our empathy."

"To continue using us," she agreed coldly.

"For their private passion, while they masquerade as rivals, catering to their bases."

"Yet as long as this is the case, they won't terminate the mortal realm," she said. "We can keep our looks and powers, and visit the children."

"And make love," he agreed. "That is the rest of it. They are offering us a deal we can't refuse."

"We can't refuse," she echoed grimly.

"Appreciating our shared abhorrence, shall we express ourselves again?"

"Our shared outrage," she agreed, embracing him. "As soon as we clean their disgusting leavings off our bodies."

"But I think we need not relate sexually, at this time," he said.

"Because that aspect has been corrupted, at least for the moment," she agreed. "Let's indulge in pure celestial love."

"Amen!"

But it got away from them. Soon they were, on a far lesser scale, emulating the recent joining of the deities. No mountains shook, but it was bearable, considering.

* * * *

As with many of the stories, this one started with an essential idea – in this case, the apt Hell Recruiter – and developed as I addressed the subject. Just garnering more souls wasn't enough of a story. Suppose she fell in love with a recruit? But why should she? Unless Heaven intervened. Ah, there was the potential for a real story.

Some readers may be upset with the portrayal of the supreme deities. This borrows somewhat from the ancient mythologies, where the gods were very like regular mortals, only more so, with their special passions and powers. Why should they fool around with the mortal realm at all, unless there is something there that interests them? Such as emotionally virginal mortals. It works for me.

About the Author

Piers Anthony is one of the world's most prolific and popular authors. His fantasy Xanth novels have been read and loved by millions of readers around the world, and have been on the *New York Times* Best Seller list twenty-one times. Although Piers is mostly known for fantasy and science fiction, he has written several novels in other genres as well, including historical fiction, martial arts, and horror. Piers lives with his wife in a secluded woods hidden deep in Central Florida.

Printed in the United Kingdom by
Lightning Source UK Ltd., Milton Keynes
139532UK00001B/11/P

9 781594 267246